SEKENRE

THE BOOK OF THE SORCERER

SEKENRE
THE BOOK OF THE SORCERER

DARRELL SCHWEITZER

For Jennifer
Darrell Schweitzer

WILDSIDE

SEKENRE: THE BOOK OF THE SORCERER
Copyright © 2004 by Darrell Schweitzer

Acknowledgements:
On the Last Night of the Festival of the Dead first appeared in *Interzone* #90, December 1994. Copyright © 1994 by *Interzone*. *The Sorcerer's Gift* first appeared in *Worlds of Fantasy and Horror* #4, Winter, 1996. Copyright © 1996 by Terminus Publishing Co. *King Father Stone* first appeared in *Interzone* #103, January 1996. Copyright © 1995 by *Interzone*. *The Giant Vorviades* first appeared in *Interzone* #99, September 1995. Copyright © 1995 by *Interzone*. *The Silence of Kings* first appeared in *Weirdbook* #30, 1997. Copyright © 1997 by W. Paul Ganley. *Vandibar Nasha in the College of Shadows* first appeared in *Adventures in Sword and Sorcery* #7, Summer 2000. Copyright © 2000 by Double Star Press. *In the Street of the Witches* first appeared in *Weird Tales* #320, Summer 2000. Copyright © 2000 by Terminus Publishing Co. *The Lantern of the Supreme Moment* first appeared in *Space & Time* #93, Spring 2001. Copyright © 2001 by Darrell Schweitzer. *From Out of the Crocodile's Mouth* first appeared in *Weird Tales* #325, Fall 2001. Copyright © 2001 by Terminus Publishing Co. *Dreams of the Stone King's Daughter* first appeared in *Weird Tales* #330, Winter 2002-2003. *Seeking the Gifts of the Queen of Vengeance* first appeared in *Odyssey* #2, 1997. Copyright © 1997 by Darrell Schweitzer. Copyright © 2002 by DNA Publications, Inc. *Lord Abernaeven's Tale,* first appeared in *Weird Tales* #334, January-February 2004. Copyright 2004 by DNA Publications, Inc.

For David Pringle, Patron of the Arts

Wildside Press, LLC
www.wildsidepress.com

First Wildside Press Edition: 2004

Contents

"The sorcerer is always a phantom, like a dark moth flitting through profoundest dreams. His book, likewise, is a phantom, opened and read in a dream." —Julna of Kadisphon

ON THE LAST NIGHT OF THE FESTIVAL OF THE DEAD

"... then all things which have been begun shall be finished."
— *The Litanies of Silence*

ON THE FIRST night of the Festival of the Dead, they were laughing.

All the capital rang with mirth; fantastic banners and kites festooned the towers and roofs of the City of the Delta. The streets swarmed with masked harlequins bearing copper lanterns shaped like grotesque faces which *sang* through some trick of flame and metal. That was a kind of laughter too.

On the first night, Death was denied. Children crouched by the canals and floated away paper mummies in toy funeral-boats. Black-costumed skeletons ran from house to house, pounding on doors, waving torches, shouting for the living to emerge and mingle with the dead. Revellers swirled in their shrouds, their death-masks revealing their ancestors, not as they had looked at the close of life, but with rotten features hideously, hilariously distorted.

That was the joke of it, that everyone was masked and no one knew who anyone else was. All gossip and insult and roguery might be done with impunity. Nothing mattered. Death itself was a jest. Surat-Hemad, the crocodile-headed Devourer, god of the Underworld, could be mocked.

But it was nervous laughter. Inevitably, even on the first night of the festival, some of the restless dead actually returned from their abode in *Tashé*, that shadowy country which lies beyond the reach of the deepest dreams. So the possibility was always there, however remote, that the person behind the mask, either speaking or spoken to, might actually *be* a corpse.

If not something far stranger.

"IS THIS the house of the great Lord Kuthomes?" the person who had knocked at the door said, holding out a small package wrapped in palm fronds.

That was all the two servants who answered could remember: the soft voice, the diminutive messenger with long, dark hair; probably a child, gender uncertain. The mask like a barking dog, or grinning jackal, or maybe a bat. Plain, scruffy clothing, maybe loose trousers or just a robe; probably barefoot.

They'd merely accepted the package and the messenger ran away.

Their exasperated master took it from them and ordered them beaten.

Lord Kuthomes tore the fronds away and held in his hands a small wooden box, cheaply made of scrap materials, without any attempt at ornamentation.

The box vibrated slightly, as if something inside it were alive, or perhaps clockwork.

Thoughtful, ever on guard against the trick of some enemy — for he *was* a great lord of the Delta and he had many enemies — he carried it to his chamber. As he entered, living golden hands on his nightstand lifted a two-paneled mirror, holding it open like a book.

Kuthomes sat on a stool, a candle in one hand, the parcel in the other, gazing at the reflections of both in the black glass.

The hands shifted the mirror, showing the image in one panel, then the other.

As he had so many times before, Kuthomes searched for some hidden clue which might reveal treachery or useful secrets. He was a magician of sorts, though not a true sorcerer, wholly transformed, reeking of poisonous enchantment. His art sufficed to unravel such lethal puzzles as one Deltan lord might design for another. In this mirror, he had often learned the weakness of some rival. Once he had even reached *through* the glass and torn out a sleeping man's heart.

He hefted the box. It weighed perhaps two ounces. But he had an instinct about such things. He sensed strangeness, and in strangeness, danger.

But when he held the box up to the mirror, even with the candle positioned to shine through the delicate wood, he saw only his hands, the box, and the candle's flame. The depths remained inscrutable; they did not even reflect Lord Kuthomes's silver-bearded face.

The box stirred, humming like one of those metal lanterns the harlequins carried. For an instant, Kuthomes was furious. A festival night *joke?* He would have crushed the thing in his hand and hurled it away. But that same caution which had made him a great lord of the Delta again prevailed.

He placed the object down on the night stand, took a delicate calligrapher's knife, and, by candlelight, began to chip away at the thin wood. There were no envenomed needles, no springs, no magic seals waiting to be broken. The fragments fell away easily.

Inside was a sculpture about two inches high, of a laughing corpseface, its head thrown back, gap-toothed mouth stretched wide. Inside the mouth, a tiny silver bell rang of its own accord. Kuthomes touched the bell with the tip of his knife and the ringing stopped.

Outside, the mob laughed and roared. Drums beat faintly, muffled, far away.

He laid the knife down on the table top, and the ringing resumed. It wasn't a matter of a breeze or a draught. He placed the whole object under a glass bowl and the bell still shivered.

He knew, then, that this was no thing of the living world, but a deathbell, manufactured in *Tashé* itself by dead hands, then borne up, like a bubble rising from a deep, muddy pool, through the dreamlands of *Leshé,* until it was present, very substantially, at the doorstep of Lord Kuthomes of the Delta. It was a token, a summons from the dead.

"Whoever has sent this," he said aloud, "know that I shall find you out and wrest your secrets from you, though you be already dead. You shall learn why Kuthomes is feared."

He rose and prepared himself, performing the four consecrations, forehead, eyelids, ears, and mouth touched with the Sorcerer's Balm, to shield him from illusion. His midnight-black sorcerer's robe came to life as it closed around him, its delicately glowing embroideries depicting a night sky never seen over the City of the Delta; the stars of Death, the sky of *Tashé.*

He regarded his reflection in the mirrors, only the robe visible in the darkness, like some headless specter.

The original owner of that robe, he recalled, had been headless toward the end, but well before he died, before others carried the remains away and finished the unpleasant, perilous business. He knew that to kill a sorcerer is to become one. The contagion flows from the slain to the slayer. Therefore a sorcerer must be disposed of carefully, by experts, not such dilettantes as he, who might occasionally require that the serpentine motif on a jade carving come to life on cue, or a sip of wine paralyze the will, or the face of a one man be temporarily transformed into that of the other. These were stock-in-trade for any lord of the Delta, to be applied as deftly as a surgeon's knife.

But no, he was not a sorcerer.

Therefore he also carried a curious sword in a scabbard underneath his robe, its strong steel blade inlaid with intricate, ultimately mystifying silver designs. It was the weapon of a Knight Inquisitor, one of those fanatic warriors from the barbarian lands across the sea, a sworn enemy of all gods but the Righteous Nine and especially of the Shadow Titans, who breathe sorcery like a miasma into the world. The sword was proof against all the magical darkness.

But Kuthomes, merely a man, had strangled the Knight Inquisitor with a cord, years ago, when he was younger and had the strength for such things.

He put on the jeweled, brimless cap of his rank and took up the death-bell in his hand, then passed silently through the halls of his own house in vigorous, graceful strides. He crossed the central courtyard. Up above, someone hastily closed a shutter. Even on such a merry night, it was ill luck to look on Lord Kuthomes in his sorcerer's aspect.

A single lamp flickered in the atrium. There were still palm fronds on the floor, and a stain where the servants had been beaten. That would be cleaned up on his return, or made larger.

He slipped out into the street.

BY NOW the night was almost over. Stars still shone overhead, but the sky was purpling in the East. He found himself in an utterly dark street, without a single lantern hanging from a doorway, a channel of featureless exterior walls. Higher up, the balconies were empty, the shutters invariably locked.

He stretched out his palm and held the death-bell up level with his face. It laughed at him, but slowly now, the faint tinkling interspersed with silence.

Several streets away, someone shouted. A horn blew a long, trailing blast that began as music and ended in flatulence.

Something fell and broke, probably crockery. Then silence again.

He walked confidently along that dark street until he stumbled, cursing, over what looked like an enormous, long-legged bird left broken and sprawling.

But Kuthomes did not fall. He regained his footing, crushing the death-bell in his hand. The thing felt like a live wasp, scraping to get free.

Hastily, he opened his hand, then stood still, gasping.

Gradually he made out an inert reveller in some absurd costume: trailing cloth wings, tatters and streamers, a crushed and shapeless mask. There must have been stilts somewhere, or else a crowd had carried the fool aloft.

In his younger days, Kuthomes might have given the fellow a kick to the ribs, but now he merely spat, then continued on his way.

He tried to follow the delicate voice of the bell, turning where it seemed to ring louder or more frequently. But his ear could not actually tell. He wandered through the maze of streets, once or twice passing others, who hurried to get out of his way.

In a market square, he faced the East. Dawn's first light sufficed to reveal the solitary figure standing there: very short, clad in shapeless white, arms akimbo, bare feet spread apart, face hidden behind some cheap animal mask.

"You there!" Kuthomes dropped the insistent bell into his pocket and stepped forward, but the other turned and ran. For an instant he thought it was a dwarf, but the motion was too agile.

A child then. He couldn't tell if it was a boy or a girl.

He pursued until his breath came in painful gasps and it seemed his chest would burst. Again and again he saw his quarry, near at hand but out of reach, vanishing around a corner at the end of an alley, on the other side of a courtyard, or gazing down on him from a balcony or from a bridge over a canal.

"Do not dare to trifle with me!"

Bare feet padded on cobblestones. Hard boots clattered after.

But in the morning twilight Kuthomes could go no further. He had to sit down on a stone bench and lean back against a wall, gazing out over the central forum of the city. All around him the temples of the major gods faced one another. The rising sun made the rooftops and the many statues gleam. Divinities, kings, and heroes lining those rooftops and perched on pillars and ledges seemed momentarily alive, gazing down benevolently or wrathfully, each according to their nature. Yawning peddlers opened their stalls. A flock of pigeons stirred, murmuring on the steps of the temple of Bel-Hemad, the god of new life, of springtime, and forgiveness. But the house of Surat-Hemad, the lord of Death, was still a mass of shadows and black stone, the eyes of the carven crocodile head over the doorway aglow like faint coals with some mysterious light of their own.

Kuthomes half-dozed, exhausted, enraged that he had been the object of a *joke* on the first night of the Festival of the Dead. He set the death-bell in his lap, and still it rang, a far more serious matter than anybody's joke. He laid the sword of the Knight Inquisitor across his knees, and the ringing stopped. When he put the sword away, it resumed.

He couldn't think clearly just then, weary and angry as he was, but he was certain that he was proof against illusion, and that there was an answer here somewhere, in the haze and dust and fading shadows. If he concentrated hard enough, he would have it, and his revenge, later.

Was he not Lord Kuthomes, feared and respected by all?

Eventually he fell asleep on the bench and dreamed, strangely, that he, the feared and respected Lord Kuthomes, had ventured alone into the city at night, and that the city was empty. All the revellers, soldiers, courtiers, even the Great King himself had fled before him, and Lord Kuthomes's heavy footsteps echoed in the empty palace, even in the vast Presence Hall where he mounted the throne with the double crown of the Delta and Riverland on his head.

He sat still and silent in his dream, the crown on his head, crocodile-headed scepter in his hand, gazing into the empty darkness, until he heard the sound of the tiny death-bell approaching.

Someone shuffled and emerged from behind a column. Kuthomes stiffened and beheld a tall, cloaked figure approach the throne slowly, tottering like a very old man; no, swaying side-to-side like a crocodile reared up, imitating a human walk.

The thing opened clawed hands when it stood at the foot of the throne. The face beneath the hood was indeed that of a crocodile. In the open hands, nothing at all.

Here was one of the *evatim*, the messengers of Surat-Hemad, whose summons may never be resisted or denied.

Kuthomes shrank back in his stolen throne, knowing that all his magic and even the silver sword were useless.

But the other tore off a crocodile mask, uncovering a laughing corpse face identical to that which held the death-bell, head back in a paroxysm of hilarity or terror, mouth agape. In the unimaginable depths of its throat, a tiny bell rang insistently.

Then the apparition breathed *laughter*, neither harsh nor exactly gentle, impatient, with a touch of petulance, and at last a voice spoke from those same black depths, soft, definitely feminine, a young woman's voice, maddeningly familiar.

In his dream, it was too much effort to recall. He almost recognized the voice, but not quite.

"Do you not know me?" the other said.

"No," he replied.

"Ah, but you did once, long ago."

"How long ago was that?"

She only laughed for a brief instant. Then the laughter was gone and the bell rang.

Lord Kuthomes shook himself out of his dream and found himself on the bench at the edge of the dusty forum, in the blazing mid-day sun. The bell, in his lap, still rang. No one had dared to disturb him, of course. Those who gaped in wonder suddenly turned their faces away, pretending not to have seen.

He took up the bell again and lurched to his feet, shouting for an old woman to fetch him a litter. When she had done so, she held out her hand for a coin. He patted his pockets, found nothing, then scowled and spat, tumbling into the litter, drawing the curtain behind him. The bearers set off, the litter lurching, swaying. Kuthomes felt sick by the time he reached his house.

Inside the atrium, the palm fronds and the stain on the floor were still there.

Later. There would be time for that later.

ON THE second night of the Festival of the Dead, they were dancing.

This was a more somber time. The streets and rooftops echoed with stately music. Paper masks from the first night floated in the canals or littered the streets. Now people wore beautifully carved and adorned wooden masks, ageless, ideal visages which did not so much hide the identity of the wearer as abstract it, like a name written in intricate, illuminated letters.

Musicians, clad in dark cerements and masked in imitation of the *evatim*, moved slowly from house to house, to palace and hovel alike, excepting no one, summoning the inhabitants to dance, to mingle in the wide forum before the temples of the gods. On this night the dead would truly return in great numbers, out of the dreams of *Leshé* and the darkness of *Tashé*, climbing up from the Great River and the city's many canals to walk among the living. It was a night of portents and revelations, of sor-rows and bittersweet joys, reunions, secret dooms, and frequent miracles.

Lord Kuthomes had rested and bathed. He had pored over such books of sorcery as he owned and could read, unable to find any answer to the riddle before him, but still certain some enemy had laid a trap.

He would be ready. Once more he anointed himself four times and put on his sorcerer's robe. Once more the silver sword pressed against his thigh. This time even he wore a mask, beautifully wrought, set with gems and feathers until the features of Lord Kuthomes had been transformed into some fantastic, predatory bird.

When the revellers reached his door, he gave them such coin as custom required, then stepped out into the throng, moving along the dark and crowded streets, into the forum where moonlight shone on the roofs of the temples and the many bronze and golden statues. The gods seemed to be watching him alone, waiting for something to happen.

Even the Great King, Wenamon the Ninth, was there with all his lords and ladies, all of them masked, to do homage to Death.

Kuthomes took his rightful place in the great circle of their dance. Once he held the warm hand of Queen Valshepsut, who nodded to him, and he to her, before he yielded to the King. Around and around dancers turned, as the musicians followed, pipes skirling, drums beating stately, muted time. Acolytes with lanterns or torches pursued their own paths at the periphery, the intricate revolutions imitating the cycles of the universe. In the center, priests of Death stood motionless in their crocodile masks.

Or were those perhaps the true faces of the *evatim?*

The fancy came to Kuthomes that many of the faces around him, in the royal circle, in the crowd, were not masks at all.

In the midst of them was one who did not dance, who clearly did not belong: some scruffy urchin in a paper mask that was probably supposed to be a fox, in shapeless white trousers and shirt, bare feet spread apart, arms this time folded imperiously.

He could see the figure clearly.

He broke through the dancers. "You there! Stop!"

But the boy was gone.

Then someone, whose touch was very cold and dry, whose grip was like a vise, took him by the hand and whirled him back into the dance.

He hissed, "Who *dares?*"

But the other merely bowed, with both arms spread wide, then straightened and stepped back, in a half-formed dance step. He discerned a slender lady in rotting funeral clothes, but that meant nothing on this night. Her mask was plain and featureless white, with mere round holes for eyes and mouth.

Now the rhythm of the dance changed. The music slowed and the circles broke apart. Dancers clung to one another, drifting off in pairs into doorways and alleys, beneath canopies, there to unmask.

The stranger led Kuthomes into the darkness beneath a broken bridge, far from the crowd, into silence. They stood on a ledge above the black water of a canal. The other lifted Kuthomes' mask off and made to throw it away, but he snatched it back and held it tightly against his chest. She twirled her own white mask out over the water, where it splashed, then drifted like a sparkle of reflected moonlight.

"Do you not remember me?" she said, speaking not Deltan but that language universal among the dead, yet known only to sorcerers among the living and never uttered aloud. Kuthomes could make out enough: " . . . your promise . . . long ago. Our assignation. Complete what you began."

He cried out. He couldn't break free of her arms. Her breath was foul. Her filthy hand pressed over his mouth.

When she let go, he managed to gasp, "Name yourself . . ."

"Remember poor Kamachina . . ."

Then she was gone. He heard a splash. The black water rippled. He stepped out of the shadow of the bridge, into the moonlight and stood still, amazed and afraid.

The absurd thing was he didn't know any Kamachina. It was a common female name in the Delta. There must have been hundreds of servants, daughters of minor nobility, whores, whoever. He searched his memory for a specific Kamachina. No, no one. He tried to laugh, to tell himself this was another, tastelessly misconceived joke, that even the dead could blunder.

But then he got the death-bell out of his pocket and held it on his palm. The bell still rang.

ON THE third and final night of the Festival of the Dead, those who had received special signs assembled in silence on the steps of the black temple of Surat-Hemad, who created the crocodile in his own image.

The temple doors formed the Devouring God's jaws. Bronze teeth gleamed by torchlight. Within the great hall, two red lanterns burning above the altar were the all-seeing eyes of Death. In the vaults beneath the altar, in the belly of Surat-Hemad, dead and living commingled freely, and the waters of dream, of *Leshé,* lapped against the shores of the living world those of the land of the dead. On this night, of all nights, the borders were freely crossed.

The doors swung wide. Twenty or so pilgrims entered.

Dark-clad, bearing the death-bell and his sword, but unmasked, Lord Kuthomes filed in with the others, circling thrice around the altar and the image of the squat-bellied, crocodile-headed Surat-Hemad, then descended into the deeper darkness of the vaults. He walked among stone sarcophagi containing the mummies of great or wicked men, who might return at any time they chose to inhabit such earthly forms.

He placed his hand on the carven effigy of some lord of centuries past. The mummy within stirred and scratched.

His mind was clear, though he had not rested after the second night. He had searched his books and gazed into his mirror for long hours, coming up with no revelation at all. He knew, then, that he could only confront the dead and allow them to speak. His fate, perhaps, was no longer in his own hands.

All things return to Surat-Hemad, so the prayer went.

Yes.

Still he could not remember a specific Kamachina. He didn't know who the boy was either. The child's significance, in particular, eluded him. He did not fit.

All things —

He had even consulted a true sorcerer, an ancient creature deformed and transformed by the magic within him, who walked in swaying jerks like a scarecrow come alive in the wind, whose head flicked constantly from side to side like a bird's, whose noseless face was a mass of scars, whose metal eyes clicked, whose hands were living fire. The sorcerer laughed slyly in a multitude of voices, and turned away.

A priest of Bel-Hemad had merely shaken his head sadly and said, "By the end of the third night, you shall know who this lady is. I am certain of that."

Kuthomes had offered a fantastic sum of money, enough to startle even the priest.

"What is this for?"

"Help me escape. There must be a way."

The priest had merely shrugged, and Kuthomes stalked away from the priest's house, muttering to himself, striking people and objects in blind rage, pacing back and forth to fill the hours until the sun set and the third night of the Festival of the Dead began. The waiting was the worst part.

Dread Surat-Hemad, may all things be completed and finished and laid to rest, the prayers went.

Lord Kuthomes did not often pray.

Now he walked among the tombs of the ancient, sorcerous dead, the carven, laughing corpse-face in his hand, the tiny bell in its throat tinkling. Like all the others, he followed the sputtering tapers held aloft by the masked priests of Death, until all had gathered in an open space before a vast doorway.

A priest touched a lever. Counterweights shifted somewhere.

Stone ground against stone, and the doors slid aside. Cold, damp air blew into the musty crypt, smelling of river mud and corruption.

Here was the actual threshold of the world of the dead.

Beyond this door, he knew, down a little slope, black water lapped silently. Funeral barges waited to carry the dead — and the living — into *Leshé*, where madmen, visionaries, and sorcerers might glimpse Lord Kuthomes passing through their dreams.

Kuthomes hoped they would know and remember whom they had seen.

At the threshold, the tiny death-bell stopped ringing.

Kuthomes threw it away, certain it was of no further use.

He reached under his robe and drew out the silver sword.

"You won't need that." A warm, living hand caught his wrist.

The voice was soft, but not feminine, speaking Deltan, accented very slightly. The boy.

Kuthomes slid the sword back into the scabbard. "Who are you?"

"One who will guide you to your trysting place. Lord Kuthomes, the Lady Kamachina awaits."

"Explain yourself, or die."

"If you kill me, you will never know the answer, will you?"

"There are slow methods, which inspire eloquence . . ."

"But hardly worth the exertion, Lord. Come with me, and all will be made clear."

Kuthomes hesitated. Slowly, the other pilgrims crossed the threshold. What could he do but follow? The boy was waiting.

Hand-in-hand, the two of them passed through the door and into absolute darkness, where not even the priests with their tapers dared accompany them. The only sound was the sucking of boots in the mud. The boy seemed to know where he was going.

Kuthomes allowed himself to be led. They groped their way into a barge and sat still, among many other wordless pilgrims.

Then they were adrift, and gradually stars appeared overhead, not those seen over the Delta on any summer night, but the stars of Deathlands, of *Tashé*.

He discerned crocodile-headed things in the river, thousands, floating along like a great mass of weed; but their bodies were pale and human, like naked, drowned men. These were the true messengers of Death, the *evatim*.

Someone in the company shrieked, stood up, and did a frantic, whirling dance, hands waving and slapping as if in an attempt to fend off invisible hornets. He fell into the river with a splash. The *evatim* hissed all as one, the sound like a rising wind.

Someone else began strumming a harp. A song arose from many voices, a gentle, desolate lyric in the language of the dead.

From out of the air, from far beyond the barge, more voices joined in.

Many wept. Kuthomes was unmoved, impatient, tensely alert.

The boy took his hand again, as if seeking or offering comfort. He couldn't tell which.

They were deep into Dream now, and the visions began. Some of the others cried out from sudden things Kuthomes could not see; but *he* was able to behold vast shapes in the sky, half human, half-beast, like clouds moving *behind* the stars, pausing in some incomprehensible journey to glance down at those in the barge below. These might have been the gods, or the Shadow Titans, from whom all sorcery flowed. Kuthomes had no idea. He did not choose to ask the masked boy beside him, who, he was certain, *did* know.

From *Leshé*, Dream, as they passed over into the realm of Death, the rest of the adventure was like a dream, inexplicable, without continuity.

Once it seemed that he and the boy sat alone on the barge.

The boy closed and opened his hands, and blue flames rose from his scarred palms. Kuthomes removed the boy's shabby mask, tossing it out among the *evatim*. By the blue light, he could see a very ordinary face, soft, beardless, with large, dark eyes; a man-child somewhere in the middle teens, with tangled, dark hair. Part of one of the boy's ears was missing. That struck Kuthomes as merely odd.

"Who *are* you?" he whispered in the language of the dead.

In that same tongue the boy replied, "A messenger."

"One of the *evatim* then?"

"What do you think?"

"You seem alive."

"Death, also, is a kind of life."

In another part of the dream they walked on water, barefoot because the river would not hold up Kuthomes as long as he wore boots. Ripples spread on the frigid surface. They walked through a dead marsh in wintertime. Among the reeds, skeletal, translucent birds waded on impossibly delicate legs.

Later still, the sky brightened into a dull, metallic gray, without a sunrise, but with enough suffused light that Kuthomes could see clearly. He and the boy walked for hours through sumptuous dust, until they both were covered with it. A wind rose. Swirling dust filled the air. By tricks of half-light and shadow, in the shifting dust, he seemed to make out buried rooftops, part of a city wall, a tower. But all these crumbled away when he touched them, then reformed again somewhere nearby.

Sometimes he saw faces on the ground before him, or in walls or doorways. He made his way through the narrow streets of a city of dust. The boy led him by the hand.

Here was the silently screaming dust-face of Lord Vormisehket, stung by a thousand scorpions; and here Adriuten Shomash with his throat still cut, sand pouring out of the nether mouth beneath his chin. Lady Nefiramé and her three children confronted him. She had hurled herself into a well with the children in her arms. So many more, faces and bodies sculpted out of transitory dust, forming and reforming as Kuthomes passed, dust-arms and hands reaching out for him, crumbling, reaching again.

He saw many who had been useful to him for a time, then inconvenient: Akhada the witch; Dakhumet the poisoner, who hurled tiny, darts fashioned like birds; even the former king himself, Baalshekthose, first and only ruler of that name, whose sudden ascent and descent both

Kuthomes had brought about.

The boy dragged him on, pulling at his arm, completely plastered with the gray dust so that only his eyes seemed alive.

Kuthomes felt indignant anger more than anything else. Why should these phantoms accuse him? Such deeds were the stuff of politics. Those who wielded power must be, by the nature of that power, above the common morality.

It was only when they came to a halt by a broken bridge over a dust-choked canal that Kuthomes recognized where he was. Here, in dreams and dust and ash, was a replica, shifting and inexact but a replica never-theless, of the City of the Delta, of a disreputable district where, many years before, he had promised to meet someone by that bridge.

In this place of dreams and death, amid the dust, the memory came back to him, clearly, like a book opening, its pages turning.

She was waiting for him, tall and slender in her dusty shroud. He knew her even before she spoke, before the caked dirt on her face cracked and fell away like a poorly-wrought mask to reveal empty eye-sockets and bare bones.

Her voice was gentle and sad and exactly as he remembered it. She spoke in the language of the dead.

"Kuthomes, my only love, I am your beloved, Kamachina, whom you once promised to marry and make great."

He could not resist her embrace, or her kiss, though both revolted him.

"I never knew what happened to you," he managed to say at last.

He had been seventeen, an upstart from outside the city, youngest of many sons, driven out of his village with few prospects, ridiculed by the great ones of the Delta, desperate for recognition, for a position of any sort. He had dallied with a girl, the daughter of a minor official. Already he was precocious in the ways of the court, though he had yet to set foot inside a palace. His lies had the desired effect, with hints of plots and of suppressed factions soon to rise again; with the implication that Ku-thomes was not who he seemed at all, but perhaps a prince in disguise, whose true name would make the mighty tremble. With this and more he secured introductions, a position. In exchange for the favor of the girl Kamachina, he promised to make her family great.

Later, when she pressed her claim and became inconvenient, he put her off, all the while whispering that she and her father were both mad,

obsessed with absurd plots. At the very end, there had been the assignation at the bridge. The two of them would exchange marriage vows but
keep them secret until the time was right for the revelation.

"But you never came," she said. On that final, sacred night of the Festival of the Dead, when uttered vows are binding forever, he had betrayed her, and, in her grief, she had flung herself into the canal and
drowned.

"I truly loved you," she said. "You were my every, my only hope."

"I . . . did not know."

"I was great with your child. Did you know that?"

"I . . . had not seen you in several months."

"I could hardly confess such a thing in a letter."

"Someone might have intercepted it," he said.

She dragged him to his knees, then lay by his side in the cold dust.

At last he broke free, stood up, and brushed himself off.

"But all this was almost *forty years ago*. How can it matter now?"

She reached up and took him by the hand. "Among the dead, time
moves much more slowly."

He looked around for the boy and saw him crouching nearby in the
dust, hands folded over his knees, watching dispassionately.

"Is that your son?"

"I have no son," said Kamachina, reaching up for Kuthomes.

"My child is still within me, waiting to be born." Once more she
dragged him down into her irresistible embrace, pressing her corpse-
mouth against his.

Kuthomes screamed. He fought her, drawing his silver sword, striking
her again and again, slashing her head off, hacking her body to pieces.

But it was no use. She merely reconstituted herself, a thing of dust
and dead bones, sculpted by some magical wind.

She caught his wrist in her crushing grip and made him throw the
sword away.

"I'm sorry," he said. "I did what I had to do. I didn't know . . . If I
could help you, I would, but it's too late . . ."

"What is begun on the last night of the Festival of the Dead," she said,
embracing him once more, "is sacred, inviolate, and must always be con-
summated."

$$\star \qquad \star \qquad \star$$

SO IT was that Lord Kuthomes came to dwell in the country of the dead with his Lady Kamachina. He was mad with the terror of it all for a long time. It seemed that he sat on a throne, and ruled as emperor among the corpses, but slowly, subtly, they turned from him, perverting his every command, until at last he was cast down, reviled, trampled into filth. He shouted that he was a great lord, that he was *alive* and they mere corpses, but they only laughed at him.

Dead hands tore his entrails out of his body, lifted his bleeding heart up before his face; dead lips drank his blood and devoured him. So it seemed, in his madness, though each time he awoke, he found himself whole.

He tried to bear all this in the manner of a great lord, silently plotting his revenge, but that was absurd, and before long he too was shrieking aloud at the hilarity of the idea.

"How shall I be revenged against myself?" he asked the ghosts. "How?"

They could not answer him.

All the while Kamachina was with him, touching him gently, whispering of her love. She alone did not mock him, nor injure him in any way, but her love was the worst torment of all.

In his madness his mind opened up. The speech of gods and of the Titans poured into him. There were many revelations, passed through Kuthomes into the dreams of men who awoke in the living world.

Gradually his pain and his madness lessened, and it seemed he had merely backtracked along a path he had once taken, then set out on another. His old life became the dream, the fading memory. Now he came to see himself dwelling, not in dust, but in an austere palace of massive pillars and black stone, there waited upon by ghosts, while his wife's belly swelled with his child.

"Is it not the duty of a lord," she said, "to provide for the comfort of those beneath him?"

He supposed it was. He didn't know anymore.

He sat with her in her garden of leafless trees and brittle stalks, listening as she spoke or sang softly in the language of the dead. He learned to play a strange harp made of bones as delicate as strands of silk. He came to behold the growing life in that dead garden, the nearly invisible leaves and blossoms like sculpted smoke, and he ate of the fruits of the trees, which tasted like empty air, and was sustained by them. After a while, he could recall no other taste.

She was delivered there, in the garden. The mysterious boy appeared once more, to assist the birthing.

"Who *are* you?" Kuthomes asked. "Can you not tell me at last?"

"I am the sorcerer Sekenre," the boy said.

"But, but, one so young —"

"For sorcerers too, as for the dead, time moves differently. I was fifteen when my father caused me to slay him, filling me with his spirit, and the spirits of all his victims, and the victims of his victims, all united in one, who must sometimes struggle to remember that he was once a boy called Sekenre. My voices are like a flock of birds. We are many. But for three hundred years and more, my body has not aged. I have learned and forgotten many things, as you, Kuthomes, have learned and forgotten."

"I too have a hard time remembering who I am sometimes," said Kuthomes. "We are alike."

"You are the loving father of this child." The boy Sekenre reached into Lady Kamachina's dead womb and lifted an infant girl out in his hands. Kuthomes thought his daughter looked more like a delicate carving than a child: skin translucently white, eyes open and unblinking, the expression severe.

Sekenre passed the baby to Kuthomes, who rested it in his lap.

"The world shall fear this one," Sekenre said, "but not for any evil in her. She is a mirror of the evil in others. In a hundred years' time I shall need her as my ally, against an enemy yet unborn."

"Therefore you have directed all these things, my entire life, to your own purposes."

"Yes, I have," said Sekenre.

Kuthomes shrugged. "I suppose one has to do such things." He felt, vaguely, that he should be angry, but there was no passion left in him.

Kamachina smiled and took the child from him.

Ghosts gathered around them, whispering like a faint wind.

ON THE last night of the Festival of the Dead, Lord Kuthomes emerged from the vaults beneath the temple of Surat-Hemad in the City of the Delta. He had grown very old. His once tall, vigorous figure was bent, his silver beard now purest white. No one knew him, or the bone-pale girl he led into the world.

His daughter clung to his arm, her eyes dazzled even by the gloom of the inside of the temple; amazed at everything she saw, whispering to him, for comfort, then out of excitement, chattering softly in the language of the dead. The grave-wrappings she wore had partially fallen away, revealing almost transparent skin. She seemed more to float on the air than to walk.

Outside, she had to cover her face from the starlight.

Kuthomes found a discarded mask for her.

They walked through streets he remembered now only from his dreams. She had so many questions he could not answer. He took her tiny hand in his and led her to a place he had dreamed, where a certain magician was waiting. This man would nurture her for five years before an enemy killed him, bore her off, and came to regret the prize.

But these things were Sekenre's business.

Kuthomes departed without even bidding his daughter farewell, then hurried back to the temple of Surat-Hemad, and descended into the vaults, so that what had been begun on the last night of the Festival of the Dead could at last be finished.

THE SORCERER'S GIFT

LADY HANSHERAT was already a phantom dwelling among ancient tombs, already dead in her own mind and in the minds of all who had ever known her, certainly mad when she came to possess her "child."

Her story is familiar. The tragedy based on her life, *The Fatal Stroke*, first performed at the court of Angzerab IV, will live long in memory.

Everyone knows how Hansherat's young husband, Valpetor, was murdered by certain great lords of the Delta, by hawk-faced Andraxes, silent Belphage, and mocking Ruaine; how his body was burned in secret without any rites, so that his soul was trapped in *Leshé,* the twilight borderland between dreaming and true death, whence it returned each night into Lady Hansherat's bedroom to shriek its despair.

But the murderers underestimated her. Somehow, steady-handed as any sorceress, she captured Valpetor's soul in a glass bottle, shaped the bottle in fire, and the slain husband seemed returned to life, to confound his enemies. How they scattered!

Thus Hansherat and Valpetor were restored to the Great King's favor, rising higher than before in his service, the Lady waxing ever more proud, always quick to remind Valpetor that he had *her* to thank for his rescue, until one day she forgot herself and struck her husband across the face with her fan in the midst of some trifling quarrel. The glass broke and his soul escaped, howling into the rafters and dark corners of the palace, from which it could only be exorcised, never recovered.

And Lady Hansherat, her clothing rent with grief, all hope and fortune lost, appeared one last time before the Great King, declining to kneel, merely saying, "When my son is at my side, I shall come again to this place." She did not know why she said this. The words seemed to be whispered into her mind by another and she repeated them, without any volition of her own.

Of course she had no son. Andraxes, Belphage, and Ruaine, now returned from exile, ridiculed her, saying, "Let the headsman clean this trash away, if he will deign to soil his axe with it."

"Because she is mad, she cannot be harmed," said the Great King. "That is the law."

Hansherat smiled at her enemies, perhaps slyly, then departed, "like a star fading at dawn," and there the poet ends his tragedy, the prophecy unfulfilled, an inexplicable mystery.

But that is not the end. Listen. There is more:

Hansherat wandered south. Soon she became a familiar figure glimpsed at the Great River's edge in the evening, her fantastically colored tatters trailing behind her. She spoke with spirits. She kept the company of ghosts among the reeds. She appeared many times in the dreams of the dying.

And she often knelt in the shallow water, or on the muddy bank, calling on Shedelvendra, the forgiving goddess, but also addressing certain other powers, even the dread Shadow Titans whom the gods themselves fear. In the night, she thought she saw the starry sky ripple like sea foam and part, revealing a deeper blackness within which the faces of the Titans slowly appeared. Perhaps it was merely her madness. Perhaps, too, she actually saw them.

More often, in her own dreams, she beheld the broken glass face of her husband and heard his soul howling like the wind in a ruined tower; and again the hawk-visaged Andraxes, the silent, cruel Belphage, and the mocking Ruaine returned to torment her.

"Where is your son?" they would ask. "Your son. Your son. Where?"

She would wake up screaming.

At last she came to that many-named place beyond the river's Great Bend, where the water runs straight again, and only rough grass and thorns hold the desert back from the very banks. There she took shelter among the ruined tombs of forgotten dynasties, in the company of ghosts, stone kings, and carvings of fabulous beasts. Offerings from river travellers sustained her. She learned to wade out as far as she could go, shouting praise or prophecies or even curses at passing vessels, then gather the baskets left floating behind. She became a kind of oracle, described in guidebooks, the subject of many stories, though few knew that this was Lady Hansherat, who had once been such a power in the court of the Delta.

Sometimes the gods truly spoke through her.

So she lingered, alone with her sorrows and memories, searching her dreams for her husband's soul, and for some trace of that son whose advent she had inexplicably foretold.

★   ★   ★

ONE NIGHT a cold hand touched her on the shoulder.

She shrugged, taking it for another dream, or a draught from some

deep vault, and merely pulled her tattered garments more tightly around herself.

"Come," said a voice like the wind and sand whispering together. "Rise up."

She rose and followed what might have been a black vapor or an animate bundle of sticks and rags out into the desert, beneath a moonless sky. Possibly her guide wore an almost featureless mask cut out of black paper. She couldn't tell. The stars revealed nothing.

At last the hand touched her once more and the voice said, "Dig here."

She squatted down and dug with both hands, burrowing like an animal until her bony fingers clutched a marble casket so small she could lift it up in the palm of one hand.

"Your son awaits beyond this small door."

She thought she understood. What had been just one more dream suddenly became desperately, immediately urgent. Trembling, she unlatched the lid and dumped out into her other hand what felt like a dried, gnarled root.

She looked up at her guide, bewildered and angry, but at that very instant, in the first light of dawn, her husband appeared to her as he had been in life. Yet there was no pain in his expression, only a resigned sadness, as if he were now, somehow, at peace.

Then the sunlight shone through him and he vanished. Weeping, Hansherat cradled the shrivelled thing in her hands. Her tears fell on what might have been a tiny face. To her astonishment, two eyes opened, then a mouth.

"Help me," the thing said.

THAT DAY, among the tombs, her madness receded somewhat. She worked with deliberation, even cunning, as she drew from her stores a small flask of wine and poured out a few drops in libation to Shedelvendra and also to the righteous Nine Gods. But she also cut her finger with a sharp stone and offered her blood to the Titans. Then she dipped her bleeding finger into the wine and touched both blood and wine to the object cupped in her other hand.

That afternoon, she left it resting in the box while she searched for fish among the shallows. When she returned, the box was tipped over and the slowly writhing thing lay on the sand beside it, too large to fit back inside.

She picked it up and tried to nurse it at her breast, but she had no milk.

Each night, free of dreams now, her mind clear, her thoughts on the present and the immediate future. She tended her charge, easing wine or bits of meat or breadcrumbs between the tiny, cracked lips.

It was no infant, she understood soon enough. By the light of the waxing moon, delicate limbs rapidly lengthened, but remained skeletal, gnarled, like sticks of driftwood, the skin rough and hard to the touch, like ancient, cracked leather. It reminded her of an insect breaking painfully out of a chrysalis.

She measured its progress and made her plans.

But in the light of the full moon, the skin was smooth and the joints supple, and the face, at least, had filled out. *It* had become *he.*

She laid the boy out on a stone slab, regarding him.

He stared up at the sky, naked, shivering in the night breeze.

"Are you really my *son?* Truly?" She touched him gently on the forehead, then ran her finger over a white mark there, like a burn scar.

If only he could be her son, then, through him, something of Valpetor might live again.

He rose on his elbows, his back arched, rigid as he spoke in many voices, in many languages, addressing invisible presences in the air. She feared to listen, but she did listen, ever attentive as he called out Balredon and Talno and Lekkanut-Na and many other names, as many spirits seemed to contest the mastery of this single, small body.

"No, no," she said at last, shaking him. "Speak to *me.* Tell me who you are."

The fit passed. He lay still again, then clung to her hand with surprising strength. She eased him off the stone, onto the warmer sand. There they huddled throughout the night, while he sometimes wept, sometimes shouted in anger, and still spoke only to the unseen others.

At times, she was certain, voices replied out of the darkness.

But in the dawn's light he curled on his side and slept with his head in her lap. She could see him clearly now, narrow-shouldered and slender, paler than most people of the Delta, emaciated, every rib showing. He had a round, soft face. A tear streaked the dirt on his cheek. His age she guessed to be somewhere between twelve and fifteen.

She couldn't be sure. She wondered if he were a child at all, or some other being, in the form of one. Again, she was desperately afraid that all had been for nothing, that he was one more ghost among so many. He shouldn't have been alive, criss-crossed as he was by scars betokening wounds no one should have been able to survive, as if he had been torn apart by beasts and pierced through the body with spears. Part of his right ear was gone too. That, she thought wryly, reminded her of a tomcat who had been in one fight too many.

But he lay calmly in her lap, warm to the touch. He turned in his sleep, mumbling something.

She shook him awake. He opened his seemingly huge, dark eyes. She reached down to touch his chin. He struggled free of her and lay gasping from the effort, peering up at her inscrutably.

"I won't hurt you," she said.

He sat, and drew his legs up, trying to cover his nakedness. She noted, intrigued, that he was blushing.

"Give me something to wear," he said, speaking her own language, that of the Delta, but with a distinct upriver accent.

She had only her own rags, but offered him some of those. He did what little he could, then moved further away and sat still, hugging his shoulders, staring at her.

She couldn't meet his gaze for long. She shook her head and blinked.

"Shall I . . . name you?" she said, carefully focusing her eyes, not on his face, but on his knees. He looked so frail. His thighs were scarcely thicker than his calves.

"I already have a name."

"A name can be a powerful thing," she said. "Is it your soul's true name, or just a name?"

"I am called Sekenre."

"Which name is that?"

He shrugged, his expression seeming to say that none of this mattered. He seemed very young then, a genuine child. Then his face went slack and he seemed about to faint. She took him into her lap once more and folded her arms around him, rocking slowly back and forth.

Again he slept. Again she woke him.

She weighed her words very carefully.

"Sekenre, where did you come from?"

"From out of a dream inside another dream dreamt within a third. I am not sure where the dreaming stops."

She took one of his hands between both of hers, spreading his delicate fingers apart. The palm was seared a pale white.

"You've stopped dreaming, Sekenre. This is the waking world now." She squeezed his hand until he winced.

He made no reply, but drew away from her, sat up once more, then folded his hands together. When he opened them, blue flames flickered from his palms.

"Ah," she said, certain she had been afforded some profound insight, if only her thoughts could quite encompass it. It was like a distant mountain glimpsed through fog.

He closed his hands and the flames vanished.

"Sekenre," she said, once more considering every word with painstaking deliberation before speaking it. "I helped you this far, and I shall help you further. Will you, in return, help me?"

He affixed her with that almost hypnotic, wide-eyed stare, but with true child-like seriousness said, "Yes. I promise."

He opened his hands, revealing only scarred palms. Then he tried to stand up, but his legs wouldn't support him and she had to catch him before he fell.

So they lingered three more days and nights among the tombs. She fed him from her meager stores. Once she went off to the river to prophesy, and when she returned she found him writing something with his finger in the sand. At her approach, he quickly erased what he had written. She didn't ask about it. She knew how to wait. During those days and nights he told her scraps of stories about a childhood in the City of Reeds, upriver, as his accent suggested. It wasn't a happy beginning: a mother murdered early in his life, a father who deteriorated terrifyingly into a lunatic sorcerer who still claimed he loved his son while the house shook with thunder and corpses wandered the halls at night. But there were quiet moments too, games, mysteries, explorations among the forest of pilings that held up the city; even what must have been moments of fumbling, boyish comedy, the occasional prank.

But at times Sekenre seemed to confuse his own life with others, with other times and places. Sometimes he lapsed into foreign languages.

But she never contradicted him, never questioned deeper. He gained strength quickly, almost by the hour.

On the third night, he slept huddled against her side for warmth, while she lay awake. She fancied that Andraxes, Belphage, and Ruaine sat nearby, playing a game with ivory pieces on a painted board.

They looked at her in sudden alarm.

"You! You are dead!" they said in unison.

"I am returned," she said, laughing, and her laughter was a mighty wind, upsetting the board, scattering the pieces, swirling her enemies away like dry leaves.

She awoke suddenly and realized she had been dreaming after all. She slid her arm over Sekenre's bony shoulders, running her fingers gently through his tangled hair. She was certain that *he* had sent her that dream. Yes, she was certain now, he was her own son, begotten on her by the ghost of Valpetor.

He was her treasured, secretly guarded instrument of vengeance.

IN THE morning, the two of them went to the river to bathe, made offerings to the benevolent gods, and began their journey north, following the river, resting every couple of hours because the boy still needed it. He collapsed at midday, prostrated by the sun. She carried him in her arms to the shelter of a grove of palm trees, finding him surprisingly light. She too was a stick-figure from her privations, but iron hard, she decided, made of metal rods. He was a thing of reeds.

So they rested again until sunset. He seemed content to listen while she told him of the royal court in the Delta, of the ceremonies and banquets there, the great spectacles performed before the gods, of the king and queen and their palace filled with riches, and of the splendid company who dwelt with them there.

She left out quite a lot, making no mention of her husband's murder, her own disgrace, of her three foes. As she listened to herself talk, her own account seemed far more fantastic and fragmentary than his, but he did not contradict her, nor question her any deeper.

They walked a mile or so further in the cool evening, then sat down, ate of their meager stores, and slept. She dreamed only of his wide, dark eyes, staring at her.

In the morning twilight, they rose and walked only a short distance to a walled town. The last stars were fading from the sky. Watchlights still burned over the barred gate. As the two of them approached, a guard shouted for them to go away, saying no beggars were welcome here. Caravaneers, encamped around the gate waiting for admission, stirred.

Sekenre made fire with his hands and held it aloft. The gate opened, whether of its own accord or because the warders feared him, Hansherat could not be sure. Like everyone else, the guards, the caravaneers, sleepy-eyed townspeople, she merely followed the bluish white flame and the nearly naked, sunburnt boy who carried it through winding streets, beneath archways and leaning houses that nearly touched overhead, shutting out the sky, until they emerged into the central square of the town. There Sekenre dropped on his knees before an image of the god Bel-Hemad, the Lord of Spring and Rain and the Master of Sparrows.

Sekenre heaved the flame into the air, where it vanished with an audible pop, then turned and sat cross-legged at the god's feet, drawing strange signs in the dirt.

Quickly Hansherat elbowed her way through the crowd and stood over Sekenre, announcing that he would prophesy, holding out her cupped hands for coins.

A priest arrived, but said nothing. A whole company of elders with long silvery beards and ankle-length red robes stood between Sekenre and the crowd, to witness while the boy divined the futures of many citizens, and foretold strange things to come. All the while Hansherat could only think of her enemies, of Andraxes, slack-faced with terror, Belphage whimpering aloud with fright, and Ruaine, mocking no more.

Yes, she would help Sekenre and he would help her. Mother and son they were, and the firmest of allies.

The elders argued among themselves in urgent whispers. The priest made a sign, both as a blessing and to ward off evil.

HANSHERAT AND Sekenre sat side by side in the upper room of an inn. Two lamps, dangling from the ceiling, swayed slightly, sending shadows drifting. Moonlight shone through the carven screen set in the room's only window. A gentle breeze blew. Hansherat listened to the sounds from the town below: voices, a cart rumbling, horses' hooves clopping on stone, an angry camel braying; unchanging, commonplace things, reminding her of the old life she had once lost and now hoped to regain.

She wore soft leather shoes and a plain dark robe, clean and comfortable. For now, she could imagine nothing better. Fine gowns and jewels, even crowns would come later.

Someone had given Sekenre baggy white trousers which had to be cut off at his ankles so he wouldn't trip over them, and an ornately embroidered silk tunic, also much too large, dropping down below his knees. He could hide his hands in the billowing sleeves or wear them rolled up. He seemed unduly fascinated by the design: birds and flowers and serpents intertwined on a black background. Hansherat wondered if there was something in it she couldn't see, some hidden, magical symbol.

She regarded him as he sat there fingering the silk, oblivious to her, his grubby feet dangling where he couldn't quite reach the floor. She still could not fathom the mystery of him. He seemed both an ordinary young man — closer to middle teens she decided, just very short and thin — and completely inexplicable. He was her son. She was certain of that. She clung to that like a drowning woman clutching a floating log. But he had come out of a marble box two inches square. The ghost of Valpetor begot him, but he seemed to remember different origins, a Reedlandish childhood in some detail, and fragments of others. At times, she thought, he was still that shrivelled thing she had found, hard and dry and very, very ancient.

"Sekenre," she said. "What are you, really?"

His stomach rumbled loud enough for Hansherat to hear.

He shrugged and said, "What you see."

"What *can* I see? Only the surface. But inside, are you divine? Can you truly prophesy?"

He stared at her, his face expressionless. "Can you?"

After a moment of silent confusion, she spoke to him again with painstaking deliberation, studying him for any reaction.

"I think my powers of prophecy, such as I ever had, have left me now. The gods no longer find a voice in Hansherat."

Because Hansherat is no longer mad, she added silently, because Hansherat has recovered direction and a goal, because the gods speak through those who are lost, whose minds achieve the same randomness of clouds, or birds in flight, or the delicate contours of wind-shaped sand, from which, likewise, much can be divined.

That brought her one more moment of despair: what if Sekenre were merely insane, divinely insane perhaps, but still useless?

But he smiled at her, and his smile wasn't that of a mischievous child at all so much as that of an old and practiced rogue.

"I was just doing tricks. We needed the money, don't you think?"

"But you *are* magical." That was not a question. It was more of a demand.

He shrugged again, once more assuming that off-putting aspect of a genuine child.

She got out the marble box and flipped it open, holding its emptiness up to him. "Remember?"

He reached over and closed the box, his movements now assured, even authoritative, as if, as quickly as that, he had become a different person. He pointed a finger at her as if he were the adult giving correction.

"Do not try to understand me," he said. "Merely trust and hope and be certain that I shall serve you as you have served me."

"Trust and hope," she said softly.

"And be certain." He paused, listening for something she could not hear. "Your faith may be tested . . ." Again he paused, listening. She heard only the town noises, coming in through the window. ". . . far sooner . . ." There. Yes. She heard it too. A footstep shuffling in the corridor outside. ". . . than I had expected."

The door to the room opened and a serving girl came in with a tray, which she set down on a small table in the far corner, then carried both table and tray over to where Hansherat and Sekenre sat.

"Your dinner, compliments of the master of this house," she said, bowing slightly, "who is honored beyond words by your holy presence here, Sir." She nodded slightly to Sekenre and curtseyed to Hansherat.

Lamplight revealed cups of wine and two fine meals. Hansherat realized with discomfort how long it had been since she had eaten anything like that.

"I thank you," she said to the servant, "and your master too."

Too hungry to wait any longer, she took a candied plum on her fork.

But Sekenre merely said, "Girl, come here. There is something I must tell you."

Holding the plum, Hansherat watched as the servant leaned down to hear what Sekenre would whisper into her ear.

With a sudden, violent motion, Sekenre grabbed the girl by the hair and yanked her down into his lap, while snatching a knife from the table. He cut off her head with a single stroke. Hansherat screamed. She froze in amazement at the sight of the girl's headless body, which did not fall, but righted itself, and stood before the table, swaying in a slow circle.

There was no blood.

Sekenre held up the still living head. Its eyes rolled up until only the whites were visible. The mouth muttered something unintelligible, but definitely spoke.

Now Sekenre addressed his captive as Hansherat had never heard him speak before, his voice breaking, like a boy imitating a giant, his thin chest unable to sound the thunderous tones, but the manner, the diction, the accent were *not* those of Sekenre at all, but of another speaking through him.

"So you have discovered my stratagem. My hiding place is found out. I had thought to attack. Now I am to defend. So be it. I am not afraid."

He breathed into the girl-thing's face and it blackened, smoked, and shrivelled, like a ball of crumpled paper at the edge of a fire. He threw it across the room, then stood up, reached around the back of the still standing body and snatched out a red, beating heart.

He held it up to Hansherat, still speaking in that harsh, fierce way. "This alone of her is alive. The rest is a construct, a fabrication, as you see, hollow behind, its flesh only covering front and sides, filled with air. When the *heart* dies —" He stabbed it with the knife. The heart exploded, splattering both of them with blood.

Then he dropped the knife and sat down. He seemed like an awkward boy again, unsure of what to do now that he'd made such an obvious mess and soiled his new, silken tunic.

The serving girl's body collapsed in on itself like melting wax.

"Well, you see what happens," Sekenre said in his familiar, soft voice.

Hansherat put down her fork even before she noticed that the plum was now offal and most of what she could recognize on the plate was mud and sawdust.

Suddenly, the two lamps dangling from the ceiling twisted wildly on their chains as if the room were filled with a whirlwind. But she felt no wind. Shadows flickered crazily. The wooden screen in the window rattled.

By moonlight she watched in horrified fascination as Sekenre stripped off tunic and trousers, neatly folded them under the bed, and began to trace intricate patterns on himself with the girl-creature's blood.

The air became so cold her breath, and his, came in white puffs. She could tell he was shivering and sweating at the same time. Still he worked steadily, covering himself with designs she could not make out. Then he made a circle in blood on the floor and wrote something around its rim, what might have been a single, long word in looping script which joined back into itself.

He made fire with his hands and touched the circle. The unbroken script glowed a brilliant white. The light spread up his arms, until the traceries that covered him glowed faintly blue, like luminous tattoos. The room grew ever colder. His whole body shook violently. His breath sounded hoarse, labored.

"Sekenre?"

He looked up at her.

"Sekenre, please tell me what is going on."

"My enemies have found me sooner than I thought they would. I can't explain now —"

"But later —?"

"Later. If I win."

Hansherat's first impulse was simply to run away, to get out of that room and forget about Sekenre and the Delta and the king and even Valpetor's ghost, and run screaming into the night, back to her tombs and madness and prophecies.

But she could not desert her son. Sekenre was her son, somehow, inexplicably. She stayed where she was, hugging her knees.

The two lamps went out, one after another, as if smothered by an invisible hand. The "wind" stopped. The lamps hung straight down on their chains, motionless.

Sekenre stood up in the bitterly cold air. Faint vapor rose from his skin. Delicate patterns of blue fire outlined his face, his front, sides, arms and legs; but he hadn't been able to reach his back, so he, like the serving girl, seemed hollow behind.

The circle on the floor burst into flames, roaring, but still giving off no heat at all.

"They're coming," said Sekenre. He shoved the table to the far side of the room. Dishes and cups clattered. Hansherat drew back onto the bed, her back against the wall, watching as a pair of eyes like deep red embers rose into the air within the burning circle and a dark form slowly took shape, something like an old, hideous man who was half insect. His shoulders gleamed, black and smooth as metal. Countless hairy, spiked limbs wriggled out of his belly. His pale face sagged to one side, like a mask of dead flesh clumsily stretched over something it would never fit. Only his arms, his bare blue-veined legs, and his narrow buttocks were completely human.

Sekenre paced around the circle, always keeping his back away from it. The thing turned to follow. Something else formed next to it, a horse-headed man, muscular, naked, covered like Sekenre with swirls and strange patterns, but set into his skin with red-hot bits of metal. Hansherat could feel the heat of them and smell the horse-man's searing flesh.

Still Sekenre paced. The two followed him, around and around. A third foe appeared, standing between the other two, a male dwarf no more than two feet high, either clad in or covered with feathers, his huge eyes aglow with reflected light. A human owl, Hansherat thought.

"Now is the time for Sekenre to truly die," said the owl-man. "Now shall Balredon and Talno and Lekkanut-Na and Tannivar pour out their secrets. Now shall even Vashtem be summoned into endless torment."

"Now," said the horse-man.

"Now," said the insect.

Still Sekenre paced in silence. The apparitions turned, angrily. The insect-thing noticed Hansherat on the bed and chittered.

"We'll devour Sekenre's wench."

"When we are done with her, yes," said the horse-man.

"Tear her apart while still she lives," said the dwarf.

The horse-headed one roared in a voice like raging thunder, shaking the room, deafening Hansherat, the force knocking her back against the wall hard, nearly squeezing the breath out of her. What followed was confusing. One moment Sekenre stood between her and the bed and the monster roared. Then she could not see him. She sat up groggily, *on the floor,* and drew her hand back in sudden terror from where she had almost smeared the scripted word at the circle's edge. That, she was certain, would have been fatal to them both.

"Help me," Sekenre gasped. She saw him now, on the floor, wrestling in the coils of what might have been an invisible serpent.

"What can I do?"

"Go to the window! Open it! Go!"

Hansherat lurched to her feet just as the horse-headed one roared again, sending her tumbling, away from the circle this time. Her head slammed into the wall below the window. She sat up, dazed, dimly aware of blood streaming from her nose and ears. She tried to rise, but got no further than her knees. The intricately-carven wooden screen still filled the window, but the light streaming through was blinding, as if the window looked out into the heart of the sun.

She closed her eyes as hard as she could, turned her face away, and fumbled for the screen, swimming in light and terrible heat, screaming in her own agony.

The screen came away in her hands. Fire poured into the room, washing over her. She had the brief impression of living flame, fiery birds, monsters without any shape she could define, and, at the end, an enormous face, the face of a god, gazing up at her from somewhere far below, from some universe of infinite fire.

And then, darkness. For the longest time she sat with her back to the wall, eyes too dazzled to make out anything but drifting splotches of light. Her ears rang. But there was no other pain. She wasn't burnt. The air was cold again.

Then some of those light-splotches moved. It was Sekenre. The blue light of his body markings drifted like clouds of fireflies. But the circle on the floor flickered with reassuring steadiness, its heatless flames no more than an inch high, like hundreds of tiny candles. A blackened horse's head lay smoldering in the center of it.

"Sekenre?" she whispered. "Is it over?"

He made no reply, but began pacing around the circle again, his bare feet padding, the floorboards creaking.

"Sekenre?"

She groped along the wall, keeping well clear of him and the circle, seeking the darkness and comfort of the bed once more. Her hand found a wooden leg. She hauled herself up. The room swayed around her. Sekenre was chanting or reciting something she couldn't make out. She let herself fall face-down onto the bed.

But its surface was alive, cold and greasy, heaving. Her right hand was inside a *mouth*, which closed on her like a vise, crushing her wrist. Another set of teeth fastened onto her chin, grinding from side to side. She felt a shock of pain as what might have been a clawed hand tore her robe from her shoulders.

She wriggled her face free and screamed. The second mouth had her by the hair now. She tried to pull her hand free. The whole mass oozed onto the floor, dragging her with it.

Then Sekenre was standing above her, commanding the thing into the circle. It released her, drifted like a cloud across the burning letters without smearing them, then sank down through the floorboards like a crocodile into river mud.

He helped her up. She stood unsteadily, vaguely aware that the whole back of her robe was sticky with blood, that she might be badly hurt, even dying. But Sekenre merely said, "Go back to the window and tell me what you see."

She staggered, caught hold of the windowsill, and leaned out, blinking. There didn't seem to be any town below, only the night sky, above and below both, filled with an infinity of stars. That was impossible, she tried to convince herself. But she saw. She lost all sense of up and down and felt sick, as if she were falling.

"Just stars," she said weakly. "Just stars."

"Good. Stay there."

So she clung to the windowsill for what seemed like hours, peering out into the firmament of heaven, while behind her Sekenre recited something very slowly, pausing for the count of four or five after every word. Once she glanced back over her shoulder and saw him tracing fiery symbols in the air with his finger.

And again, someone was in the room with them, a woman dressed in scarlet, holding a lantern and a sword. Then a clap of thunder. Then something hunched and massive like a lion with serpentine arms flailing, cracking in the air like whips. It reached out of the burning circle and caught Sekenre across the bare back, whirling him around, another limb sweeping his feet from beneath him. He fell, struggling as the monster dragged him toward itself.

She cried out, but he shouted, "Stay where you are!" and in another instant the lion-thing was gone.

She saw the stars ripple like luminous foam. She turned back into the room to tell Sekenre, but instead watched him confront a naked black man covered from head to foot in glowing symbols. Sekenre's own markings, she saw, were damaged, many of them smeared or gone altogether. The rest seemed to give off less light than before.

But she could only watch helplessly as the black man reached for Sekenre and Sekenre reached for the black man, neither touching the other, as if, Hansherat thought, there were an invisible barrier between them with equally invisible holes in it, and the winner was the one who found the way through first.

Sekenre found it, wiping the black man's chest clear, then reaching up and ripping out his throat with a single, violent jerk. Once more, blood sprayed over the walls and ceiling. The black man vanished.

And again, a bald, fat man in an iridescent blue robe sat cross-legged in the middle of the circle, writing on a tablet in his lap with a quill. Sekenre also had a tablet and pen. The fat man held up what he had written. Sekenre gasped, as if struck a heavy blow. The fat man grinned. Then Sekenre held up his tablet, and the other scowled, drawing back in fear. He scribbled some more, but before he had finished gave up, cast his tablet aside, screamed, and vanished, darkness closing over him like the cover of a book suddenly snapped shut.

It went on for hours, Sekenre's enemies appearing in countless forms, sometimes vanishing again too quickly for Hansherat's eyes to follow. Sometimes she wasn't sure it was Sekenre who fought them. His form, too, flickered into something else. More often he spoke to recited or cried out in voices she didn't know, in strange languages.

Fascinated, she watched, clinging to the windowsill, the view beyond the window forgotten, while frigid wind blew in over her.

"Look!" Sekenre shouted at last. "Look out again! What do you see?"

She screamed at what she saw, and her mind could not grasp, nor could her words describe as the rippling tapestry of stars tore apart like a curtain, the very heavens trailing in streamers against a greater darkness, and out of that darkness the Shadow Titans appeared, equal and opposite to the gods, whom even the gods feared. They opened their eyes and beheld her spying on them. They opened their mouths to devour her with their speech. She fainted.

"YOU HAVE won, Sekenre. It's finally over."

Hansherat sat up in the darkness, leaning painfully against the wall beneath the window. It seemed that someone else spoke, not her.

"It's safe now. You may erase the circle."

The voice sounded so familiar.

Hansherat shook her head, forcing herself awake. She saw Sekenre on his knees before the circle, his back to her. He didn't seem to be in any ritual position, but, instead, too weak to stand. She could see the dark gouge across his back where the lion-creature had struck him. He was covered with blood. Very few of his protective markings remained.

Inside the burning circle stood a perfect replica of herself, a false Hansherat, duplicated down to the torn, bloody robe and lacerated shoulders.

"You are my son," this other Hansherat said. "I am your mother.

Come to me now."

Sekenre lurched unsteadily. "My mother died," he said. "A long time ago."

"No, I am your mother. You are my son. Come." The false Hansherat held out a hand.

And he reached for it. "I want to stop," he said, sobbing. "I just want to stop."

"No! Sekenre! No!" Lady Hansherat screamed.

Sekenre turned, that lost-little-boy expression on his face. He held a long copper knife in his hand.

"Behold your final enemy!" said the thing within the circle, pointing at Lady Hansherat. "Kill it and you'll be finished. Don't you see? That's the only one left."

Sekenre crawled toward the window, the knife scraping the floor, his eyes wide, staring.

"No, Sekenre!"

He didn't seem to hear her. The apparition in the circle laughed. He was almost in reach when Hansherat found the strength to heave herself to her feet, easily evading the clumsy swing of his knife. The boy rose to his knees, trying to stand, turned to follow her, but fell over on his back with a yelp of pain as he hit the floor. Hansherat snatched the knife out of his hand, ran to the flaming circle, stepped inside, grabbed the false image of herself by the front of the robe with one hand while driving the knife through its back with the other.

The back was open, hollow. Meeting no resistance, the knife pierced the thing's heart, burst out through its chest, and cut Hansherat's own wrist. Startled, she dropped the knife. The false Hansherat disintegrated into fine, swirling dust.

The circle was empty now, and broken where Hansherat's foot had smeared it. The fires burned lower, then went out. Tiny trails of smoke rose in the freezing darkness.

She stood still, shuddering.

Sekenre coughed. "You're not finished," he said. She turned, startled, only able to make out a few glowing swirls and points of light moving as he approached her. Quickly she snatched up the knife again. "Victory can swiftly turn into defeat if you're not careful. Give me the knife. It's more essential than you can ever imagine. "

She backed away.

He shuffled toward her. "Give it."

She clung to the plain wooden handle with both hands. How strange that she should notice such a detail in such circumstances: It was no magical implement, just a carving knife from the table setting.

"I'm afraid," she said.

He put his hands on hers. "Not of me. You should never be afraid of me."

He took the knife from her unresisting fingers. The remains of the impaled heart crumbled at his touch, dry and brittle and impossibly light, like an old wasp's nest you find in the winter.

"You see?" she said. "She was like that other one, the servant girl, hollow behind, just like you said."

She couldn't really follow what he was doing. It was too dark. He knelt down, back to her.

"You've ably destroyed the unliving *device*," he said. "Now let's finish off the one who devised it."

Grunting, he drove the knife down through the floorboards. A shrill, warbling shriek sounded from below. For just an instant, a flabby, glowing face rose up out of the wood. Sekenre twisted the blade. Black blood poured from the screaming mouth. The face sank down and vanished.

Then it was Sekenre who was screaming, in the same warbling voice. He thrashed over the floor, clawing at the wood.

Hansherat crouched beside him, holding him by the shoulders until he was calm again. He was slick and clammy to the touch, but she felt his heart racing within his thin chest. When he spoke, he seemed barely able to form the words, but it was his own voice. She knew it was Sekenre and no one else who whispered, merely, "Thank you."

IN THE gray dawn, Hansherat looked out the window, over the rooftops of the town. Two soldiers of the watch strolled lazily below, their pikes over their shoulders. Somewhere nearby, a rooster crowed.

Hansherat called for the landlord, who came to her door, yawning, lantern in hand.

"Didn't you sleep well, Reverend Lady?"

"You mean you didn't *hear* anything?"

"Hear what?"

Then the man's eyes widened as he saw the burnt horse-skull in the middle of the floor, the smoke trailing from the magic circle, the knife still embedded in the floorboards, and Sekenre lying there, naked and bloody.

"Merciful gods! Oh merciful gods!" The landlord kept repeating that over and over. But Hansherat had to give him credit. He didn't run away. Instead he helped her carry Sekenre to the bed, and the two of them examined him. The wound across his back was huge and deep. He was going to have another massive scar from it, she realized.

The boy moaned and started to struggle. She held him firmly in place.

"Sekenre, you ought to wear armor while doing this."

"No," he said, his words muffled in a pillow. "If the sigils are covered up, they have no power."

His had been covered up with his own blood.

Calmly, methodically, she examined him, finding burns, welts, and gashes all over, but no deep punctures; a lot of bruises, and, she suspected, a one or two broken ribs, but nothing worse than that. His face was puffy and red, his lips split, one of his eyes blackened. She saw him right then as a child who needed her help and nothing more.

She sent the landlord out for water, ointments and bandages. He went, closing the door behind him, shouting to the servants to stay away.

When they had finished and Sekenre was sleeping peacefully, the landlord said, "Merciful gods, this will never do. It'll bring a curse on my establishment. You two must go *at once.*"

Angrily, Hansherat made what she hoped he would take for a magical gesture. "My son and I are both sorcerers," she said in a low voice. "You can see that. If you do not let us remain until he is able to travel, *we* will most definitely put a curse on your establishment."

"Oh merciful gods —"

"All that you have seen shall remain a secret. Tell the others only that the holy prophet and prophetess require seclusion, that no one may come up here."

"Oh merciful — I shall try —"

She made another sign in the air. The landlord flinched.

"You will *succeed.*"

★   ★   ★

TEN DAYS later they left, secretly, in the evening just before the town's gates closed. Both wore plain, loose robes and sandals, carrying provisions, money, and extra clothes in satchels. Sekenre held his bundle in his arms, in front of him. It was still too painful for him to carry anything over his back.

In the darkness, beneath the clear and starry sky, somewhere along the river, they camped beneath a cluster of palm trees. Sekenre made an ordinary fire by rubbing sticks together. The two of them sat leaning over it for warmth. The desert night soon grew quite cold.

Hansherat finally said what she had been longing to say.

"Sekenre, you have a lot of explaining to do."

He replied slowly, almost solemnly, but in his familiar voice. She knew it was truly Sekenre speaking.

"Yes, I do. Very well then, know that I am Sekenre the sorcerer, called the Illuminator. I am nearly three hundred years old. For a hundred of those years, I lay in the box, as I was when you found me. Know, too, that we sorcerers fight strange wars, over the centuries, across many worlds, in *Leshé* among the ghosts, in dreams, in the sky and under the earth. In the course of these, my rivals became too strong for me and there was no other way to escape them but to lie in that box, to become a seed which might one day be replanted and grow again into Sekenre. In the intervening century, the others battled among themselves, and were weakened, but not as much as I had hoped. It was a near thing. You saved me, Lady Hansherat of the Delta. I owe you my life."

She wanted to weep. He still had that little-boy manner, the wide-eyed, innocent expression. She wanted him to be her son, but even she, even mad, ragged Hansherat knew that she could never be the mother of the three-hundred-year-old sorcerer Sekenre. That was impossible. That delusion was gone.

"But *why* do sorcerers do it?"

"Fight, you mean? Because they are afraid. They fight to be free from fear. They become disfigured, grotesquely transformed, but they can't stop. They mutilate themselves, becoming ever stronger in their pain. They carve signs into their flesh. I knew a sorcerer once who tore out his own eyes so that molten metal serpents could inhabit the sockets. They served him well until somebody poured a bucket of water over his head and they shattered."

He paused. Hansherat supposed he was remembering strange and terrible things from long ago, which even he could not bring himself to describe. "This wasn't even my quarrel, you know," he said at last, shuffling closer to the fire. "One of those within me, Balredon or Tannivar, one of them — they can still hide secrets from me — someone made an enemy, who was aligned with another, who betrayed a third. It goes on and on. I think you know this already. Whenever a sorcerer is killed, the slain one becomes *part* of the slayer. Thus we devour one another, filling ourselves with the souls and memories of our victims. Sometimes, for a sorcerer, death is a kind of escape, as it was for my own father, when he induced me to murder him. He hoped to hide from his enemies in the body of his own son. That was how I began. Oh, I contain multitudes and mysteries, Lady Hansherat. Everyone my father ever killed, everyone each of *them* ever killed, many more I've acquired along the way —"

For just an instant she felt absolute, abject terror. She covered her face with her hands, then let out a whimpering cry. "Do you mean . . .? If I had finished what you finished —?"

"Absolutely. When I drove the knife through the floor, I merely added to the number of the already varied company within me. But if *you* had done it, *you* would have become a sorcerer too. That I would never wish upon you."

He paused to untie his sandals, banging them together to shake the sand out. He lay back on the sand and stretched, wriggling his toes. He seemed, Hansherat thought, terribly, deceptively *human* when he did things like that.

She hardened her thoughts, recalling her own purpose.

"Sekenre, if you cannot stop doing what you do, it won't matter much if you do it one more time —"

"I am trying to find a way. More than anything else, I'd like to stop."

"But before you do, I remind you of your promise to help me as I helped you."

He sat up and remained silent again for a very long time. The fire burned down. He poked the embers idly with a stick. Hansherat shivered in the night air. Somewhere along the river, geese honked.

Sekenre sighed. "I won't do it."

Very coldly, she said, "Would you break your promise? Have you no honor, no gratitude? Should I have left you where I found you?"

"I have gratitude," he said. "Possibly even honor of some sort. But I will not do what you want."

"Then I have lost my only hope."

"Doesn't that depend on what you were hoping for?" Now he spoke, not like a boy at all, but like a wise old man who just happened to have a boy's voice. "Lady, I am grateful to you for saving me. You even, many times, tried to comfort me. You did that of your own will, not because I tricked you or magicked you into it. I still know what such things mean, despite everything I have become. But I also know what you want —"

"I haven't told you —"

"Let me guess. You want me to return you to the capital, kill all your enemies, restore you to power and riches, maybe even make you queen —"

"But I didn't tell you this. How could you know?"

"I'm a sorcerer, Lady. But, even if I were not, you are completely transparent."

"Then, yes, that is what I want. Let that be my reward for saving you."

He took her hand in his. He gazed into her eyes.

"Don't ask this. Please, don't. I performed such a favor for another exile once. She got to be queen, all right, but ended up with her head nailed over the city gate. In the process, a lot of people got killed, including several sorcerers, strangers, whose powers and old feuds I acquired. That is how it continues. Each new atrocity requires vengeance, each act of vengeance a fresh atrocity. As it is with sorcerers, so with queens. But the way to *stop* is by halting right here, right now. You don't have to forgive your enemies. Merely live beyond the hurt they have done you. Vengeance might hurt you even more."

Hansherat struck the ground with her fist, feeling helpless and foolish.

"But I swore before the king that I would return with my son . . ."

"And it was I who put that thought into your head. It was merely a stratagem. I wish it were not so. I wish I truly could be your son."

"You put —?"

"As I slept in the box, my spirit wandered in *Leshé,* among the restless dead. There I met your husband's ghost. He told me everything. I sent him to you, directing you to uncover the box. Then I whispered into your mind, and caused you to prophesy before the king."

It was too bewildering. It didn't make sense. "But, but . . . I spoke to the king *before* Valpetor's ghost led me to the box."

He smiled that disarming smile of his. "It was I, too, who entered your dreams and instructed you in the art of capturing a soul in glass. Remember? No, you do not. I covered over the memory, like drawing a curtain, before I left."

"Can you travel in time, then?"

"There is no time in sorcery, nor in dreams, nor in death. Therefore, once my purpose had been served, I led Valpetor into *Tashé*, the realm true death, where he is at rest, whence he cannot be recalled because he is beyond time."

Lady Hansherat wept long and hard. "For that, I am truly grateful, Sekenre," she said at last.

"Nevertheless, it is I who am in your debt, and I shall give you adequate recompense before we part."

HE TRAVELLED with her for many years, wandering from place to place, working small miracles to sustain them. He was her companion who pretended to be her son.

They came into Reedland, to the quaint and tumble-down City of Reeds, a place of wooden houses tottering on stilts, of watery avenues, docks, and endless fish smells.

"This is where I grew up," he said. "I was a real boy here. But it was so long ago, no one will recognize me now."

So they dwelt there in one of the rickety houses. He spent long days in his sunlit study, wrapped in that oversized silk tunic (which he wore into rags; she used to chide him about it), working magic with parchment and pens and colored paints, painstakingly illuminating, symbols, words, the story of his life, and hers. He explained that it made him whole and real. He defined himself that way.

While in Reedland, he was her son in public, but in private, her husband. She was still young enough. He gave her a true son whom she named Tuolas, which means, in the Deltan tongue, "Autumn."

But a sorcerer, of course, does not age. He cannot change, except to die. Sekenre had to present his own offspring as his younger brother, then his elder, and finally, his father. When Tuolas married and the circumstances became too strange for the growing family, when Hansherat could not bear to look on Sekenre but would never say so, he went away, so the rest of them might live ordinary lives.

He visited Hansherat only once more, when she was very old, and Tuolas was nearly sixty himself. The sorcerer paid for their passage on a ship, and the three of them sailed downriver to the City of the Delta, where the ancient lady beheld one last time the palace of the king, the houses of the great lords, and the many temples of the gods. There had been a change of dynasty. Hawk-faced Andraxes, silent Belphage, and mocking Ruaine were long dead, executed for treason.

But Hansherat did not announce herself to the new king. No one knew that she had indeed returned to the capital with her son, as had been prophesied.

"Such is my parting gift to you," Sekenre said. "Don't you think it was better this way?"

The legend is very old, but that is how the story of Lady Hansherat really ends. I know it and I tell you, for I am Sekenre who writes this.

KING FATHER STONE

King Father Stone, under the earth, swimming in blood to give
    himself birth.
King Father Stone, under the sky, gobbled three sons, but
    won't let them die.
    —Anvastou children's rhyme,
    recorded in the notebooks of Sekenre the Illuminator.

DARKNESS and thunder.

King Hrosan raged in the night, against the rain and wild wind, against his traitorous sons and their armies arrayed before him. He could not allow the battle to end, not now, not like this. But, in the pouring rain as the darkness closed in, the shield-wall broke and the royal troops scattered, streaming from the field into the adjoining woods, pursued by yelling cavalrymen.

Now the slaughter had truly begun, and the night was filled with the frenzy of it, a second storm of death amid the surging elements.

He cursed his sons' names. He shouted, facing into the wind.

No one could hear him.

The realization that all was lost hit him like a fatal blow, numbing him at first, even as wounded soldier is sometimes numbed for a few minutes before the pain comes and his blood pours out.

The king tore off his purple cloak and threw it aside, drew his sword for the last time, and plunged into the oncoming mass of his enemies, striking this way and that, like a swimmer laboring against an impossible tide. In a flash of lightning he saw the mass of struggling men heaving up, washing over him, as ten thousand voices cried out. Trumpets spoke, before the thunder came.

Ahead of him, somewhere, infinitely far away yet almost within reach, swayed the huge, golden standard of one of his sons. He couldn't tell which. Possibly Hrosanian, the eldest, whom the king had once bounced on his knee, whom the king had trained in horsemanship and war, whom the king had discreetly advised in the matter of his first murder.

Or it might have been Hrosantae, or Hroso, or even Delmantine, who was only four years old. It didn't matter. They were all monsters.

He had sired them.

They would tear the Pentarchy of Anvastou to shreds fighting over it.

By the Nine Gods of Righteousness, he cursed them all.

It was time to die.

Something hit him squarely between the shoulders and he sprawled forward. His shield buckled and was torn away. His sword flew from his hand. He rolled over stones, into mud, fumbling for the sword. Someone snatched the crown from his head and he tried to grab it back, but caught hold of a soldier's belt and was dragged some distance through the mud before the man fell down on top of him, dead.

Incredibly, though, King Hrosan did not die. What followed, he tried to convince himself, must have been a dream.

It felt as if he lay in the earth for a hundred years, raging against his sons, while battle sounds filled his ears.

Slowly the torrents of blood and the screaming voices in the wind and the footsteps of countless armies wore away the dirt above him, until he looked out on the night sky again, amazed to see the stars.

He lay on a hillside above a battlefield, and wore the fields and forests like bedclothes. His struggled to rise, to break free, brimming with unslaked rage. The earth shook. Stones tumbled and rolled away.

Far below, barely visible in the darkness and rain, two tiny figures were climbing up the grassy slope toward him.

He closed his eyes, commanding himself to awaken from this dream.

Now he lay under a heap of corpses. One by one the corpses were dragged away, and then someone was tugging at his boots.

He raised his head to see what was happening, and tried to laugh, but only managed a coughing snort. A boy was carefully unlacing the purple boots that only a king may wear.

"Don't steal those, child. They're much too large for you."

The boy looked up. The lightning of the fading storm still flickered in the sky, revealing the field strewn with the dead.

Squatting down among them, the robber boy — thin, ragged, and barefoot, no more than thirteen or fourteen years old — worked at the king's boot-laces.

About the same age as Hroso, the third of Hrosan's despicable princes, who would strip his father's corpse even as this boy did.

Dark eyes gazed up at him from a soft, round face. Lighting flickered once more, then darkness came, and the boy held up a cupped hand. Blue flames burned there, sizzling in the rain.

Not a robber then. A ghoul.

Hrosan struggled to get away.

"No, don't," the boy said.

The king wriggled backward through the mud. The boy crawled to follow, holding on to his boot-laces.

"I've come to help you," the boy said. "You don't have to die."

His words were strangely accented, but it was the sense of what he said that made him hard to understand, not his pronunciation.

"What?"

The boy repeated himself.

"This is crazy," said the king. "I am already dead."

The boy shrugged and went on methodically unlacing the king's boots. He pulled off one and tossed it aside, then started working on the other.

"Well, *suppose* you weren't going to die then?" the boy asked. "What would you do?"

Hrosan could not believe he was having this conversation. He couldn't take it seriously. "I'd have my revenge," he said. "No matter how long it took, I'd rip my damned brats from their stolen thrones and grind them up —"

"In your teeth?"

The king laughed. "All right, in my teeth."

"And would you swallow?"

Lunatics speak thus, the king thought. *To them such details are terribly important. Therefore, let one lunatic say to another:* "No, I would spit them out." He spoke this aloud.

"Ah. So you say. I am not so certain."

Even coming from a lunatic, that made no sense.

The boy threw the other purple boot away. He reached up and pulled the signet ring from Hrosan's finger, tossing that away too. The king was too bewildered to resist.

"If you would achieve your worthy and much yearned-for goal, you must be more than a king, other than a king. Come on. I'll help you. Get up."

Hrosan struggled upright, swaying, his bare feet sinking ankle-deep in mud. He shivered in the wind and rain, coughing.

This was all a dream, he told himself again, all some absurdity seeping into his brain as he lay dying. He looked around for his own corpse, but did not see it.

Yet if he were to escape the field alive, from the midst of his enemies,

it *would* be a good idea to get rid of every badge of kingship, cloak, crown, ring, purple shoes. That single thread of rationality was more frightening than all the craziness, because it suggested that this might really be happening.

The boy took him by the hand and pulled him along. The boy, too, was shivering.

"What are you, child? What really? Some sort of imp?"

"I am the sorcerer Sekenre and I am not a child."

Hrosan laughed. "If you're a sorcerer, then I'm the master of all the earth. No, you're mad and I am dead."

The boy shrugged. Again, he shivered. "Believe what you want."

They walked on, their feet making sucking sounds in the nearly frigid mud.

"Gods! It's cold!" said Hrosan.

"Flesh must touch, for magic to be true."

This wasn't a dream, Hrosan decided. It was a true vision, such as came to prophets from the gods. It was his task, then, to puzzle out the hidden signs and know the way of destiny.

He walked barefoot in the mud, leaning on Sekenre. Sometimes other stragglers surrounded them in the darkness between the trees. Once, on a forest path, enemy horsemen burst into view, howling through the silver face-pieces of their helmets like metal demon-statues come furiously alive, cutting down stragglers like sodden stalks. But Sekenre opened his hand. A blue flame danced there, and no one molested them, as if they were invisible.

It seemed that for a time that a dead chiliarch walked beside them, his almost severed head rolling horribly, his shattered neckbones grinding while blood streamed over the sunburst-embossed cuirass of his rank. He spoke not from his mouth but out of the gaping wound in his neck, in that universal language of the dead, which somehow Hrosan understood.

Sekenre joined the dead man in conversation, speaking fluently in that same tongue.

The dead man mourned unfinished lives and cataloged the sorrows of this night, remarking how so much suffering, so many deaths, might gather in one place, swirling like a great storm, and assume its own, miraculous life.

He turned away from Sekenre, his head dangling like a sack slung from his shoulders, and to Hrosan said, "My suffering has not ended, Great King. Know that it continues still."

Hrosan replied angrily, "I don't know what you expect me to do about it." He turned to Sekenre for some reassurance, but the boy merely held a flame in his hand and trudged silently.

Then that part of the vision ended, and it was dawn. The rain had receded into drizzle, and the air was thick with slowly rising mist. The boy led Hrosan up a hillside, stepping over corpses, the both of them slipping and sliding in the mud. They caught hold of the stiffening dead to steady themselves, the both of them trembling, exhausted by the cold, their breath ragged and hoarse; both of them utterly caked in mud from head to foot.

Crows gathered on the battlefield, cawing.

Once in a great while, a wounded soldier cried out.

In the dawning light, Hrosan recognized this place. He saw where the enemy's standard had been. He had been walking in circles all night. He regarded Sekenre, who looked like any other urchin, his eyes wide in his muddy face. He yanked the boy to a halt.

"You had better explain yourself."

"I already have. I, a sorcerer, offer you, formerly a king and in your own estimation a corpse, a chance to become something more than a corpse. Do not question. Merely accept."

"You are hardly a sorcerer, child!" King Hrosan swore an angry oath by the Nine Gods of Righteousness.

"You are hardly righteous." Sekenre opened his hand once more. Fire danced on his scarred palms, but without burning him.

"Then again, you are hardly a king anymore, and your sons are hardly model princes. Yet they seemed so, outwardly, did they not?"

"All right. All right. I'll do what you want. If only —"

"No *if*. No conditions."

Hrosan thought of his sons and their treachery. His rage swelled up. He ground his teeth. "Yes. Do what you will."

Now the vision frayed apart, like a tapestry coming unwoven.

Contradictory things happened. He saw Sekenre holding strands of light, twisting them, casting them away. Sekenre got down on his knees and began to dig in the earth with his muddy hands. He bade Hrosan help him, and the two of them dug a shallow grave. Sekenre helped the king into the grave, and covered him cover. Hrosan struggled for breath. He felt the mud in his nose and mouth. He was floating under the ground. It seemed that the limp hands of the slain soldiers reached down and brushed across his face as he passed.

And, dreaming in the earth, Hrosan saw himself and Sekenre kneeling on either side of his grave, in mud up to their elbows.

The boy said something he couldn't make out.

And he looked down on two tiny figures, from where he lay at the top of the hill. In the dawn's first light he spied Sekenre and Hrosan, standing over the grave, then making their way onward, up the slope.

He in three places at once, observing and dreaming: walking with Sekenre up the slope, kneeling by the grave, and in the grave.

His numbed feet could not find purchase. He fell many times.

The earth shook slightly. Stones rolled past.

"Look," the boy said, pointing.

He looked. Among the massive boulders at the top of the hill, overlooking the battlefield and the forest, a face was revealed, carven there or formed by some impossible freak of nature. He didn't know which. He had no time to consider. He screamed at what he saw.

The face was his own.

It spoke with the voice of thunder. The hillside rippled like a blanket thrown back. Sekenre lost his grip on Hrosan's hand and went tumbling down somewhere out of sight.

The stone face rippled too, and fell down on him, like a tapestry suddenly cut loose.

Hrosan screamed once more, as the great jaws ground him up.

Darkness and thunder.

HE LAY in the earth, but he did not die. He lay in the earth, having been swallowed by earth, swallowed by stone, swallowed by himself, but still he could not die.

He lay in the earth, listening to the voices of the land, to the rain caressing it, to the wind, to the rivers flowing. Time passed as a dream and he did not dream; his eyes truly opened as a prophet's are opened, seeing all that the earth had hidden, as he lay in the earth.

He spoke with the dead in the language of the dead.

He raged, and the ground shook. He turned in his slumber.

City walls fell. Houses folded in upon themselves.

He raged, because he could hear the voices of men, saying, "The old tyrant is gone. Good riddance." No one mourned the apparent passing of King Hrosan.

No riddance at all, he said, within the earth.

The seasons turned, and in the darkness, in the depths of winter, Sekenre came to him again, walking barefoot on the snow like a ghost, leaving no footprints, blue flame cupped in his hands.

The boy crouched down, and whispered at the grave of King Hrosan, telling him how his sons had fallen to warring, and now Hrosantae and Hroso had allied themselves against Hrosanian their elder brother and now besieged him in a castle far to the north, high in the mountains, where the marches of Anvastou end in utter desolation and the sun never truly rises.

So Hrosan followed Sekenre for long miles, drifting in the earth beneath his feet, in dreams which were not dreams. Sekenre passed through the besiegers' camp as if invisible. The occasional tent-pole swayed and toppled as Hrosan slid beneath.

The castle gate opened for them. Sentries cried out in alarm and rushed to close it, but no one saw Sekenre pass through. His bare feet moved silently up stone stairs. Hrosan swam in stone, in the stairs and walls and floors, and the castle trembled very slightly. They passed more sentries in the halls, who did not challenge them. They entered the king's chamber.

It was Hrosanian who called himself king now. He wore his father's crown. He had laughed at his brothers, as Sekenre had told the tale, tapping the crown on the edge of a table to show it was a solid thing, not to be divided lest it no longer be a crown, only scraps of metal.

Now Hrosanian wasn't laughing. He sat on a wooden bench before a table, by a fire, his most trusted knights with him, a map spread out on the tabletop. He looked miserable and cold, though wrapped in a bearskin.

The new king and his knights were discussing the battle which must come soon, because the garrison had run out of food.

The room suffused with blue light. Hrosanian looked up.

To Hrosan, this was the truly impossible part: He was not dreaming, but in that room, physically, yet not in the flesh. His body was made of stone, living and naked, carven, ripped from out of the earth, massive and invincible as his hatred. He bellowed as he rushed forward, splintering the table, seizing the knights as they tried to defend their lord and breaking them like wooden toys in his stone hands.

He closed his hands upon his eldest son, upon Hrosanian who called himself king, and he devoured him with his stone mouth, grinding him between stone teeth, while his stone ears reverberated with the sound of screaming.

Once he happened to glimpse Sekenre huddled by the fire, wrapped in the bearskin, shivering from the cold. Then, for an instant, Hrosan stood alone in the room, as the fire burned down.

Not even Sekenre was there. Outside, sentries banged on the door and shouted.

ONCE MORE King Hrosan lay in the darkness, naked and cold, his body incorruptible and unchanging.

His son Hrosanian lay with him.

"Father, I cannot describe how much I hate you."

"And I hate you."

"You taught me by your example, how to grab what could be mine and make it mine. You taught me that a king does what he must and will, and makes the laws afterward, fitting them to himself like a cloak."

"You have learned well, and become a king, and therefore I must hate you endlessly, my son."

The father Hrosan rolled over in the darkness and devoured his son Hrosanian once again, until he felt the other's anguish within his mind.

The two of them fused into one, became one being, filled with hatred and with rage, like a storm colliding with another and doubling in strength.

But he was not otherwise changed.

The king's mind filled with memories that were not his, with lusts and fears. But he understood them. They were like enough to his own.

Then he lay in the earth for another year, dreaming, listening to the snows melting, to the rivers swelling in their courses, to the sowers in their fields, to the beasts driven to pasture, and to the tread of soldiers as the armies of Hrosantae and Hroso marched down from the mountains after their inexplicable victory.

THAT SUMMER, Sekenre appeared in the forum of the Eastern Capital, a ragged, muddy-footed boy with tangled hair. The townspeople ignored him, and chattered on of prices and crops, and of politics: how Hrosantae and Hroso had divided the kingdom and would probably be at war soon. Nobody knew what would become of Delmantine, the youngest son, or of his mother, the old king's second wife, Queen Theodatas. Somebody would probably kill them.

Sekenre sat among the beggars on the steps of the temple of the Nine Righteous Gods, a tiny knife in his hand as he carved a piece of wood. He ignored the passing traffic and did not call out, until at last he had finished his work. Then, without a word, he held up his finished carving for a richly-clad lady to see. It was a delicate bird, lifelike in every detail. When he touched the tail, the wings opened. The lady exclaimed in delight.

"That's very pretty," she said. She took it and gave him a silver coin.

He turned the coin over in his hand after she was gone. The image on it was that of King Hrosan, and the inscription on it celebrated his eternal victory.

On the following day, Sekenre carved a wooden fish with a jointed tail and a mouth that opened and closed.

The day after that, a frog. Then a mouse. Then a tiny man who played a flute. Sekenre showed another lady how to hold the wooden man into the wind to hear the music of the flute.

Then a master carver came to him and examined his latest work, a wooden skull the size of a grape with a hinged jaw and every tooth carefully detailed. "Young man," he said. "You are very talented. Come and be my apprentice. You shall work in my shop."

Sekenre smiled and shrugged his shoulders and went on carving.

"Don't you know," the carver said, "that I am carver to the king? I provide him with sacred images for holy festivals. An apprentice of mine can go very far indeed."

"What king might that be?"

The carver was taken aback. Then he said, slowly, "I can tell that you are a foreigner. Yes, I see it in your face, and I hear it in your voice, certainly. Know, then that our king is the noble and righteous Hrosantae, second son to the former king, Hrosan."

Sekenre did not ask what had happened to the first son.

Instead, he put his knife and the wooden skull away and went with the carver. He dined in the carver's house that evening.

But first the carver's wife insisted Sekenre have a bath.

She had her maid fill the tub. Sekenre waited for both women to leave the room, but instead they pulled off his clothes and the maid threw them out the window into the rubbish heap behind the house. Then they shoved him into the tub and scrubbed him with a brush so hard that he yelped.

They paused, clearly disturbed when they saw that he had scars all over his body, as if he had suffered terrible wounds, that the palms of his hands were seared, almost featureless, and part of one of his ears was missing. The maid seemed about to say something, but the carver's wife merely shook her head, made a *tsk*ing sound, and went on scrubbing.

"Where are you from, Sekenre?" the lady asked.

"From very far away."

"And how old are you?"

"You wouldn't believe me if I told you."

"And your father and mother?"

"Both dead . . . My mother, yes, my father, sort of."

"Well, either people are dead or they aren't."

"Sometimes."

She looked at him strangely, then dried him with a towel, while the maid fetched one of the carver's old shirts, which Sekenre could wear as a robe, with the sleeves rolled up. It came down past his knees.

The carver's name was Rogatis, his wife Godfinna. Sekenre became the most brilliant apprentice Rogatis had ever seen. The delicacy of the boy's carving, the detail he could bring out in wood or ivory or even stone, was truly incredible.

"You are already a master," he said. "How did you learn so much?"

"I practiced for a long time."

"But, one so young —?"

"I had a long time."

When the summer festival arrived, Rogatis and Sekenre dressed in their finest clothes, Godfinna endlessly fussing to make sure Sekenre was presentable, and the carver and his apprentice carried the products of their labors on special trays, to be offered to the king.

"What sort of man is this king?" Sekenre asked, as he and Rogatis made their way through the crowd, toward the special pavilion which had been set up in the city's forum. There King Hrosantae sat on a golden throne, the temple of the Righteous Gods at his back.

"They say that our lord is a hard man, one who has been forced to do many grim things, but sometimes he sorrows at the memory of what he has done, and his future actions are moderated.

More than that . . . it is not wise to say."

"Ah."

One by one the craftsmen of the town presented their gifts to the king, to be paid, blessed, or driven out by attendants with clubs.

Rogatis knelt before the throne, bowed his head, and offered up his tray. An attendant carried it to the king, who removed the cloth covering and beheld a wooden locust, ten times life size, with jeweled eyes. As he watched, it came alive, stirring. It rubbed its legs together and sang.

"We are pleased," said King Hrosantae, "if a bit puzzled. What does this thing signify?"

"It is hard to explain," said Rogatis, who could not explain it at all, because it was Sekenre's work he was passing off as his own.

"My Lord," said Sekenre, interrupting, then continuing before anyone could hush him for speaking out of turn, "there is no explanation to be had, nor any needed. The thing is merely a marvel, and the delight is in its construction. That delight, then, is conveyed to you."

"You are a bold one," said the king.

A courtier paid Rogatis several gold pieces and ushered him away. Then Sekenre offered up his own tray, speaking again out of turn. "But this, Lord King, has a more obvious and immediate meaning."

The servant carried the tray to the king and the king removed the covering.

He screamed. The stone carving he beheld was the perfect image of his father's face. It opened its eyes, and the eyes were filled with fire, as if a tiny furnace raged within. The thing spoke in a voice he had not heard in a long time outside of his nightmares, saying, "Second of my brats, I come for you."

And it swallowed him, sucking him into its stone mouth as if he were made of smoke, grinding him in its stone jaws.

The wooden tray and the king's crown rattled to the pavement before the throne.

BENEATH THE earth, old king Hrosan conversed with his second son.

"I truly hate you."

"And I hate you, Father, but I wish it were not so. I reigned long enough to learn that a king is a kind of slave, bound by his throne and his crown as if they were chains, while all men flatter and secretly abuse him. It wasn't worth murdering you."

"Is that supposed to be comforting? Am I supposed to embrace you in a flood of tears and beg your forgiveness even as I offer you mine?"

"I only wish it were so, Father."

Hrosan rolled over in his sleep, in the darkness, and devoured his son once more, and the two of them become one, fusing together, and a new voice awakened in the king's mind, a voice which rebuked Hrosanian, the eldest, who was already there, and filled the king's mind with fears and doubts, even with tender memories. Hrosantae returned again and again to the quiet hours as he lay beside his wife and queen, whom he truly loved, and whispered to her that the evil was all past, that it was no longer necessary for him to be cruel.

"I wish it were so," she had said, and Hrosantae, the second son, and Hrosan, the father, both wept at the memory of that, while Hrosanian, the eldest, scorned them both.

In his unending dream, old Hrosan saw Sekenre before him, swimming in the muddy earth. "Have you had enough?" the boy said.

"Is your revenge complete?"

Hrosan did not answer for a long time. He too was like a swimmer, fighting against a tide of memories and sorrows and hesitations that were not his own. He clung to the memory of who he had been, old king Hrosan, father to four sons who had betrayed him and overthrown him in a battle, one night in the rain.

Remembering this, he at last was able to say, "No, my revenge is *not* complete," while that part of him which was Hrosanian laughed mirth-lessly and that part which was Hrosantae wept.

"My work isn't complete either," said Sekenre.

"WE all know what must be done."

The conspirators met in a vault below the palace in the Western Cap-ital. Gorhinglas, a great lord, spoke for them all.

"We cannot have civil war again. Already, the barbarians press us hard. Nor can we afford a regency, which will only mean weakness and further division. Therefore the child Delmantine and his mother, the former queen Theodatas, *must die.* Our Lord Hroso must sit on the throne *alone,* or we are all done for."

The others nodded in agreement.

"My boy is the key to it," one of them said. "My stepson, Sekenre, an orphan whom I found it useful to adopt. He has become young Delman-tine's playmate. He can get us into the right chambers. He can steal keys and open doors. If necessary, he can do the job himself."

All this while the boy Sekenre sat on a stone bench nearby, idly playing with a cup-and-ball. He paused. "Oh yes, Stepfather. I will finish everything for you if you want me to."

Therefore, that same evening, Sekenre went to the carefully-guarded wing of the palace where the queen's chambers were. This was all that remained of her kingdom, the only place where she could feel safe, sur-rounded by her few loyal followers.

King Hroso would never dare storm the place, for fear of the outcry. It was officially given out that he shared the diminished Diarchy of An-vastou equally with his half-brother, Delmantine, and honored the boy's mother, Theodatas, as if she were his own.

In fact the two were Hroso's prisoners, though he had not figured out how to dispose of them.

His loyal courtiers proposed to solve the problem for him.

So Sekenre went, dressed in an embroidered blue robe, white leg-gings, and silver slippers, with all the appearance of a prince, for Del-mantine had given him some of his own clothes. The supposed stepson of a minor lord, he was deemed harmless enough.

He said he was fourteen. The young king Delmantine was now twelve, fatherless under circumstances best not discussed, for eight years.

Sekenre was the boy's only playmate. The two of them studied together. They shared games and secrets. Sekenre told the most amazing stories, to Delmantine alone, and performed even more amazing tricks, but only if Delmantine swore never to tell his mother.

Further secrets, which Delmantine offered to Sekenre in exchange, included knowledge of numerous sliding panels and hidden passage-ways, and the possession of a set of keys.

Now Sekenre slipped into one of those passageways, opened a panel, descended a marble, spiral staircase fashioned like a writhing serpent, unlocked a door, and admitted Lord Gorhinglas and the twelve other conspirators, including Ouen, his own stepfather, into the crypts below the queen's suite. All of the noblemen carried drawn swords.

"We'll gut him like a sheep," somebody said.

"Don't relish it so. It's a horrible thing we must do," said Lord Ouen.

"But necessary," said Gorhinglas. Turning to Sekenre, he said, "Lead us on, boy. Do not lose your courage and do not think to betray us. There will be a great reward for you when this is done."

Sekenre knew that most likely the reward included being gutted like a sheep, but still he led them among the tombs of kings, past effigies of conquerors who had made Anvastou great.

He turned another key. A creaking door swung wide of its own accord, and all of them but Sekenre had to duck their heads as they crowded into a low-ceilinged chamber where unfinished tombs lay open and empty. It was a musty, damp place, with no sign of recent construc-tion, though the carvings were only half finished, and marble chips and abandoned tools lay all about.

"Why have you brought us to *this* accursed place?"

Gorhinglas demanded.

Indeed it was accursed, for these tombs had been prepared for the most recent rulers. Here, stretched as if asleep, lay the image of the oldest son, Hrosanian, but the tomb was empty, because Hrosanian's body had never been recovered. And no one had figured out what become of Hrosantae either, for all there had been witnesses, many of whom went mad with fright at the memory of what they had seen. So the second brother's tomb was hardly begun, the image on it no more than a scratched lump, and a sigil was cut into it, to ward off evil.

The conspirators made gestures with their hands, for luck.

Nearby were smooth, unadorned tombs where one day, quite soon it was earnestly hoped, Queen Theodatas and her son Delmantine would rest, without ceremony, hastily buried and forgotten.

"Again I asked you *why* you have brought us here?" said Lord Gorhinglas. He looked angrily at Ouen first, then raised his sword to threaten Sekenre.

"My Lord," the boy said, "Delmantine and I come here often, to play our games."

"I always knew the brat was unwholesome," one of the assassins said.

"Here especially is our *favorite* place." Sekenre brought them to the tomb of King Hrosan, where a huge stone effigy of the king's face seemed frozen in the middle of a great shout. "This is part of the game." He put his head into the gaping stone mouth, and his voice suddenly came from several directions at once. "You do it. Try it yourself."

Sekenre drew his head out again and turned to Lord Gorhinglas. Several of the assassins eyed the stone face uneasily.

Gorhinglas paced back and forth testily, ducking his head.

"I don't have time for stupid games. Now you say that Delmantine will meet you here this night?"

"Yes, Lord, very soon. All you and your friends have to do is hide yourselves and wait. But first, come and look inside here. You must, to understand a very great secret."

Gorhinglas sighed and put his head into the stone mouth.

The stone eyes opened, burning with blue fire.

The other lords screamed as the stone jaws ground to life, as the mouth closed and the headless body of Lord Gorhinglas flopped to the floor, spouting blood like wine from a ruptured skin. It was too late for any of them to escape. The stone face spoke with thunder, stunning them all, pronouncing their individual dooms. The castle shook. Stone and plaster rained down from the vaulted ceiling. The walls came alive, the other crypts bursting open as stone hands reached out to seize each of the twelve.

Then King Hrosan sat up, bursting through the lid of his own tomb, grown hideous and huge like a scuttling, misshapen thing with twelve arms.

He devoured what he had caught.

WHEN SEKENRE entered Delmantine's room, the young king rushed to embrace him.

"What's happening? What's going on? Mother is so afraid."

"It's just the earth trembling."

"No, it's more!"

Then Queen Theodatas came in. She embraced both Delmantine and Sekenre. "Righteous Gods protect us! I sent one of my maids to King Hroso, but she couldn't get in. The soldiers were all running around. She heard the king *screaming,* she said. Oh! It is the end of the world!"

"He is not screaming anymore," said Sekenre.

Queen Theodatas let go of Sekenre. She looked at him strangely and drew her son away.

"No, I suppose he is not. But how do you know, Sekenre?"

Outside in the corridor, the footsteps of something far heavier than a man thundered nearer and nearer. Guards shouted.

Metal clanged on stone. Men screamed.

"Sekenre!" the queen shouted. *"What* do you know?"

He held out his hands to show that they were empty, but they were not empty, and blue flames danced on his palms. "I only know that this is the end of what began eight years ago."

The queen screamed as the door splintered and the astonishing, marble monstrosity which wore her late husband's face clawed its way in. Its lips, chin, and many fingertips were smeared with blood.

Even Sekenre turned away from the sight.

Once more, in a voice like wind and thunder, King Hrosan pronounced inexorable doom. He stepped forward, the floorboards straining beneath his weight.

Sekenre turned back to look, and several things happened at once. Delmantine drew a dagger and stood in front of his mother to protect her. But Queen Theodatas shoved him aside and hurled herself into the monster's arms, shouting, "No, husband! No! He is too young. He is innocent! Take me instead!"

In the frenzy of his rage King Hrosan took her, his stone jaws grinding until his whole face was covered with her blood.

Delmantine shouted something and struck with his dagger. The blade broke. He cried out again, and held up his arm in a useless attempt to shield himself, but then paused and lowered his arm, because the monster did not attack him. Instead, it paced back and forth, turning from side to side, its hands waving chaotically, tears flowing from its stone eyes. It bowed down, hunched beneath the ceiling of the chamber, and the stone face spoke his name, and said something more, in a voice which was his father's and wasn't, in many voices at once. He couldn't make it out.

He thought he heard the word "forgive" before the floorboards snapped and the stone thing crashed into the vaults below.

The young king reeled back from the edge of the broken floor. Sekenre caught hold of him. The two of them struggled, rolling at the edge of the opening. Delmantine held the broken stump of his dagger to Sekenre's throat.

"Don't do that," Sekenre said. "If you kill me, you will become as I am."

★   ★   ★

SEKENRE SWAM through the earth and whispered in King Hrosan's ear, where he lay turning in the sleep which partook of both death and dream.

Hrosan wept, grinding his teeth. A babble of voices came from his mouth.

"I am a father who devoured his sons. I am a mother who died for her own. I am Gorhinglas. I am Ouen. I am Hrosanian, Hrosantae, and Hroso. I loathe the evil within myself, the thing that I was and have become. Merciful Sekenre, help me. Let this thing end, now. Please."

"It's not so simple, mighty king, is it? You are all those things, all those persons. King Hrosan remembers them, and they remember what Hrosan remembers. All of you are mixed together, like differently colored paints stirred into a pot. The color of Theodatas is the color of genuine love, and that, King Hrosan, is beyond your imagining. Your son Hrosanian was just like you. Hrosantae resembled you much, but he had a conscience. Hroso whimpered like a beaten animal, fouling himself in terror. That, too, O king."

"End my pain. What can I do?"

"Delmantine still lives. Is your revenge complete? Do you want me to arrange something?"

King Hrosan screamed in his own voice now. Far above, rivers leapt their banks and the stone faces of cliffs broke and tumbled. The skies were filled with fiery portents.

"I just want to die. I want this to be completed at last."

"No, I cannot allow that. It would ruin the project I have undertaken."

Then King Hrosan raged, and called out to the merciful gods.

They did not answer.

"As for me," said Sekenre, "I am merely a sorcerer, and not necessarily merciful."

SO SEKENRE led King Hrosan, in the dream which was more than a dream, walking to and fro in the earth and up and down in it.

Hrosan felt the rain falling on him, for the earth was his flesh.

He felt the earthquake roiling in his guts. And he felt the entire world, at his feet, spinning among the stars before the gods.

He walked barefoot on an old battlefield, where white bones poked up out of the mud, where ghosts wandered aimlessly like mist. He gathered those ghosts to himself, the chiliarch and all the rest, devouring them one by one, filling himself with the sorrows and longings and memories of ten thousand lives, growing great with pain and remembered joy, with wisdom and foolishness, until among the many voices within him, only one was King Hrosan, whom the others dimly recalled.

And they spoke to him, Hrosanian, Hrosantae, Hroso, and Theodatas, and the slain ten thousand, and they told him what he must do.

"We are alike, you and I," Sekenre said, a little later. "To become a sorcerer, you have to murder other sorcerers. Then they fill your head, and you and the others become one, and their secrets are your own. I began as a boy, tricked into murdering my own father, as part of one of his schemes, so that he might hide from his enemies in my body. Therefore I became him, and I knew all those others he had murdered, and all those *they* had murdered. We are legion, of countless names. The outward body does not change, but only after a long struggle could I sift out that memory which was the boy Sekenre, and cause the others to whisper the name of Sekenre within me, until their whispering becomes a great harmony, and I became again, at least in part, that boy who was Sekenre, who was both brave and afraid, and who killed his father and was swallowed by him."

"I am not sure who King Hrosan is anymore."

"Let him be known as the Fortunate One, for he has one advantage a mere sorcerer does not."

"What is that?"

"He can disgorge what he has swallowed."

In a dreaming time which is forever and no time at all, King Hrosan walked barefoot on the surface of the River of the Dead, with ten thousand restless ghosts in his mind and in his belly.

Sekenre walked with him a little way, but then turned back, and Hrosan continued on his own.

The dark water rippled out from his feet. The crocodile-headed *evatim*, the messengers of the Death God, hissed at his passage, but did not molest him.

He passed from the country of dream into the country of true death, which lies in the belly of the Devouring God, Surat-Hemad, whose mouth is the night sky, whose teeth are the stars. There, in the land of the dead, kneeling in the holy mud by the bank of the river, Hrosan disgorged his sons, his wife, the chiliarch, and the ten thousand, laying them to rest, to be unmade.

But when he returned from out of the god's mouth, he retained those voices and memories inside his mind, like echoes, for all he had laid them to rest.

Sekenre waited for him on the river's bank.

He spoke to the boy in the language of the dead. "Do you understand, truly, why you have done these things?"

"We are so alike. I thought that in you I would find the answer to myself."

Hrosan shook his head sadly. "We are not alike at all."

Sekenre wept. "I feared it would be so."

"But you do not regret what you have done."

Very softly, the boy replied, "No."

"Thank you, Sekenre."

The boy made a gesture with his hand, to acknowledge the presence of holiness. Then he took the king by the hand and led him up out of the earth.

In the dreaming time, this took almost forever. In waking time, a single night had passed, and just before dawn Sekenre saw the king walking in the sky, behind the stars, in the company of the gods. The Righteous Nine were there, and many more, gods and goddesses, some with the heads of animals, one with a face formed all of flowers, some who were winged.

Sekenre covered his eyes, because it was not meet that a sorcerer, who is unclean, should look upon the gods.

That morning he sat alone on an old battlefield amid broken stones, writing the tale of King Hrosan into a book. The air was cold.

> *Who comprehends The work of sorcerers? Surely not they.*
> *Most especially, not they.*
>> — attributed to Tannivar the Parricide,
>> from the notebooks of Sekenre the Illuminator.

THE GIANT VORVIADES

HE FOUND the giant crouching amid the frozen peaks of the highest mountains in the world. At that precise moment, he could remember little of his adventures coming here, of the hardships endured, and, perhaps, beloved comrades lost along the way. Even his own name seemed to shimmer just beyond his grasp.

But the voice out of his dreams told him clearly, as he led his emaciated horse onto the ledge, that what he saw across the adjacent chasm, huddled beneath the roof of the sky, was no mere pile of stones and ice. Here was Vorviades, cousin to the Shadow Titans and nemesis of the gods, devourer of light, enemy of mankind.

He made the sign of the dead for himself, crossing his arms briefly on his chest, tossing his head back to silently invoke the Righteous Nine Gods, performing, as best he could under the circumstances, his own funeral rites.

For his dreams told him that he had come to kill Vorviades, and he did not expect to survive the attempt.

Slowly the blizzard abated. The snowy curtain parted, and he beheld Vorviades, grown encrusted with centuries of waiting.

An avalanche roared into the gorge below. The monster turned its head toward him and opened its eyes. The giant's face looked like a thing of ice and stone, now torn free from the flesh of the mountains.

Calmly, the nameless man took his bags down from his pitiable horse, spread them out on the snow, and began to unpack, carefully unwrapping each piece of armor and strapping it on. Last came the ornately-inlaid, silver sword and gleaming sun-shield of the Knights Inquisitor, and his helmet, which was shaped like the face of an eagle.

Without hesitation, trembling only from weariness and the cold, he armed and bedecked himself as a champion of the Righteous Gods. He closed his visor, snapping the eagle's mouth shut. The clang echoed upward, toward Vorviades.

At the very last he removed his horse's saddle and bridle, and sent the beast down into the world wearing only a blanket.

Had the animal speech, he knew, it would be able to tell much, but the ending of the story would remain unknown, unless revealed by the Nine Gods in visions to the most holy.

For a confusing instant, he wasn't sure he even was a knight. He had

some memory of another life, of a boatman who left his work by a river's bank when a dream summoned him; of crows picking at an armored corpse by a roadside, shrieking the words of dream; of the voice in his dream commanding him to take up another man's life, and another: the boatman, a slain knight, other wanderers. Souls processed into the darkness, but each time the hero rose again and continued his centuried quest.

Perhaps it really had been that way and he was an impostor, a madman, last of a series of madmen, who had stolen armor off a corpse. He didn't know. It hardly mattered now.

He drew his sword.

The snow in the air swirled away, revealing blue sky. The sun gleamed on silver blade, golden shield, and on the icy face of Vorviades.

"Do you not fear me, little man?" The giant spoke with the voice of wind howling among skybound crags.

The knight's waking dream told him not to fear, and he did not.

Vorviades slid down into the chasm in an even greater avalanche, the whole mountain seeming to split apart as his thundering limbs stretched themselves for the first time in countless years. Snow, ice, and powdered stone filled the air like spray, concealing the giant entirely.

When the knight saw Vorviades once more, the monster had donned a mask of battered, mottled silver. It rose out of the tumultuous snow-clouds like an ominous moon.

"Do you not fear me?"

For an instant the man was afraid, for he felt the voice within him quaver, as if the unseen and unknown sender of the dreams actually feared Vorviades.

Then the fear was gone, like sound cut off by a door suddenly shut.

The silver mask hovered before him, rising out of the abyss. He struck at it with his sword. Sparks flew. The mountains echoed the sound, and with the giant's laughter. Vorviades stood up to his full height, swelling like smoke, filling the entire sky, blotting out the sun.

"Do you not fear me?"

"No," the man gasped, unprompted by any dream. "I do not." Indeed, it was entirely too late for fear.

The giant crouched down again, but the sky remained dark. Somehow hours had fled away. Stars gleamed. The knight could barely make out the rough, hunched shape of Vorviades, diminished considerably but still huge, climbing up out of the chasm onto the ledge. Chivalry bade him wait until the giant was on the ledge before him.

Vorviades loomed perhaps forty feet above him.

"You have reason to fear me," he said. "Fear me when the cities are crushed beneath my tread. Fear me when the plains tremble, when the seas rise up and wash over the lands because I am wading."

"Not if you die here, on this ledge," said the knight.

"Not then, I freely admit."

The knight struck the giant again, but was brushed aside with the flourish of an enormous hand. He sprawled in the snow, perilously close to the rim of the ledge, rolling over on his back, his shield upraised to protect himself. He paused as he saw that the giant had diminished once more, and now was no more than fifteen feet tall.

"I have seen your death in my dreams, Vorviades. Many times. It must be true."

"Aye, true. But is it true *now?*" The giant rushed at him. The knight leapt to his feet and struck again. He felt the blow connect, but found himself hurled through the air. Once more he rolled, at the edge of the abyss.

When he beheld Vorviades again, the giant was no more than ten feet tall, and seemed to be bleeding.

"I think it is true now."

"I myself have awakened *into* the dreams of many men," said Vorviades, "to bring them terror. I don't think it is over yet."

They fought on, the giant's fists crashing into the knight's shield, the silver sword flickering like a serpent's tongue, finding blood until the snow was splattered with it.

Now Vorviades was only a head taller than the knight, broad of girth and shoulder, but human-sized.

"I think it is over," said the knight.

"For you it is."

The giant had disappeared. The knight turned this way and that in the darkness, but could not find him. Then came the piercing, crushing pain from below and behind and he was hurled through the air once more, clear of the ledge this time, into the gorge below. His mind couldn't sort it out: the mountains and sky whirling, the clanging, crashing impact, pain spreading like the blood spurting inside his armor. In one dream he seemed to imagine the giant shrunken down to the size of a dwarf, calmly snatching a dagger from the knight's belt and ramming up into his groin before shoving him off a cliff.

He lay broken on the rocks far below the ledge. No, he could not accept such an ending. The dream had to be torn and rewoven.

He dreamed of Vorviades, grown huge once more, his mottled mask like the rising silver moon, reaching down tenderly, lifting up the dying knight, peeling away armor and flesh with surprisingly delicate fingers.

The knight wept, but for joy, for this was a hero's proper death.

Vorviades wept too, but only for an instant. Then he spoke as if he were addressing to someone else entirely, the dead man in his hand already forgotten.

"Dream of me, and fear me. I am coming for you, no matter how many such you send against me."

Vorviades sighed, and blew the knight's soul away as one might puff on a dandelion; and the man who still could not remember his own name sailed off into the darkness, to be judged and to dwell far to the south among the crocodiles, in the belly of Surat-Kemad, the Dreaming God, Lord of Death, whose mouth is the night sky, whose teeth are the number-less stars.

THE DREAM-SENDER, dreaming, sat up with a shout, but did not wake. His voice echoed in the stillness of his tomb, and his dreams were filled with fear. He felt the earth tremble as Vorviades strode down from the mountains and began to cross the plains.

Therefore the Dream-Sender searched his dreams once more, franti-cally, to find another champion.

AFTER KING Angharad the Great had conquered all the lands between the northern forests and the Crescent Sea, fathered many sons, and brought peace to his wide domains, he was still a vigorous man, and it was assumed that he would reign for years to come.

But one night in his banqueting hall, before all his warriors and the ladies of his court, the king slowly poured out his winecup in libation to the gods and said, "I am summoned to conquer Vorviades, for I fear him."

At once, all were filled with consternation, that King Angharad could be afraid.

His queen, seated beside him, said, "Surely this was only some idle fancy of sleep, and you need not heed it."

But the king said, "I have dreamed truly."

That very evening, messengers came with the news that a city in a distant province had been overthrown.

"It was an earthquake," they said.

"It was Vorviades. The earth trembles when he walks."

Who knew of Vorviades? The historians searched the name out of books, but, but such books were old and filled with obscurities. The poets knew of him, but only stories. Hadrondius the philosopher, chief of the royal counselors and reputedly a wise man, merely said, "Lord King, you must defeat whatever it is you fear."

Therefore the king summoned his armies, and in the days that followed the earth indeed trembled, with the tread of King Angharad and ten thousand soldiers, off to battle Vorviades. They covered the hills like dark locusts. They looked down on the broken columns of the fallen city, and the king said, "Indeed, this is the work of Vorviades."

No one dared say otherwise.

The king summoned Vorviades with the blasts of a thousand trumpets. But the giant did not come.

The moon rose over the ruins, and the king declared the moon to be a silver mask, dented and tarnished, with burning eyes. He commanded his archers to shoot, and no one could say that they shot only at the moon.

In the midst of a forest, the king peered into the shadows between the great trees, and cried, "There! There is Vorviades!"

He sent his lancers charging for hours, until many were lost in the forest. Yet no one reported that they were chasing only shadows.

When a fire burned a whole district, Angharad said, "Vorviades has breathed."

When crops withered, he said, "Vorviades was hungry." Not even Hadrondius could make the king see otherwise.

Only when the army attacked a river with their swords and the soldiers began joking about baths and rust did anyone mutter anything, or look to the king and shake their heads sadly.

In time, though, everyone concluded that King Angharad the Great was mad. His courtiers slipped away, and his soldiers went over to his too-numerous sons, who fought over the pieces of his kingdom. Angharad watched the final battle from a hilltop, weeping, a ragged beggar now, alone and forgotten by the contending armies. In the end, two of his sons were beheaded. Two more died on one another's swords. The old queen perished before his eyes when her chariot overturned as she escaped one faction and was about to be captured by another.

The king raged on his hilltop, shaking his fists at the sky, while the smoke of battle rose. In the evening, in the bloody sunset amid the dust, he saw the giant Vorviades, clearly outlined against the sky.

"You!" he shouted with the last of his strength. "Why did you never fight me?"

The giant turned his masked face, which now gleamed like a second sun. He spread his hands.

"I have fought you all this time, and behold, I am victorious. Have I not destroyed everything you arrayed against me?"

"You never fought against *me!*" the king shouted. He reached for his sword, then fell to his knees sobbing when he found that he had no sword.

"Yes I did," said Vorviades, hurling his spear, which was the thunderbolt, to transfix the king.

THE DREAM-SENDER cried out in agony as if he himself had been pierced, but still he did not wake. His tomb resounded like a great, echoing bell. Once more he whispered into the minds of men, commanding that Vorviades be opposed. But, in his own dream, he saw his champions like wooden statues, fierce enough, impressive enough in the darkness; but when the moon rose — and the moon was the mask of Vorviades — they were revealed to be only carven wood, useless as Vorviades knocked them down one by one and drew ever nearer.

Dreaming, the Dream-Sender cried out in his dream —

IN A parched land, to the south and east, the boy Anzaxos lay down to sleep in an olive grove on a mountainside overlooking the crescent sea. On that bright, quiet day, when the air was still, the birds fell silent, and the sea gleamed like a warrior's shield, Anzaxos dreamed of Vorviades standing astride the mountains, reaching up to seize the sun in his hands.

Vorviades seemed to notice the boy as he lay there. He turned toward him, and his hands poured out blood and fire, until Anzaxos drifted in crimson depths, remembering lives which were not his own: a knight who died by the side of the road; another, pieced from below on an icy ledge; a king who went mad and saw his sons perish.

He feared the giant then, but some other voice spoke to him of glory, and of the path of the hero.

Anzaxos awoke and ran to his village to tell his parents, scattering sheep.

When he had told his story, his mother took him in her arms, rocking him side to side, saying only, "Small boys have big dreams sometimes, but they are only dreams."

He asked his father, "What *are* dreams?"

"Vapors in the head. You're better off ignoring them."

But Anzaxos could not ignore his dream, or forget it, and he spoke of it often, boasting that he would be a hero one day and kill Vorviades. At first people laughed or turned away, but when a traveller knelt before him and said, "You who dream true dreams, prophesy for me," he began to do so, repeating things the giant had told him in his dreams.

His mother cried out in fright. His father commanded him to be silent, but it was too late. The high priest's servants seized him and carried him off to the temple, and, while he sat trembling and afraid in a dark vault beneath the temple, his mother wept, his father pleaded, and a great deal of money changed hands.

Then the high priest announced that a little boy had been telling lies, no oracle had been discovered, and the gods had not spoken.

But before he was allowed to go home, Anzaxos fell asleep in the dark vault and dreamed that Vorviades leaned over him and whispered through his silver mask, "If not you, another shall come after you to fight me." Then the giant departed, laughing.

Anzaxos's father took him out to a shed behind their house and beat him with a rod until he swore that he was only telling stories and would tell no more. Then his family had to leave, because their farm had been sold. They begged by the roadside for a time, until a rich man hired them and to work his land as tenants.

The boy grew up alone and silent, toiling in the rich man's fields, never telling stories, nor pausing to hear when others repeated old legends of the battles of Vorviades or the madness of King Angharad. His father and mother both died, exhausted and sorrowful, but never angry, as if somehow they knew that it wasn't their son's fault, that he had dreamed truly of Vorviades and now all their misfortunes were the giant's revenge. The giant wanted to fight, so the stories went. Combat was his only pleasure, the object of his lust, and when he was denied it, he grew very angry indeed.

When Anzaxos finally married Dera, the third daughter of a poor family, and begat three sons of his own, he did not tell his boys any of those stories, nor did he mention his dream of Vorviades. He raised them to work the fields, hoping that between the efforts of the four of them, they might one day get out of debt and buy their own farm back from their master.

But Velatin, the eldest, preferred to run. He ran along the dusty roads and over the hills without ever tiring or suffering thirst. When his father demanded of him why he ran rather than worked, he called back, "I am chasing Vorviades."

Anzaxos fell to his knees and beat his fists in the dust, remembering what the giant had said, that it would be either he or one who came after who would go off to fight.

And in those days there was war in all the lands. Velatin, the Swift, ran in the service of his king, bearing spear and shield and wearing a crested helmet, as messenger, as soldier, sometimes finding time to write home to his father that he spied Vorviades beyond the horizon, in the sunset or the moon's rising, and ran to meet him.

Dera said sadly, "Vorviades has claimed our firstborn."

Tired, gray, Anzaxos could only shake his head and remember his dreams.

Still the wars continued. Velatin, boldest of all the youths of his country, saw the giant Vorviades above the enemy hosts, or looming in the smoke above a burning city, and raced to battle him.

Then, one night the silver moon-mask of Vorviades appeared to Anzaxos, hovering beyond the bedroom window as he sat up in bed, and his wife slept beside him.

"Velatin is impaled on a post. Crows peck out his eyes," the giant said.

"This is just vapor in the head," Anzaxos said. "Go away."

The giant went, but Anzaxos wept until dawn.

His second son, Kalo, likewise left for the wars. He worked a huge device called a scorpion, which hurled a flaming spear.

"I'll use it to shoot Vorviades," he said. "I'll avenge my brother's death."

Anzaxos only wept more, and when word came that Kalo, too, had perished, he could not weep any longer, and accepted the news in silence.

His wife sickened. His third son, Naius, tended her lovingly, but one day he too came to his father and told how he had dreamed of Vorviades, and understood that he must be the champion of mankind against this monster. Naius was twelve years old. In those hard years, he had gone hungry a great deal, and was small and thin. From an accident in the fields, one of his legs was crooked. In his piping voice, holding back tears, he said, "I have to go, Papa."

At last Anzaxos was truly angry. His shame and his hatred of Vorviades overcame any fear. Trembling, afraid he would strike out in his rage and injure his sole surviving son, he said merely, "No, I shall go in your place, as I should have gone long ago."

Then he put on the plumed helmet Velatin had once worn, and took up his spear and shield. Around his waist he strapped Kalo's sword. He bade farewell to Dera, who, in her delirium, did not know him and babbled of Vorviades.

"I dreamed truly," Anzaxos said to all he met as he took to the road. "The only lie was the deny that I had seen Vorviades. Look. The signs of his passage are all around us."

Old as he was, tired as he was, he ran, as Velatin had, not as far, not as fast, but he crossed old battlefields and saw the bones of the slain, noting the mark of Vorviades. He slept nights in ruined cities, listening to the giant's laughter on the wind. When he reached the shore of the sea, the sun was setting into the water, and there, amid the red and orange clouds, far over the sea, stood Vorviades, surveying all he had wrought.

Anzaxos caught the fading sunlight flashing on his shield. He shook his spear over his head. Vorviades gazed upon him.

"You!" Anzaxos shouted. "If you do not fight me, men will say you are afraid."

When the giant replied, storm clouds darkened the sky. The raging sea crashed upon the shore.

"At the Tarasian Gates, then, I shall meet with you in mortal combat, in one day's time."

Anzaxos was outraged. He was being mocked. "Coward! Your legs might be long enough, but you know I can't run that far in a single day. You're trying to escape me!"

"When the sun rises one more time," said the giant.

Anzaxos began to run, bearing his shield and spear, his helmet's plumed crest waving in the storm winds; ever eastward he ran, with the sea on his right. The greatest miracle was not his strength, his tirelessness, or how fast he ran. The storm ended, and the night continued. The stars turned in their courses, once, twice, five times and more, and the sun did not rise. Still Anzaxos ran, his endurance beyond anything human, beyond exhaustion or pain, in a kind of dream where he dreamt that he lay in a dark vault, far beneath the earth. At times he was not sure which he was, the dreamer or the runner, or the dreamer dreaming he was running.

The Dream-Sender said to him, many times, "You are my last, my best hope. You must prevail."

Anzaxos gasped, "Tell me of Vorviades. What are his strengths? What are his weaknesses?"

"His strengths are numberless and indescribable. He is the fury of mankind, which even the gods fear. His weaknesses, I have never been able to discover."

"That's not much help."

"I cannot help you. You must help *me*. My dread of Vorviades is unendurable, for I know that if you do not win he will find my hiding place and tear me out of it, and rend me to pieces in the light on the sun."

In darkness, what should have been ten days and nights passed, and by starlight Anzaxos came to that place where the Tarasian mountains part like gates swung wide, revealing the southern lands beyond. There he paused. He drank from a stream and waited.

In time he noticed that the stars were being blotted out, as if ink had been spilled over the sky, spreading relentlessly toward him. A dark shape rose up. Its silver mask gleamed so faintly he could barely make it out.

"Ah, Vorviades. I have waited all my life for you."

"Now let us finish this."

"Yes, now."

There was no combat. The giant reached down and snatched him up, as a child might a particularly curious and cumbersome beetle, then hurled him far out to sea.

THE DREAM-SENDER screamed one last time, a wailing, despairing cry. The tomb resonated like a gong. Dust trickled down. Surely, he realized in sudden, hideous terror, Vorviades had heard and would be coming soon.

Yet he did not wake. He commanded the dream to continue, and reached out in it, cupping Anzaxos in his hands, forbidding him to die, summoning a great whale to bear him on its back.

Vorviades *did* find him, in the dream. The silver moon-mask rose out of the sea. The terrible, burning eyes opened. The storm wind spoke.

"Enough. Every time you try to repel me, you draw me ever closer. Surrender to me at last."

Now the Dream-Sender tried to end the dream. He dismissed the whale and summoned a storm to drown Anzaxos, lest Vorviades follow him and be led, inevitably, to the crypt of the Dream-Sender.

Now it was time to hide, to be silent, to become invisible, that not even the Shadow Titans, or Vorviades who was their cousin, could find him in the darkness.

But Vorviades breathed on the sea and calmed it, and blew again so that the wind carried Anzaxos all the way to the southern shore, where he was cast up in Riverland, near the City of the Delta.

ANZAXOS AWOKE from a dream of his own death. He sat up, coughing, his throat fantastically parched, his limbs weary beyond imagining.

"There's some wine in the jug," someone said.

He blinked in the bright sunlight and groped for the wine. As he drank, he slowly took in his surroundings.

A tent-flap swayed gently in a sea breeze. Beyond it, he could make out swaying grasses and a sandy beach. The whole front of the tent was open to the sea, to let the cool breeze in.

The speaker, who had offered him the wine, was a child. A pang of remembrance came: his own sons, little Naius, who was paler, but not much smaller than this boy. His host could have been no more than fourteen or fifteen, with a soft, round face, large eyes, and unkempt hair. He wore what must have once been a plain white robe and sat cross-legged on the ground, writing in a book in his lap, every once in a while reaching for or replacing one of the pens and brushes he held between ink-splattered toes.

Before Anzaxos could question him, the boy turned his book around, displaying with obvious pride two pages of beautifully intricate calligraphy. It was an indecipherable script, all whirls and flourishes.

"Do you like my story? It is all about the giant, Vorviades."

Anzaxos tried to draw away from him, but was too weak.

"Don't be afraid of me," said the boy.

"I . . . I don't understand. All my life . . . Who *are* you?"

The boy placed a sheet of blotting paper over the page he had been working on, then closed the book. "To answer your last question first because it is the easiest, I am the sorcerer Sekenre. Whether I am the author of this story or merely one who records it, I am not at all certain. But I know that I shall profit from it, and find its meaning."

"But . . . it's not just a *story!* I have *lived* —"

"All that suffering, all that dying, did it happen because I wrote it down, or did I write it down because it happened; or is there a third explanation which only Vorviades can give us? This is a further mystery. I have pondered it for at least fifty years."

Cautiously, Anzaxos took another sip of the wine, then wiped his mouth with his hand.

"You're crazy, child. You can't be that old."

The boy began to pack his pens and brushes carefully in a case. As he worked, he spoke, and somehow seemed to change, not in physical appearance, but in manner, in voice, in presence, until Anzaxos had the impression that someone else, that a whole legion of others in turn, wore this boy's body like a garment, and now someone else entirely shared the tent with him. "Know that when one sorcerer murders another, the murderer *becomes* his victim, who lives on in the body of his murderer, but subject to him as a slave to his master — supposedly, though it doesn't always work out that way — and perhaps in the company of many more. Thus the power of the sorcerer grows. Sekenre, when he was truly young, started by murdering his own father."

The voice and manner changed again. "But his father wanted him to, and contrived it."

And another. "We are many."

Yet another. "The body does not age, but the culmination of our selves is very ancient indeed."

Anzaxos asked, "Do any of you . . . remember . . . or dream about Vorviades, or of some *other* who is his foe?"

Now the boy wrapped his book carefully in an oilcloth and put it in a shoulder bag. He seemed himself again, as if nothing had happened and he did not remember what he had just said. He got to his feet and stepped out of the tent, leaning over backward to stretch. He turned around to look at Anzaxos.

"Yes, I have dreamed of both of them, but only recently. I think I know how the story ends. Come."

Anzaxos tried to rise. "I'm so tired."

"You were always tireless before."

"Yes. And I think I can manage to be one last time."

Sekenre helped him to his feet.

THE DREAM-SENDER came to them every time they slept, screaming in terror of the giant, warning that Vorviades was right behind them, pointing into every shadow, into the palm trees where moonlight flickered and exclaiming, "There! There is Vorviades! I beg you, go away and do not lead him to me!"

But Anzaxos and Sekenre journeyed ever southward, along the left bank of the Great River, to a place of pillars, where the tombs of ancient kings lay half buried in the sand. They camped there, seeking the final solution to the puzzle, the way into a maze which could be found only in dreams, despite the Dream-Sender's every effort to conceal it.

The Dream-Sender appeared to Anzaxos, walking across the moonlit river, ripples spreading from his path. He pointed a bony finger. His bird-faced mask gleamed. His iridescent blue robe wavered like water flowing over him.

"You! You *are* Vorviades! You've changed your form once again, but I know you!"

He raised his staff as if to strike, but at that moment Anzaxos awoke, and beheld only the river, the dawn sky, and herons wading by the shore.

Each night, as they slept, Anzaxos and Sekenre both dreamed of an ancient city of high, white, marble walls and golden rooftops, and of a time so near the beginning of the world that the gods themselves walked the streets of the place; for the world was new then, and the very gods had only just awakened from their birthing-places in the Great River's mud. The first of mankind lived there, and had the gods as their house guests. A certain sorcerer dwelt among them, but apart. When the gods stood up and saw their likenesses in shadow, and these shadows sprang to life to become the Shadow Titans, making the very gods afraid, it was with the shadows that the sorcerer conversed. He invited them into his secret chamber and conferred for long hours. From them he gained certain powers and many, many secrets. He was the first and greatest of his kind.

Each night Sekenre and Anzaxos dreamed too of corridors and doorways, of passages turning, of hidden stairs. Sometimes they found such things, and moved their camp accordingly. Sometimes they understood what they had seen to be only symbols.

This went on for twenty years, during which Anzaxos grew older. Sekenre did not. Anzaxos, dreaming at night, began to prophesy by day, and travellers from the river stopped to hear him. Sekenre served as his attendant, gathering the offerings the travellers left. When the spirit left Anzaxos, and he no longer prophesied, flocks of birds swarmed over the ruins every day at sundown, leaving fish and fruits and grain scattered about. Thus the two of them were sustained. Perhaps Vorviades sent the birds.

The sun and wind darkened and gnarled Anzaxos, until, when he went to drink from the river, he beheld the reflection of what looked like animate driftwood with a wisp of white hair at one end. Sekenre merely darkened. The two of them were almost naked now, their clothing having fallen to tatters. Anzaxos saw that the boy's body, youthful as it was, was covered with intricate scars, like the elaborate calligraphy of a manuscript page, or the inlay on a warrior's sword. He understood that Sekenre was not young.

Sometimes, by day, he would dream — or remember; he wasn't sure which — another life, which was filled with glory and battles; and also of working fields and raising sons, who went away and died, first the eldest, then the second. He didn't know what happened to the third. He couldn't remember his wife's name. He was certain this was one more trick of Vorviades.

Sometimes he awoke cursing Vorviades.

Sometimes he seemed to be the Dream-Sender, peering fearfully into the world, certain that Vorviades was near.

Every day, Sekenre wrote in his book, and questioned Anzaxos about what he had dreamed.

Anzaxos felt that he was at sea again, drifting on the waves, carried along by the wind as if he were a feather, dissolving into nothingness. He forgot his anger. He felt only a fading regret and longed for release.

Then Sekenre found the way into the maze.

By torchlight, the two of them descended into the tombs. Sekenre touched a stone or spoke a word and some panel swung aside or a lion-headed god receded into the floor, and they climbed down further. Into the carven darkness they went, between huge pillars, through vast stone chambers, like insects crawling among the bones of a corpse.

In a low, narrow vault they found a sarcophagus; on its lid carven the image of a man with the face of a bird. Sekenre, for all his sorcery, wasn't very strong and needed Anzaxos to help him slide the lid off. The two of them grunted and heaved and the lid crashed to the floor.

The vault reverberated like a gong.

Within lay a man in an iridescent robe, wearing a bird mask, like the one depicted on the stone lid. Around his neck was a tarnished silver medallion of the moon.

"Behold the most ancient of sorcerers, Vorviades," said Sekenre.

"I don't understand."

"Nor do I, entirely. Come. Help me lift him up."

The two of them carried the stranger — sleeping or dead, cold to the touch, no heavier or lighter than a man should be — all the way back to the surface. All the while Anzaxos felt his mind overbrimming with terrors, with dreams hurled at him like the waves of a storm-tossed ocean. But the dreams were formless things and had no power over him. Instead he concentrated on memories of his past life, of his home, and tried to imagine what sort of man he might have become if he had never heard the name Vorviades. This left him angry, sad, and resigned all at once. He merely did what Sekenre told him to.

By the river's edge, in the bright moonlight, they laid the stranger out on the sand. Sekenre removed the mask, his hands trembling with excitement, his whole body tense with expectation.

But then he merely sat quietly while the ancient face revealed crumbled away into bones and dust.

"I think I understand," Anzaxos said.

"Do you?"

"You wanted to murder this sorcerer, so all his secrets would be yours."

Sekenre paused, as if deep in thought, then handed the mask to Anzaxos. "The bird is called Hennet-Na. It seeks immortality by flying ever eastward, into the sunrise. But it never catches up with it. Eventually it flies all the way around the world and is burnt to death in the sunset. But that takes a long time. The mask of Hennet-Na may delay death for centuries, even as sorcery does, but neither is truly eternal. In the very end, Vorviades knew he was dying as even sorcerers must. He had mastered dreams, truly mastered them, so that what he dreamed became real. He was almost a god when he was young. He could create worlds. The giant which shared his name was merely his own implacable death, given shape by his dread of it. Now that his dreaming has ceased, the giant is no more."

"When you took the mask off —"

"I did not murder him. He merely *ended.*"

"And what of those who fought for him, against his own dream?"

"Merely implements, like brushes to write the story with."

"To be discarded when you're done with them?"

"Brought into existence for that sole purpose."

Anzaxos thought of his wife and his sons. So many wasted lives. He wept and laughed at the absurdity that a discarded, worn-out implement should be able to do either.

"Come and assist me one more time," said Sekenre.

Together they cut reeds and to make a funeral boat. As they worked, it seemed to Anzaxos that a third person crouched with them, stirring impatiently in the shadows of the tombs. When they finished, and the bones of the dead sorcerer were placed in the boat, this additional presence was gone.

They waded out into the river, Sekenre shoulder-deep, until the boat caught the black current which flows upstream and they both felt the cold wind that blows out of the land of the dead. The boat drifted out of their grasp.

"I cannot accept this," Anzaxos said. "I am more than an old brush you throw away."

"What then?"

Anzaxos wept and raged. "I don't *know!* What life can I return to? I beg of you, please, help me."

Sekenre reached under the water and took the old man's hand. He squeezed hard. "I cannot help you. But you can help yourself."

"How?"

"You need Vorviades. Go after him. You'll beat him yet."

"But he is gone. You said so yourself —?

"Believe in him again. Dream him back. Remember."

"I —"

"Find the dream. Look!" Sekenre pointed to the sky. "There! Do you see him?"

Anzaxos saw only the darkness, but he remembered knights and kings and a boy who had had a dream once, lied about it, and spent much of his life denying it until it would not be denied. Awake and yet dreaming, he was Velatin, who ran, and Kalos, who hurled spears with a device called a scorpion. He rose up and ran on the surface of the river as on smooth stone. He overtook the funeral boat, snatched the moon-medallion from among the piled bones, and put it on.

And he saw the giant Vorviades towering above the world, gazing down from behind the stars.

He shouted and he cursed and he ran, calling on the giant to come down and fight.

LATER, Sekenre climbed up onto the shore, dried himself, and began writing in his book. He left several pages blank because he did not know how the story was going to end.

THE SILENCE OF KINGS

THERE IS A special silence only kings know, because only kings feel the need for it and only kings seek it out. For the holy man in his desert cave, the silence is everywhere. It is sound that startles. But the king's life is filled with noise, for the king is never alone. When he sleeps, the guards outside his door make their rounds, and servants are with him, asleep at his feet like dogs. His bath and his breakfast are ceremonial occasions. His dinner is like a parade. Even when he begets a royal heir, the multitudes await, just beyond the door, just beyond the shadows, speculating anxiously in muted voices.

These things the prophet told King Ekitares, as he paused by the Great River's bank in the evening.

"Yes, yes, I know all that," said the king.

"His death, too, is but the final tableau in a very public pageant."

Ekitares watered his horse, and drank, then mounted once more, and his army followed him, like a vast, lumbering storm, filling the sky with dust.

The prophet ran to keep up with the king, gasping for breath, as he was an old man, but the king rode on, and merely leaned over to listen.

It is when the king goes forth alone into a special place that he hears the silence, the prophet told him, *when he must consult with the gods on the weightiest matters, when the destinies of nations hang in the balance and the doors of heaven swing open so that the gods may speak. There, the king's minions do not interrupt. Even the assassin follows him not, for fear of the gods.*

"But if the gods are speaking, that is hardly silence, is it?" The king laughed and spurred his horse to a trot. The prophet caught hold of the king's saddle and kept apace.

And he bade the king appreciate the exquisite irony that the revelation comes only if the heavenly doors swing ajar and the gods aren't home. Then the king partakes of divine silence, and its wisdom is profound as anything spoken from the lips of the gods. But this happens only once, at a special place, at a special time.

"How will I know this place and time?" said King Ekitares.

"Sire, you will know it. Trust me. You will."

The king merely shook his head with contempt, and spurred his horse on. The prophet let go, doubled over with hilarity as the army passed, for he was one of the Laughing Sages, to whom enlightenment comes as a joke.

The soldiers, as they marched, sang the song of the Nine Righteous Gods, and drowned out the old man's laughter.

BUT WHEN the king came to the ruined gardens of Okishere, which lie at the desert's edge within sight of the City of the Delta, he heard that special silence. He knew. This was the place. That the prophet had told him so was itself a portent.

Therefore Ekitares the renegade pretender, who had come to cleanse the Delta of its multiform wickedness, of its thousand idols; he who had come to claim his birthright and his revenge; went alone into the empty garden to hear the silence.

And it came to pass that the armies of Righteous Ekitares shook the earth and spread over the plain before the city like a darkening tide, the gleaming armor of the Knights Inquisitor among the host like flecks of foam; and the trumpets sounded, and the false king Wenamon VI and all the sinners knew that their doom was at hand.

Yes, yes, the chroniclers were already beginning to tell it that way. Ekitares could already hear the thunder of their prose.

But he listened to the silence, alone in the evening, as once more he explored the ruined villa, the outbuildings, the remains of the garden which were little more than half-buried irrigation ditches, stone stairs, and walls.

For an instant he thought he saw someone running ahead of him, a short, slight figure, leading him deeper into the garden. A boy perhaps, running barefoot and noiselessly in the sand. Or a ghost. He followed. The other vanished, one more portent, the meaning of which, he was certain, would become clear eventually.

It was enough for the moment that he knew this place. He had come here often as a child. It was a secret then. As a child he had slipped his fingers into the deeply cut letters on the pedestal of a broken statue which spelled out THE GREAT LORD OKISHERE. Now his fingers were too large. The inscription was filled with dirt. Two enormous marble feet remained, snapped off at the ankles, all that was left of Great Okishere, who had been, perhaps, some king or noble, or even a god, in the time before the present kingdom. In one of those leisure moments kings enjoy as often as silence, he would someday find out who Okishere was.

But not now. Armed for war, but carrying his helmet in his hand, King Ekitares walked through the garden. Above, the sky deepened from orange into purple, then to velvet black. The full moon illuminated every detail of the gardens of Okishere, banishing shadows, giving birth to more.

"The silent moment is a contest," the prophet had said, "in which the king may be challenged. He may battle his foes with the sword. Or, he may win or lose a kingdom by picking up a pebble. Everything is a symbol, a glyph."

The prophet had babbled quite a bit more.

On the morrow the City of the Delta would fall completely and suddenly, like a tent cut loose from its stakes. 'Let the streets run red,' commanded the dread king, and they would run red, and the insult to his family would be avenged, the bitterness of his exile erased, and the land would be cleansed of all unrighteousness, the false gods toppled from their thrones in their temples, and only the Holy Nine set up, like sentinels above the world.

Yes, the chroniclers would write it that way.

But for now, silence. The doors of heaven were ajar. King Ekitares listened. The silence itself was a challenge, a question. It was for him alone to riddle out its answer.

The answer came in a coarse bellow that might have been the sound of an ox being tortured, or of someone singing very loud, and very, very badly.

"Oh my name it ain't nuthin' if you don't want my love.

If my kisses are misses, just give me a shove —"

Filled with rage, the king put his helmet on and drew his sword. He crashed through dead branches in the direction of the sound. *Who dared?* Who *dared?*

In the darkness he lost his way. Somehow the shrubbery closed out the moonlight. Not all of it was dead. Furiously, he hacked through thick, clinging vines. He felt a breath of damp air on his face. He thought he heard water splashing, which was quite impossible, of course.

Then he calmed himself. This was a test, a kind of battle, each thing he saw and heard part of some mysterious script which would reveal the way to victory.

Once he thought he saw a maiden bearing a lantern, clad in diaphanous white, gliding like a cloud. Or it might have been a cloud.

Once a lizard scurried across the path in front of him.

The bellowing continued.

Someone, tall and dark, either clad in armor or possibly made of metal, stood nearby, with a fire burning inside his heart like a tiny furnace. The figure vanished suddenly, by some trick of the light.

Clouds covered the moon.

For an instant he saw the ghosts of dead soldiers, tens of thousands of them, filling the garden like smoke. He stood unflinching before their onslaught, and they passed over him like a breeze, whispering in his ears.

Groping blindly, he tore through a flower-screen and came face to face with a pale, dark-eyed boy seated cross-legged on the grass. The boy had been writing something in a book by lamplight, his pens and brushes carefully arranged between his toes. He looked up at the king, expressionless. Then the clouds drifted away from the moon, light and shadow shifted, and the boy was gone.

The king stood very still, waiting for the gods to speak.

Instead, that caterwauling voice.

He pressed on, through hedges shaped like fantastic beasts. Only briefly could he marvel that by moonlight, in the darkness, the dry, dead garden had come alive again. He didn't have time for that. He would never hear the holy silence like this, as long as the "singing" (if such a word could apply) persisted.

He rounded a corner and came upon a pool, where an enormously fat man sat in the water, splashing.

The king stood breathless from his exertions. The fat man stopped singing. The two of them stared at one another. That bloated face, balding head, and scraggly beard seemed to hover before Ekitares like something out of a faintly ridiculous nightmare, some memory suppressed more out of embarrassment than fear.

"*You!*" was all either of them could say, simultaneously.

The other stood up, swaying in the shallow pool. He was almost naked, but for a cloth about his loins; his belly like a huge, risen moon, his breasts almost as pendulous as a woman's. He tilted his head to one side, as if to frame a question, then scratched himself under the arm, and squinted.

"Yes, yes, old friend," he said at last, "I *have* changed a lot since we last met. So have you."

"*Why* are you here?"

The fat man shrugged. "What can I say? When the gods arrange these things, it's a gift. Don't refuse it."

"But *you*, here, like this. It is absurd."

"The absurd and the sublime are two sides of the same coin. A prophet said that once."

"I don't doubt it," said the king. He sheathed his sword, still angry that his sublime vision had somehow flipped over into low comedy, but feeling his rage subside into mere, bewildered chagrin. Was the laughing prophet laughing now? Possibly he'd have that fellow's head on a pike sometime soon, and then ask what was so funny.

Ekitares commanded, "You had better explain yourself, Aleando. Make it good."

The other made a sweeping gesture. He nodded his head. "Pardon me if I do not bow, Lord, as there is quite a lot of me to balance, and if I tip over I might not be able to get up again. Suffice it to say that I am as surprised as you are at my presence here this night. I stepped out onto the roof of my house for some air —"

"After working up a sweat whoring, I'll bet —"

"Perhaps you'd win your bet too. Nevertheless, as I sought relief from my exertions, I stepped out, and somebody tugged ever so lightly on my arm and said, 'Aleando, come at once.' I turned. It looked like some beggar child. I thought to swat him for trespassing onto my roof. That he knew my name wasn't odd. Everybody does. But the voice *commanded.* That was intriguing, or even a little scary, so I stepped toward him, into the shadow of the awning, and by some mysterious agency found myself *here,* to which I could hardly have walked in my present condition, or been transported in a litter, a poet's poor wages being too little for such extravagances. So it has to be a miracle."

"Don't they pay you in wine? You could have *floated* here," Ekitares said.

The other belched. "You are very witty, Lord."

"Your response to this supposed miracle intrigues me," said the king. Your piety overwhelms me."

"Oh, that. Upon my arrival, nothing happened for quite some time. I was still overheated. Here was this inviting pool. Perhaps I had forgotten myself a little when you found me."

"Ah."

Aleando belched again. "Pardon me while I perform my obsequies to the god of rude noises. I am sure that if I search among the idol-stalls long enough, I can locate that particular divinity."

Ekitares stiffened at the mention of false gods. He had come to purge away such trash.

The poet reached out. "Would you help me?"

The king eased the fat man out of the pool.

"I suppose it is actually good to see you," Ekitares said, though he did not smile.

The other hiccoughed. "Yes. I suppose it is. Now what?"

"Walk with me."

The king's boots crunched gravel. Barefoot, Aleando tottered beside him, the folds of his flesh quivering like the blubber of a sea cow. *What was this supposed to mean?* The king's mind raced. *This?* A sign? An omen? Now he was *determined* to have that cackling prophet's head off at the first opportunity.

"Do you remember the first time we came here, Lord?"

"Yes."

"We were brats then. We snuck away from our nurses because you'd found the tunnel beneath the culvert. I remember I was afraid I'd get stuck, but I didn't want to seem like a sissy. You had the advantage even then, Lord. You were thin as a reed and could wriggle through anything. So off we went, under the city wall, then down by the river, and we spent all day and most of the night playing, exploring, certain we were going to be beaten when we went back, using that as an excuse to compound our mischief just a few minutes more."

"I remember the first time."

"And we really did get our posteriors paddled, but we kept coming back, because it was our secret place. Remember? We used to sail our toy boats in that very pool where you found me."

"How very appropriate." But Ekitares could not discern the meaning of this symbol. He remembered that pool being almost empty, with scummy, green water in the bottom, its sides cracked and overgrown with harsh weeds. Now, in the moonlight, the pool had renewed itself, as had the garden.

"That's how I knew it's a miracle, or a dream, or something, that we are here again. It's our little secret all over again, Lord." And sadly, Aleando continued. "I think it is so for the last time, because in the morning I shall doubtless wake up in my own bed, with or without female companionship, as I shall leave to your imagination, but just as certain to be killed when your soldiers knock down the city walls and massacre everybody."

And the king felt just a touch of sadness too, as if the great door of his anger had been left ajar, and a faint regret had drifted in.

"Then just stay here, poet. I do not require your death. I shall spare you, for old times' sake."

"I don't think it's that simple. We have to act out our roles in the miracle, or the gods will beat us like disobedient children."

"Aleando, I was beaten worse than that when my father's downfall came. I saw him tortured. My mother too, and all my uncles, everyone from our faction. They crucified my father after they'd already torn his guts out, keeping him alive by some torturer's drug. I saw the vultures pecking his face away. I had a very good view, you will recall, because I was left hanging naked in an iron cage, where I was supposed to starve to death or burn up in the sun. But there was a miracle then, too. The gods had something else in mind. One night a wind blew the cage down from its gallows. I fell at my father's feet. The cage broke open and I crawled out. I looked up into my father's ruined face, and his ghost was still there. His eyes burned like candles. His jaw fell down, slack, and there was only a gurgling sound, as if he were trying to speak, but couldn't. Therefore I went away, and sought among foreign lands for the words my father wanted to speak to me, which were commands, explicated for me by others: to live, to grow strong, to embrace the Nine Righteous Gods and come back with their power in my hand to strike down all unbelievers —"

"That's an ugly story," said Aleando. "I could have made it prettier. Given him a noble speech, something about fate and forgiveness."

Ekitares yanked him to a halt. "It doesn't have to be *pretty*. It needs to be *complete*. Tomorrow, it will be, and if you get killed in the process, that's just too mother-whoring bad."

"What if the story had a different ending?"

"What?"

"The gods can always rewrite the ending."

"What are you talking about?"

"Be quiet before you get paddled. Look."

They had walked in a circle and come again to the shallow pool. Now two boys, one of them plump like a pear with legs, the other reed-thin, lay by the water's edge, finger-pushing toy boats through the stagnant water.

"Remember?" whispered Aleando.

"I remember." Ekitares wondered if the thin one might be the same as the phantom runner he'd seen earlier. Somehow, he didn't think so.

"I asked you then," said Aleando, "what you wanted to be when you grew up. You asked me. I said I was going to be a poet. You said you were going to conquer the world. 'But doesn't that involve killing a lot of people?' I wanted to know. You didn't have any answer. But suppose, just suppose, you *did*, have an answer, that is, but not the same answer, and you decided to do something other than conquer the world. Just suppose that those two boys went home and grew up, and everything turned out differently."

"You're talking nonsense, Aleando."

"No, Great King, I am inspired. I think the gods are offering you a wonderful gift."

"Which gods?" said the king. *"Which?"*

"Any and all. Does it matter?"

"Enough!" the king shouted. He waved his arms at the two boys. "You! Get out of here! You don't belong!" He crashed through the hedges, sword drawn, dragging Aleando after him.

The two screamed and ran off.

"I remember when that happened," the poet gasped, wincing as he felt where his bare self had been scratched all over by the hedge-thorns. "I was particularly afraid of the fat giant. I used him as a monster in a poem —"

"Silence!" said the king.

"A wonderful gift. Don't refuse it," said the poet, and then he was silent.

And in the silence, the absolute silence of holiness, which is known only once in a lifetime to kings and somewhat more conveniently to prophets, Ekitares tried to understand.

ALEANDO AND Ekitares ran back to the city as fast as they could go, the fat boy stumbling in the darkness, floundering in mud so that he lost his shoes and was wallowing about helplessly trying to find them until his silent friend grabbed him by the hair and dragged him on his way. Aleando babbled of ghosts, of old Okishere come back to haunt them and curse them and tear out their eyes and eat their guts for breakfast.

"Shut up," said Ekitares, hauling him along through the reeds at the Great River's edge, impatient, cursing, but unwilling to abandon Aleando.

It was not their first visit to the secret, ruined gardens, but their last. They were both thirteen. They had decided to go one more time. They both felt a little foolish about it, for all that no one cared anymore, and they faced no beating on their return.

Now this —

They'd lost their boats. The secret place wasn't a secret anymore. It was time to grow up.

Below the window of a certain tower, Ekitares slammed his hand on the stone, once, twice, thrice, in a rapid signal.

A giggling maiden leaned out, then disappeared back inside. A rope snaked down. Ekitares caught it and climbed up into the tower, where the girl caught him and hauled him through the window. She yanked off his tunic and his shoes.

"Ugh, you're all muddy."

She covered him with kisses anyway.

"Don't leave me out here!" Aleando wailed.

Ekitares and the girl looked into one another's eyes.

"Maybe we should get him."

"In a minute."

Several minutes passed.

"Hey! Don't leave me!" Aleando yanked on the rope.

"I suppose we should get him."

They lowered a basket out the window, and, sweating and straining, hauled Aleando up.

"You're muddy too!" said the girl.

The three of them went down into the vaults beneath the tower where an illegal tap had been driven into the city's water supply. The girl pulled out the plug. Naked, the three of them jumped and yelped as cold water from the aqueduct splashed over them.

Later, right there on the wet stone floor, the girl made love to both of them.

EKITARES OPENED his eyes, squinting at the bright sunlight. For the moment, he didn't know where he was. He had dreamed of battles, of killing and glory, of toppling gods from their thrones. The dream had been so real that it took a while to convince himself that he was actually awake. He had had dreams like that for years, as if remembering another life.

He was older now, a man, old enough to have a beard.

He should have been off conquering the world. He was obscurely certain of that.

But right now the only battle seemed to be going on in his head, where armies clashed. He staggered to his feet, clinging to one of the poles that held up the rooftop awning on the house of his friend, the poet Aleando. There were cups scattered about. A table had been overturned. A couple of clay amphorae had gotten smashed somehow.

He was still, even in the morning, very, very drunk.

Nearby, the massive Aleando lay in the shadow of the awning, a naked woman resting on either arm. He snorted in his sleep, sputtering his lips to drive away flies, performing ritual obsequies to the god of rude noises.

Ekitares cursed foully, at no one in particular. He went over to a basin and washed his face with his hands. Then he dressed himself as best he could. He couldn't find his shirt, or one of his shoes. It had been one of those nights. He pulled on loose trousers and tiptoed down through the house, where other revellers still slept, the single shoe held uselessly in his hand.

Someone sat up and asked about breakfast, giggling.

Barefoot and shirtless, Ekitares stepped out into the street. People turned to stare, then looked away when they recognized him. Poets were supposed to be dissolute, weren't they? It came to him that he was a poet too, of the "School of Aleando," as some people jokingly put it. That Aleando actually wrote very fine verses didn't seem to be the point. That he, Ekitares, occasionally wrote decent ones, was not the point either.

He should be out conquering the world. Or was he some deluded maniac only dreaming he was a conqueror? And did the conqueror, in the dream, dream that he was young Ekitares, drinking-companion of Aleando, all-around good-for-nothing, the son of some minor nobleman who had been kicked out of the palace years ago for petty corruption?

Which was true? All? Neither?

In the silence known to kings, which was inside him and shut out the city's noise, he sought an answer. He walked through the streets, ignored by passers-by after a while as he reached the broad avenues where great multitudes gathered and no one paid any attention to him. A laughing

holy man walked on stilts above the crowd, his ragged clothing streaming in the wind. A peddler sold petty gods from a tray he wore around his
neck. In the street of the smiths, the air was filled with hammering, as
craftsmen labored at their work, manufacturing divinities. Again, in the
city's forum, before the huge temples of the Great Gods — the Nine and
many others — a juggler had climbed atop one of the holy statues and
was tossing balls into the air. Some people applauded. Others turned
away. A watchman shouted for him to come down. All around, servant-
women haggled over the price of fish, merchants displayed cloth, children ran and shouted, and thousands of voices joined together in a vast
murmur of mundane business which was like a endless, overwhelming
tide.

Sudden trumpets parted that tide. Iron-shot feet thundered on the
pavement in measured step. The juggler slid down from the statue. The
children stood still. The haggling women paused.

And in the silence of kings, Ekitares turned and beheld Wenamon VI,
the Great King, Lord of the Delta, parading in all his majesty, in his
golden robes and beehive-shaped crown with the eagle and crocodile
emblems on it. Guards flanked the royal litter on either side, marching in
perfect time, the plumes of their helmets swaying in the morning breeze.
While heralds proclaimed and slaves bore him, Wenamon sat motionless
in his litter like the statue of a god, encrusted in jewels, turning neither to
left nor to right. And when the procession passed out of the forum,
beneath a huge, triumphal arch, the Great King, who was not a tall man,
bowed his head as a god might when passing out the doorway of some a
temple that was too small for him.

Ekitares looked around at all the other people, who began milling
about again, their voices rising, disrupting forever that special silence
known only to kings at the moment when their destiny hangs in the balance.

He had received his answer. He understood. He was no different
from anyone else in this crowd, one more silly young man, who did not
matter in the passing of time.

In the garden, King Ekitares, the dream-king, had asked the dream-
poet Aleando, *Couldn't you just stay here?*

If Aleando could stay in the dusty garden of Okishere, and, by doing
so, not get killed when the city fell, couldn't Ekitares just stay where he
was, in this other life?

That was the miracle, the "wonderful gift." That was what the gods, in their infinitely mysterious way, offered. That was what the assorted phantoms in the garden had brought about, or come to witness. He could stay here, in the crowd. He didn't have to be a drunkard. He didn't even have to be a poet. He could marry, work at a trade, or use what remained of his father's connections and seek some minor position at court.

But if he stayed, he knew, he would never know glory. The rage that drove him through that other life would dissipate, like a storm scattered by a fresh wind. He would forget his pain. He might even be vaguely content.

But he would never hear the sound of ten thousand men marching at his back, singing his war-song. He would never topple gods. He would never sit on a throne.

As the silence known only to kings faded, he knew what he had to do.

"NO! I must conquer! I will conquer!"

King Ekitares, fully armed for war, burst through the hedges in the garden of Okishere, splashed into the pool and struck one of the toy boats with his sword. The two boys screamed and ran.

"You have chosen, then?" said Aleando.

"Yes, I have," said the king, in that grim voice which could make men fall down faint.

"The gods offered you something else. Your family wasn't murdered. Nobody suffered. But you throw away the gods' gift and cling to your pain. Why?"

"Because there is glory," said the king. "Because of that."

Aleando shook his head sadly. "For glory then."

The king turned his back on him. He was ready to leave. Unnoticed, the night had passed. It was almost dawn. The silence was only a memory now. An owl called out from the reeds down by the river.

Ekitares stood for a moment with his back to the poet. "Goodbye," he said. He spat the word out like a command.

"Goodbye," said Aleando, weeping.

And with surprising quickness and strength, Aleando the fat poet seized King Ekitares in both his hands and broke his neck. Then he dragged his old friend to the edge of the dried-out, cracked pool where once they had played. Weeping, he rummaged around in the muck at the bottom and pulled out the remains of a toy boat which had been smashed.

He held it up to Ekitares, who stared, glassy-eyed, into space.

"Remember?" said the poet. "We lost them. Years ago."

The king gasped for breath but did not speak.

Above, the sky lightened, and the last stars were going out. For just an instant, in the depths of the sky *behind* the stars, the gods appeared, towering figures like cloud-banks, some wearing featureless masks, some with the heads of birds, others looking down with pity or amusement or indifference.

In the silence, Aleando beheld the gods, not the Nine, but the Thousand, who knew when the doom of the City of the Delta was to come, but had ordained it was not yet.

Something stirred nearby. He saw, at the edge of the pool, gazing at him like reflections, the boy with the book, the white-robed maiden with the lantern, an iron-wrought thing with fire in its heart, a gaunt man whose hands seemed to be made of feathers, and many more, witches and sorcerers, seers and ghosts, drawn to this moment of silence and destiny, to observe and record, but not to alter.

The laughing prophet was there too, but soundless as the rest. He alone of those others gazed upon the gods with ecstasy and recognition on his face, for he was holy. The rest, even the boy, turned away or covered their eyes, for they were not.

This was a haunted place. Aleando was afraid, and wanted to be away.

But before he left, he rolled King Ekitares over face-down into the stagnant water, leaving him to listen to the silence of kings.

Someone tugged him on the elbow and said in a soft voice, "Come, now, Aleando. It is finished."

And Aleando wept, and resolved to make a poem out of all this, to set things right.

IT WAS early in the afternoon when Aleando stirred awake. He sat up, sleek with sweat.

His lady of the previous night had long departed. Her clothes were gone.

He washed his face in a basin and shook his head, puzzled to discover mud on his hands. He remembered some fantastic dream he'd had, which he was supposed to make into a poem.

While he was doing so, the door to his chamber creaked open and someone entered without any other sound.

Aleando looked up. It was the boy with the book. He could see him clearly in the light from the window, an ordinary street child somewhere in the early teens, very thin, dressed in shapeless, dusty clothes, his trousers torn off just below the knees, his bare feet grubby, his calves scratched as if he'd been running through underbrush.

"Would you like to see what I have written about you?" the boy said. The look on his soft, round face and in his dark eyes was completely inscrutable.

As soon as Aleando glanced at the open page of the boy's book, he knew that such exquisite, detailed calligraphy would take years to perfect, far more years than its author had apparently lived.

He looked up, but before he could say anything, the other spoke.

"You are quite correct. I am the sorcerer Sekenre and am much older than I seem. I appear as I was when first the affliction came upon me, it being the nature of sorcery that, while the soul is corrupted, the body does not age."

Aleando began to weep once more, surprising himself, embarrassed and angry, but unable to hold back his tears.

"How much of what went on was your doing?"

"A part. It was a collaborative project."

"How did you know I would do . . . what I did?"

"A kind of foreknowledge."

"Then what was the damned *point?*" said Aleando. "It was all fixed."

"No," said the sorcerer, "your friend's choice was not predetermined. That was what intrigued me. I wanted to know if he could turn his life in another direction."

"Could you turn *yours?*"

Sekenre paused. He seemed startled. For an instant Aleando thought he could see a trace of tears around the sorcerer's eyes.

"I have written whole volumes on that subject," Sekenre said at last. "You may read them if you like."

Aleando turned back to his desk. "I have work to do." For a while, the boy sat beside him, as words flowed across Aleando's own page, were sometimes blotted or scratched out, and the poem continued.

After a while, Aleando realized that he was alone.

All day, the army of the conqueror remained where it was, like a vast cloud in a motionless sky, but by evening word spread that King Ekitares was dead, and the invading host scattered, like a storm dissipated by a fresh breeze.

VANDIBAR NASHA IN THE COLLEGE OF SHADOWS

I

WHEN HIS enemy's servant gave him the bronze coffer shaped like a human hand, Vandibar Nasha accepted the gift politely. He did not have to open it to know that it contained the severed hand of one of his own servants, who had died hideously in a cellar beneath the enemy's house.

The other had taken Vandibar's piece, but the game would continue. That a little blood seeped through the hinge and stained his sleeve was the only cause for true offense. It was inelegant and unworthy, and Vandibar was, if nothing else, a fastidious man, who maintained about his person and his house a sense of unadorned, even austere, but undeniable elegance.

He gazed across the glittering sea of his guests, as they surged over the roof-garden in the twilight, beneath swaying paper lanterns. He spied his enemy, Radaces, by the punchbowl, dressed like a peacock in heat, a jumble of jewelry and multi-colored silks and, indeed, billowing feathers, his face painted and slightly streaked with intricate black and silver spirals. Radaces leaned away from the crowd, conversing with a man in a tarnished sun-mask.

Vandibar pressed gently toward them, pausing to greet guests, to laugh at their witticisms, to sample delicacies, even once stooping as a child prattled something in his ear. But still he made his way, and by the time he reached Radaces, the man in the tarnished mask was gone, something Vandibar noted with concern. He knew, though he was not supposed to, who that person was: a prince up from the Delta on an intrigue.

He confronted Radaces, still holding the hand-shaped coffer. Their eyes met. Radaces leaned forward, that none might overhear, and said, "It is death between us now."

"I know that. I've found you out."

Radaces laughed softly, and waved his hand to indicate the crowd in attendance, "But we must maintain appearances."

"Yes, of course."

So they stood together, host and illustrious guest, smiling at the assembled nobility of Elandisphon, the City of the River's Bend. Above, a brilliant moon shone. It was a Goddess Moon, Shedelvendra's Lantern, marking the springtime and the river's rising. Therefore tonight was a time of celebration, of renewals and new unions, and, especially, of maintaining appearances.

Both he and Radaces pretended not to notice a certain young couple seated among the tumbling vines against the far wall. Vashimur, who was Vandibar's son, furtively held the hand of Tatiane, daughter of Radaces.

Suddenly there came a commotion from the great stair that led up from the inner court of Vandibar's house. Everyone whirled about, including Radaces.

Then Vandibar touched his enemy on the shoulder with the brazen hand. Radaces turned, startled, and Vandibar whispered, "I think it is death coming."

Radaces's face went pale for just an instant. But everyone was laughing as eight slaves, hugely-muscled, sweat-drenched (but perfumed), bore a palanquin up among the guests, set it down, and pulled back the canopy to reveal a cooked and stuffed crocodile bedecked with pearls, crowned with a silver wreath, its claws sheathed in gold. Vandibar's crier announced the advent of Surat-Hemad, Lord of Death, the Devouring God, whose mouth is the night sky, whose teeth are the stars.

A murmur of amazement rippled through the crowd.

On this night, however, the crier continued, the Devourer was to be himself devoured, for the springtime is a celebration of new life.

Flower-masked page-boys ran through the crowd, handing out forks. One of the slaves produced an enormous knife and began carving.

At the first touch of the blade, flames exploded from the crocodile's mouth. There were astonished shouts and a couple of screams. But the slave blew the flames out in a single breath, and everyone applauded, if nervously, and began devouring the Devourer.

Radaces smiled weakly. "A brilliant jest."

"Yes. Isn't it? But more your style than mine. I designed it with you in mind."

"That doesn't change anything."

"Nothing ever does."

Much later the dance began, and a priest and priestess whirled in the circle which had been cleared for them, their respective green and yellow streamers trailing fantastically as the two of them embraced in imitation of the sacred coupling of Bel-Hemad, who brings the rain, and Shedel-vendra his consort; only then could Vandibar Nasha slip away down a marble, spiralling staircase, past a stone trellis covered with night-blooming, almost luminescent flowers, into the empty lower garden.

Only then could sorcery come to him, almost as a distraction.

Even here, in the quiet, familiar place to which he had retreated, as he sat on a marble bench by the edge of a stone pool; even here, alone in the dark, as the sounds of dinner-party faded into a murmur only occasion-ally punctuated by a voice or a note of music louder than the rest — a squeal of laughter or a cymbal clashing — even here, Vandibar Nasha maintained perfect decorum.

He sat quietly in the perpetual twilight of the garden, among the night-blooming flowers, by the edge of the pool, where the water like pol-ished ebony perfectly mirrored the sky. He did not yield to rage, or to fear, or to laughter. He sat with the bronze hand in his lap, and it seemed that, ever so subtly, something opened within his mind, like a shutter left slightly ajar; and a single dark moth fluttered in out of the night.

There. Like that.

He looked up with a start, as if he'd been pricked. But he was alone. The distant music and voices whispered like a tide. Tree branches creaked gently in the night breeze.

The stars rippled. He gazed, not at the sky, but into the pool, as if that dark thing already lodged inside him gave him this instruction, and reas-sured him that one day, but not yet, he would be ready to look up and behold this miracle directly.

For now it was as if the earth were no more than the floor of a great hall, and he had opened a portal, and now gazed into the infinity below.

The stars in the pool shone more brilliantly than he had ever seen them before. They drifted back and forth, like gems set in a dark velvet hanging which billows with a sudden breeze.

Faces appeared behind the stars, huge and fierce, wild in their aspect, with terrible eyes. He knew that these were not the gods, but the Shadow Titans, shadows cast by the gods on the first evening of creation, which rose and came to life, which even the gods feared, but which sorcerers adored, for sorcerers are abominations which serve the abominable.

He knew that if he were to turn his head and look up at them directly, he would die.

But he was already a sorcerer. That was enough.

In that instant of realization, he was exultant. He would swiftly take care of Radaces. No sorcerer would ever have to suffer such a fool.

Besides, with Radaces out of the way, Vashimur could marry Tatiane, and all the wealth of the house of Radaces would be joined to that of the house of Nasha.

Therefore Vandibar became a sorcerer, by unknown means, toward an unknowable end, and he knelt by the pool and prayed to the reflected Titans, and offered to them thanksgiving. He was not afraid.

He heard the Titans whispering. They told him what to do. He opened the bronze coffer eagerly, fumbling with the latch, heedless of any possible venomed edges or similar childish devices. He washed the severed hand of his murdered servant in the starry water. Blood swirled over the faces of the Titans, obscuring them briefly.

With an ornamental pin from his collar, he carved a certain sign and the name of RADACES on the back of the hand.

He placed the thing on the surface of the water. It stood up on pale fingers and scurried like a water-striding insect across the pool and into the garden on the other side. He heard it rustling among the leaves for a few seconds and then it was gone.

Once more he gazed into the reflected stars, and a voice within him spoke through his lips. The Titans replied in the language of corpses, that universal speech of the afterworld in which sorcerers, alone among living men, are conversant. For the moment, Vandibar understood little. He was like a small child eavesdropping on adults. Yet the understanding came, a remembrance, not of a dream, but of an earlier life *before* the dream which had been his life up to this point, from which he had now suddenly awakened.

Then the water splashed and the Titans disappeared. Someone addressed him in a soft voice, in a stiffly formal manner mimicking the corpse-language, but in Deltan with a bad provincial accent.

"Art thou, then, Vandibar Nasha, who holds the doom of Radaces in his hand?" Here what might have been an impudent snicker, and the tone and accent changed. "If you will pardon the expression."

Vandibar looked up, furious, then incredulous to see what seemed to be a child seated on the opposite side of the pool, splashing his bare feet in the water; a ragged boy of early teens, with a round face and large, dark eyes.

It wasn't one of his servants, whom he would have had beaten within

an inch of his life for such an outrage. It had to be some starveling beggar, whom he could have killed.

But he realized that he hadn't heard anyone approach, and now the boy spoke in the true death-speech.

"Thou art indeed that Vandibar Nasha, whose name is known in the land of ghosts, whose deeds are told by the dead around their cold fires."

Sometimes, Vandibar knew, when the game takes an incomprehensible turn, one must keep on playing, no matter what, merely to survive, and hope for advantage to appear later. Therefore he answered, "I am."

The boy reverted to Deltan, his accent far worse, his manner casual. "Oh, I thought so."

"But I don't understand. What deeds? What stories?"

"All that are and shall be, for among the dead there is no time, as it is for the sorcerer, who swims in eternity like a fish in the sea, rising to the surface only when he chooses."

A moment of silence followed. Vandibar closed the empty hand-coffer and floated it in the pool, rippling the surface gently.

"I am Sekenre," said the boy, "not of this place, but of Reedland, also a sorcerer and therefore an abomination as you are; perhaps your ally, perhaps your foe, but unlikely to be your friend, for it is a fantastically rare thing for a sorcerer to have a friend."

Some part of Vandibar's mind felt sudden, irretrievable loss, as if he'd just dropped a particularly precious gem into the sea without realizing he'd done so until it was too late. He was a man who loved as well as hated. Was this boy saying he was now beyond all that?

He dismissed the thought. "You could be just a lunatic."

The boy closed his hands, then opened them slowly. Blue flames danced on his palms without apparently burning him.

"I demand to know why thou hast come," said Vandibar Nasha firmly, startled that he had used the corpse-language.

Sekenre's voice shifted again. His accent was gone. Someone else seemed to speak through him. "Only to show you what you have already done, Oh dread sorcerer, Vandibar Nasha."

"What have I done? I haven't done anything."

Sekenre in this new voice replied only, "Radaces," and accented again, said, "Come with me."

Vandibar rose and followed him. The boy walked noiselessly, lighting the way with blue fire in an outstretched hand. They came to the stone trellis and the stair. Vandibar hesitated. He wasn't going to appear before his guests in such company.

But Sekenre continued, barefoot on stone, quiet as a ghost, and he could only follow.

He heard no voices, no music, no sound at all, and was astonished to find the roof-garden deserted, the canopies rolled up, the furniture cleared away. Dead leaves rustled across the pavement in a faint breeze. The moon, which had been full tonight, was now well past, and low in the east, though the hour must have been quite late.

His mind wasn't working right. He couldn't reason. He merely accepted. Such details were not clues, but portents, part of a vision.

His breath came in white puffs. The air was cold, as in winter.

Sekenre said nothing. In the moonlight, Vandibar Nasha saw that his initial estimation had been wrong. This wasn't a beggar child: skinny, but not emaciated; his trousers roughly torn off just below the knees and his tunic several sizes too large, but not ragged; his face clean and his hair trimmed. An ordinary forum brat, then; but that was one more falsehood, another mask.

And the voice of sorcery within himself seemed to ask, *What mask do you wear, Vandibar Nasha?*

Sekenre shivered in the cold, the blue flame flickering as his hand trembled. When they descended the further stairway, which lead to a covered passage bypassing the house, there was ice on the steps.

Yet when they emerged into the street, the moon was gone, and warm rain poured over the pavement in muddy rivulets, swirling around the boy's bare ankles. The fire in his hand did not go out. Vandibar followed him down steep, cobblestone streets, tier after tier, as the city extended down to the river like a carpet flung over a flight of stairs.

By the time they reached the forum, the rain had stopped. The air was hot and stifling. Mist rose from the pavement like smoke. The temples of the gods all around them silent and empty, the stone colossi on the roof-tops gazing down blindly through the thick haze. For just an instant there was a hint of a crescent moon, but then it was gone.

So the two of them reached the house of Radaces in utter darkness, but for the almost lightless flames flickering through the fingers of Sekenre's half-closed hand.

Here again, Vandibar hesitated, thinking of proprieties, imagining how ridiculous he must look in his sodden, ruined gown, with his fine shoes now muddy and squishing as he walked, his hair plastered to his face.

Sekenre, dripping beside him, sneezed loudly. "We must go in," he said.

"Yes, we must."

Sekenre touched the door with fire. The door swung silently inward. Vandibar followed, into the darkened house, through what he knew to be a gaily-frescoed atrium, where just a year earlier, it had been Radaces's turn to greet guests at the Festival of the River's Rising.

Now there was only gloom and the only sound was of his squishing shoes.

They came upon what seemed to be a naked, hugely muscled, pot-bellied man. He took it for a statue, but then the apparition lurched for-ward, drawn by Sekenre's light, and he saw it more clearly: bloated, hid-eously pale like one long drowned, wearing some kind of animal mask.

The long jaws opened, and Vandibar knew it was no mask at all, but the true face of one of the *evatim*, the messengers of the death-god Surat-Hemad, which crawl up out of the river to devour corpses. No one ever sees them except when he is about to die, or when someone very close to him as died, or perhaps in the midst of deepest sorcery.

For the first time, Vandibar Nasha was truly afraid. He wished he could go back, that the vision would end, that none of this had ever hap-pened. He was almost ready to apologize to Radaces.

Yet Sekenre pressed on. Vandibar reached out and took the boy's free hand, for comfort, fully aware of the absurdity of the gesture. But Sekenre did not pull away.

"Why hast thou come?" said the monster in the death-speech. "This is my master's house now."

"This is the house of the lord Radaces," said Sekenre, in an almost naive tone, Vandibar thought, in that barbarous up-country accent of his.

The monster seemed to understand him, and bowed with mock courtesy, continuing in the death-speech, "Then proceed, honored guests. The lord's wife and children await thee within."

"What about Radaces?" said Sekenre.

But the creature only bowed again and shuffled aside, its clawed feet scraping the tile floor, its long tail dragging.

Vandibar felt increasing helplessness as Sekenre led him deeper into the house, as if this were a terrible dream from which he wanted so desperately to awaken, and the voice of sorcery inside his heart told him, *Never, never, shalt thou awaken from this dream, even beyond thine own death, until the ending of time and the deaths of the gods themselves, a thousand times never.*

All of the lower rooms were empty, all the servants gone. They ascended a great marble stair, Sekenre silent, Vandibar cringing as his wet shoes made sucking sounds. Another of the *evatim* waited at the top, this one on all fours like a crocodile. Sekenre whispered something Vandibar could not hear. The creature shuffled aside to let them pass.

Upstairs on the landing, they found the youngest daughter of Radaces, aged four or five, torn apart as if she had been savaged by dogs. The lord's younger son hung by his ankles in the bedroom, gutted like a pig that has been slaughtered.

On the balcony overlooking the central garden, the wife of his enemy sat on a bench, gazing into nothingness, holding what must have been her youngest daughter Tatiane in her arms. It must have been that same slender girl of fifteen or sixteen, whom Vandibar's son Vashimur secretly loved. But he couldn't be sure. Her head was gone, and her blood had spread out at her mother's feet like a sea of black oil.

Sekenre stepped back to avoid the blood. He held up his blue flame. Vandibar gasped, then turned and wept as he saw that the lady's eyes had been gouged out. Her fingers were bloody. Perhaps she had done it to herself, to escape such sights. Her breath came in hoarse gasps, sobbing long since exhausted, and incredibly she began to sing almost inaudible, incoherent snatches of some lullaby as she rocked Tatiane back and forth. It was a small mercy that she was mad, but only a small one.

And Sekenre said, without irony, but in hard, unaccented Deltan,

"Are these not the fruits of victory, for which the sorcerer Vandibar Nasha has so long striven?"

Furious, his voice breaking, Vandibar yanked the boy aside and would have hurled him into the garden below.

"No! No! It's all wrong!"

"But it was all your doing."

"Liar!"

"Look for yourself."

Sekenre turned his head and Vandibar followed his gaze. Something stirred at the lady's feet, swimming in blood like an enormous and ungainly spider. It was a severed human hand. The sign and name Vandibar had cut into it now glowed blue, the color of Sekenre's flame.

Revolted, Vandibar let go of Sekenre and kicked the thing away. Then he caught the boy by the shoulder and shook him. "No. I didn't mean it this way. Take me away quickly!"

II

ALL THE while as they walked back through the deserted city, through the hot, steamy night, through the cool spring rain which sent the mud swirling around their ankles, in the chilly winter air, as the moon rose and set, crescent, gibbous, full, waning, Vandibar raved. He debated with himself. You did these things. No, you did not. They didn't happen at all. They are a dream. You can undo them. You're a sorcerer now, aren't you? No, that is a dream too.

In the midst of all this Sekenre turned to him and said in his accented, little boy's voice, "What kind of a monster is Vandibar Nasha?"

Weeping, the other replied, "A terrible monster indeed."

They walked on some more, and Vandibar's words poured out in a babbling torrent, and only after a long time did he realize that they had not seen the corpse of Radaces anywhere.

"I think he has escaped this particular holocaust," said Sekenre as if he knew what Vandibar was thinking, his voice once more hard and his Deltan flawless. "Sorcerers can be elusive."

"What do you mean?"

"It's like trying to nail down quicksilver."

"That's not what I ask!"

"You and he are evenly matched."

"Sekenre, help me!"

The boy's voice reverted to the softer tone and the accent that Vandibar had somehow come to trust. It was therefore some comfort when Sekenre said, "Yes, I'll do whatever I can."

But there was no comfort at all when the boy guided him up the last street, to the smoldering ruins of his own house, where the walls had been breached and broken, and the bodies of his servants lay beneath the fallen timbers. A part of the roof-garden remained, and there Vandibar found his son Vashimur crucified on two of those same timbers, naked and bloody and near to death, already whimpering deliriously in the language of the dead.

In that same tongue, Vandibar addressed him, gently. "It's only a dream. Think that you'll soon wake up and it'll all be over."

But the head of Takida, Vandibar's wife, glared down at him from a stake. The eyes opened and burned with blue fire. The mouth tried to form words, but lacking breath, could not speak them, yet the meaning was clear enough, and they called Vandibar liar.

All around them, the *evatim* crawled on all fours like beasts, sometimes reaching up to snap at Vashimur's nail-pierced feet.

And Vashimur spoke only one more word in reply, clearly pronouncing the name of Tatiane.

Then Vandibar covered his face with his ruined gown and allowed himself to be led into the lower garden, by the pool. Only there, out of sight of his wife and son, did he think it proper to grab Sekenre and try to break his neck. He, Vandibar, was a tall man, over fifty but still strong. Sekenre weighed nothing. He could snap him like a twig. He screamed in all his pent-up rage and tried to do exactly that, but Sekenre slipped from his grasp like quicksilver, and stood apart from him, gasping.

"Think, Vandibar Nasha. Think what it means to kill a sorcerer. His sorcery doesn't die. It lives on *inside you*. You become what you have slain, devouring your foe, so that everything you loathe about him becomes part of you."

"I loathe only myself."

"And not Radaces?"

"Radaces also."

Sekenre began to pace back and forth, hands clasped behind his back, his manner that of a much older man, and his voice changed yet again, to an accent and a tone Vandibar had never heard before.

"Ah, now we are getting somewhere. You still hate Radaces, even if you hate yourself. Yes. I cannot tell you how to undo what has been done, but perhaps it can be *deflected,* or, more precisely, *delayed* in its effects. Do not doubt that in the end you will burn for it in terrible fire, and for what Radaces has done."

"And he too?"

"You are evenly matched."

Wearily, Vandibar sat down on the marble bench beside the pool. "I see that I can't go back, only forward. Very well. Tell me more."

And the *other* within Sekenre discoursed, in a dry, stern voice, on the nature of sorcery and its relation to *time,* repeating much that had been said before, about swimming outside of the normal flow of events, or perhaps *beneath* it, only surfacing into the lives of ordinary men at chosen intervals. Vandibar understood very little, at least right away. But there was another image, which made more sense.

Sekenre worked a few tiles loose from the edge of the pool, and held them in his hand, arranged in a line, a single black tile second in the sequence among the white.

The black tile was the day of suffering, of the deaths of all Vandibar loved, and the white were the days of their lives, and his own.

Sekenre, or the person who wore Sekenre like a cloak, looked up at him and smiled, and the expression on his face was utterly inscrutable, perhaps cynical, perhaps genuinely offering hope, perhaps beyond anything he had words to describe.

The boy rearranged the tiles until the black one came last.

"You can't get rid of it," he said, "but you can place it differently."

In that instant, Vandibar Nasha heard something incredible.

Music and laughter came from the roof-garden above him. He rose from the bench and hurried away from Sekenre, and ran up the stairway by the trellis. He didn't care how he looked in his muddy gown, and when he reached the top, in full moonlight, on a warm spring night, he was as elegantly garbed as he had ever been.

He gazed in amazement at the swarming guests, at their gaudy robes and masks and feathers, and spied Vashimur and Tatiane furtively holding hands over by the punch bowl. He waded into the crowd, almost oblivious, making only perfunctory replies to any who spoke to him, and came upon Radaces seated on the bench in the shadows, against the far wall amid the vines.

He sat down beside him. For an instant, the two of them silently surveyed all before them.

"I cannot forgive," said Radaces at last.

"Not can I."

"Then we are agreed."

"It is death between us."

At that moment, the revellers broke out in riotous laughter and applause as muscular slaves delivered a stuffed crocodile, and everyone devoured the Devourer with silver forks.

Later Vandibar rose and joined with all the others, even with Radaces, in the great dance which concluded the evening, to celebrate the holy union of Bel-Hemad, god of the springtime, and Shedelvendra, the Lady of the Lantern.

The fat poet Agetirae was too drunk for all that whirling and circling. He had to be led away discreetly. Everyone else departed more graciously, presenting the host with a final gift.

Radaces gave Vandibar a coffer shaped like a human hand, which Vandibar accepted graciously.

Later still, after everyone had gone to bed, he awoke in his own bed, trembling. Takida, his wife, stirred beside him.

"What is it?" she said.

"I dreamed . . . terrible things."

"Go back to sleep. It's just vapors."

"It's probably something like that," he muttered, but he instead got up, wrapping himself in the same elegant gown he had worn to greet his guests.

He walked out onto the roof garden in his bare feet. It was nearly dawn. The moon hung low in the west, almost touching the desert beyond the river. The city lay dark and silent.

A few of his servants were still sweeping up, carrying away benches, and taking down the now extinguished lanterns.

He called a boy over to him and told him to run down into the city, to the house of Lord Radaces.

"*Now*, Master?"

"Yes, now. I want you to tell me if his house is still there and if all is well."

The young servant looked at him strangely. "They'll all be in bed."

Vandibar fished a silver coin out of his pocket, and held it up. The servant's eyes widened.

"This will be for you if you do exactly what I tell you." He picked up a slate one of the waiters had used, rubbed it clean with his sleeve, and made a sign with chalk. In some other time, in the midst of his terrible dream, he had carved that sign with a pin into the dead flesh of a severed hand. "Make this sign on Lord Radaces's door. It's a joke between us. He'll understand. Now go."

The servant took the chalk and went.

Vandibar returned to bed, then arose at the usual hour and breakfasted. But the servant did not return. In the middle of the morning, a parcel arrived, wrapped in silk, sealed with the emblem of Lord Radaces.

Vandibar took it alone into his study. There he broke the seal and pulled away the wrapping. Inside was a beautifully lacquered box. The sign inlaid on it in mother-of-pearl was that same one he had intended to be written on his enemy's door.

Inside the box was a bloody nail.

III

"SO RADACES has countered you," said Sekenre, by the pool, regarding the nail. The water rippled in the darkness, and the Shadow Titans appeared.

"You said that I would burn in a terrible fire."

"Every act of sorcery has a price, and that price is usually pain, but that pain, the consequences of your actions, can often be put off, even as tiles may be rearranged. Your son *will* one day die in great agony, as you saw him do, and he will die a young man, but this does not mean that he can't first grow to be an old one, happy and prosperous, surrounded by wealth and friends, by his sons and grandsons. It doesn't mean he can't live happily to be a hundred, only that one day, when his death is upon him, he may find himself snatched from his deathbed, made young again, and nailed to a cross. That much cannot be prevented. The rest can perhaps be contrived."

"And the children of Radaces?"

"The same for them. And for his wife. And yours. It is admittedly only a partial solution."

"But how?"

"You must counter Radaces every time."

Therefore Vandibar Nasha rose and returned to his garden party, on that spring night beneath the full moon. There he greeted his guests, saw Vashimur and Tatiane slip away as if no one had noticed them, and leaned beside Radaces against a railing, looking out over the city.

"It is death between us."

"Yes, it is."

And when the feast was done and the other guests departed, Vandibar Nasha bade Lord Radaces tarry, and led him into the house, into a large, empty room hung with tapestries to muffle any sound, and there he plunged a dagger into his enemy's back. But Radaces wriggled off the blade like quicksilver and became a serpent, whipping his coils around Vandibar to crush him. Vandibar in turn became a shaft of molten iron, and the serpent fell away, its flesh steaming. It reared up, its hood spread to reveal the face of Radaces, contorted almost out of recognition by rage.

"I . . . shall never . . . forgive."

"Nor I," said Vandibar Nasha. The injury is too great."

The serpent dissipated like smoke and was gone.

THEN VANDIBAR Nasha pored over certain arcane books, and sorcery grew within him like a cancer. Each night he slipped out of bed and went into his study, lit a lamp, and waited until Sekenre came to him, padding silently on the polished floor. Sometimes the boy brought him more books, massive codices with iron locks which could only be opened with a touch and a whispered word; sometimes scrolls which seemed to unroll out of the air into endless length, then roll up again into nothing, invisible. Or he would discourse in many voices, in a babble of tongues, all of which Vandibar came to understand.

Together they raised up spirits. Together they questioned the dead about the secrets of the living.

They prayed to the Shadow Titans, together, and then looked up into the sky and beheld them in their true aspects, not as reflections in the pool.

And once or twice, though Vandibar was sure Sekenre was testing him, the other seemed merely a skinny, scruffy boy with a bad foreign accent, who was alone and wanted company, and asked Vandibar to tell him some story of his own life, of how it was before he became a sorcerer that night in the garden.

Vandibar told such stories, though he did not know if he was giving the right answer, or what the test was.

Once Vandibar offered Sekenre a plate of particularly fine, sweet cakes. The boy sniffed them cautiously, almost as an animal would, then devoured them greedily, oblivious to all else, licking his fingers clean.

His dark eyes revealed nothing.

Many times Vandibar worked to build some apparatus, or peered into murky jars at flopping, wriggling captive things which screamed back at him in tiny, but distinctly human voices; or he merely read, and Sekenre sat across from him and waited.

Sekenre was one more riddle to figure out. The simple questions made Vandibar laugh. Why couldn't a powerful sorcerer afford shoes? Was it an ascetic discipline, or a mere disguise, since a barefoot street child would be underestimated by his enemies?

The deeper mysteries intrigued him. Once the boy had let slip that he had once met a certain king of the Delta, and the name he gave was one Vandibar knew only from history. There was also the matter of the deep scars on the boy's bare legs, which almost formed a kind of writing. And the palms of his hands were seared almost featureless, and part of one of his ears was missing, like that of an alley cat who has gotten into one too many fights.

His manner was often gentle. Certainly Vandibar never saw him angry, but at times it seemed that Sekenre, or some of the *selves* which he contained or could become, were dead to all feeling.

Often Vandibar looked up and realized it was almost dawn, and that the boy was gone.

And yet, too, as the sorcerer swims below the surface of time, and emerges into the duration of men's lives only at points of his own choosing, after long nights of labor, Vandibar Nasha awoke in bed each morning beside his wife, fully rested. Each morning, sorcery seemed a fading dream. Each day his study was filled only with familiar books and carvings. His household servants came and went. He looked out a window. He saw his son Vashimur riding a horse around and around in the exercise yard. The youth was growing tall and strong, and Vandibar was proud of him.

It was as if he lived three lives simultaneously. Each night he studied or labored with Sekenre. Each night he slept beside his wife. And each night, too, he returned to the garden party at the Spring Festival, where he stood beneath the full moon and greeted his guests, and spied his enemy among them, and the ritual words were passed: "It is death between us."

Each night the two of them fought, devising and countering new strategies. Once he found the roof garden party populated only by corpses in feathered masks. They dropped their masks at a signal from Radaces. But Vandibar caused the sun to rise suddenly, and the corpses melted away like mist. Then the ordinary guests emerged from shadows and departed, a little startled that they had let the whole night past without realizing how late it was.

Once there was only ice, the house, garden, the guests, even the moon and stars made of shimmering, almost luminous ice, and the contest between Vandibar and Radaces was to find the single tiny flame hidden somewhere, which meant both life and destruction for the whole world.

Vandibar found it rising out of the palm of his own hand. But Radaces blew on it, and the fire leapt up to devour the entire city of Elandisphon. Vandibar's mind was filled with the screams of the count-less dying. He felt each of those deaths. He drowned in remorse and pain. And he rose up, transcending any feeling at all, beyond to conscience and compassion, and rearranged the white and black tiles of countless lives into such patterns as suited him.

In some other newly-cut channel of time, he and Sekenre both walked barefoot on the surface of the Great River, in the night's darkness as the gray stars of the otherworld looked down, and they guided the souls of the slain into the land of the dead, one by one, speaking to each the words of passage.

He took aside the ghosts of his murdered servants, the one who had lost a hand, the boy who had not returned, and others. Of these, in a hushed, secret voice, he asked forgiveness.

So the people of the city both lived out their individual lives and died their individual deaths, and perished together in flames on a single night, while Vandibar Nasha held those flames back from his own house with upraised hands, pushing them back like an impossible tide.

All of these things were true at once. He understood that now.

He and Radaces directed armies against one another from atop mountains. Perched on the backs of enormous, black and silver birds, they fought above the clouds. Higher still, the gods and titans battled, like hugely-cast shadows of Vandibar Nasha and Lord Radaces. It was a combative dance between the two of them, whirling, whirling, striking out to kill or to parry, until the two became as one, and Vandibar Nasha peered deep into the mind and heart of Lord Radaces, and beheld only himself there, as if in a labyrinth of mirrors.

And, greeting one another among the guests on the rooftop, they passed between one another polite words, and treacherous gifts, and poisons.

Sorcery was a craving now, a lust Vandibar could not control. Only briefly, during half-dreamed mornings when he woke up beside Takida, could he remember that man who had once been. More briefly still, he wondered what had ever become of that fellow.

Yet when he awoke, that *other* Vandibar Nasha, who was an exemplary lord of Elandisphon, progressed through a separate life, troubled by terrible dreams of Vandibar the sorcerer.

His wife Takida grew lined in the face, gray-haired, then silver, then white. Vashimur grew to be a man and married Tatiane, daughter of Lord Radaces. The wedding feast was held at the house of Radaces, who greeted his guests in the frescoed atrium, as the benevolent gods gazed down from the rooftops of the temples nearby.

Among the gifts exchanged was a bronze coffer shaped like a human hand, which Lord Radaces presented to Vandibar Nasha.

Takida aged. Vashimur had three sons by Tatiane, all of whom were strong, wild boys who ran through the house making lots of noise. Soon the firstborn of them appeared to be about as old as Sekenre's, or even older.

Vandibar remained as he was, as did Lord Radaces. There were gray streaks in both men's beards, but not more than before. Neither lost the vigor of his stride. People remarked on this at first, then looked after them furtively and began to make signs after them as they had passed, to ward off evil. Fewer guests came to either house.

Vandibar held back the tide, but he couldn't hold it forever. One night, after the garden party had ended, when the last of the guests had departed, he came upon his wife's head impaled upon a stake, while around him the ruins of the house smoldered.

Takida opened her eyes, which burned with blue fire. This time she spoke in the language of the dead, which requires no breath to utter.

"Husband, what is this abomination that thou hast done?"

He could only reply, helplessly, in his own language, "I don't know. Once I did. It was clear. But it isn't anymore."

Radaces stood beside him. Their eyes met, but no words passed. Weeping, Vandibar covered his face with his muddy gown and rushed into the house, which was not burnt. He climbed into bed beside Takida, who stared up at the ceiling with blind eyes and muttered something in her sleep, as if she were shouting in a dream.

When he slept, he dreamt of a man — or perhaps several men — called Vandibar Nasha, but when he awoke in the morning he could not recall any of the details, distracted as he was by the discovery that Takida had died in the night and lay still, staring at the ceiling, with a tiny stream of blood staining her upper lip.

He slid his hand around her neck gently, to reassure himself that her head had not been cut off; but somewhere else, he was sure, it had, and he wept, knowing that.

Many years later, word came that Lord Vashimur, aged about seventy — that same one who was reputed to have a father younger than he, if one believed such stories — had been thrown from his horse and killed.

But Vandibar found young Vashimur amid the ruins of his house, naked and crucified, with the *evatim* at his feet.

In his final pain, the youth cried out in the corpse-speech, "Where is my father? Thou art not he, but some other, evil thing."

Radaces was there. He and Vandibar merely gazed at one another, and after a while Vandibar said, "Come with me and let us make an end."

IV

TOGETHER THEY descended into the lower garden, but the garden was dead, and the pool filled with dust. They followed that dust as the wind bore it, across an endless plain toward a bloody sun that lingered on the horizon before them but never set. Amid terrible storms they struggled, Radaces bracing Vandibar and Vandibar lifting up Radaces when he fell. It seemed, several times, that they came into various countries and settled there, living out whole lives as amicable neighbors before rising again to resume the endless quest. It seemed, too, that they were enemies and fought in the darkness, amid terrible transformations.

Yet neither could conquer the other, for all each sought out some fatal weakness in the mirrored depths of the other's soul, during those quiet times when they lived side by side and interpreted one another's dreams.

Together, they mourned murdered children and wives, and were comforted by the remembrance of the lives of those children and wives lived out to the full in some impossible interval before the counting of days came to the inevitable black tile.

"We are swimming just below the surface of time," said Radaces, "and we carried them along in the ripple of our passage."

"As long as we could," said Vandibar.

The two of them wept together, and were transformed, and fought.

"I don't know how to stop," said Vandibar.

"Nor do I."

Then Radaces told how Sekenre had come into his house each night, bringing books of magic, and Vandibar told the same. Neither raged that Sekenre was a traitor, false to both of them, for they had reached that point in sorcery which is beyond passion, which is only *doing* because there are things to be done.

When they found Sekenre at last, he was seated on a marble bench by the dry pool in a dead garden, scuffing one bare foot idly in the dust. The red sun shone dully, low in the west.

The boy sat with his other foot up on the bench. He held various pens and brushes between ink-stained toes. He was writing something in a book. When the two sorcerers approached, he held up the book to them, revealing a beautifully illuminated page of text, in swirling, delicate script.

"What kind of abomination is Sekenre?" demanded Lord Radaces.

"Indeed, that is what we must know," said Vandibar Nasha.

Sekenre closed and covered the book carefully, placing a blotting cloth over the page he had been working on. He put pens, brushes, and ink bottles away in a leather bag. Then he stared at his own hands and said, in his own, heavily accented, adolescent's voice, but in a distracted manner, "I don't think Sekenre is an abomination at all. But he *contains* abominations, and they, in turn, have committed abominations. Sekenre is a boy who never got to grow up. Did you know that in Reedland, where Sekenre was born, the children go barefoot, while the young men who have passed through the rite of manhood wear shoes? The father must lead the son, unless the father is negligent, in which case the son remains forever a child. Sekenre's father was worse than negligent, though he, or part of him anyway, loved his son deeply. Vashtem was a sorcerer of great wisdom and evil. He caused his son Sekenre to murder him. That was part of his plan. Therefore Vashtem the sorcerer awoke in the mind of

Sekenre, for to slay a sorcerer is to become a sorcerer, and Vashtem became Sekenre and Sekenre became Vashtem, and he became many others, whom his father had slain before, whom he had occasion to slay afterward. They all mixed together, like paints in a pot. Sekenre learned, slowly and painfully, that in order to remain Sekenre he had to remain as he once was. Therefore Sekenre is forever a child of fifteen who wants to be good, and who wants to grow up. It's not going to happen."

Vandibar Nasha and Lord Radaces both drew daggers, but no ordinary weapons. These were forged of that metal which only dragons may fetch from the cores of suns.

"Release us," said Radaces. "Let us be what we once were."

"Or else die," said Vandibar Nasha.

Sekenre rippled like quicksilver and stood behind them. Both of them turned. He shook his head sadly. For just an instant, his expression was that of a little boy who has made a mess and is terribly sorry, but can't do anything about it. Then his manner changed, and he seemed older, and he spoke without an accent.

"Once that single instant has passed in which you open yourself to sorcery, there is no going back. You cannot say that when this is all over you will resume your former life, because it will never be over."

Vandibar, fingering his dagger, said, "But we are still apprentices. I've read that to truly become a sorcerer, you have to attend the College of Shadows, and there take a master, learn everything you can, and in the end, as a graduation exercise, you have to overcome and kill the master, thus becoming the other sorcerer."

"Or else the master kills the student, and the result is much the same," said Radaces.

"There is one difference," said Sekenre. "The winner is the jar, containing the loser."

"I understand further," said Vandibar, "that I have been attending this college for a long time, that it is all around me, and has been ever since that first night in the garden. It is different for each individual sorcerer."

"But we have not yet graduated," said Radaces, holding his dagger in a firm, clenched fist. "I think it's time we do."

Sekenre merely shrugged and sat down on the bench again. He got out his book and pretended to ignore them.

Vandibar and Radaces both stepped forward.

"Then you must discover who your master is," Sekenre said, not looking up as the two of them paused and glanced at one another uncertainly. "Each student may encounter any number of teachers, but he has only one master, whose heart and mind he comes to know as intimately as his own, with whom he shares the great majority of exercises, sparring, countering one another as both grow in sorcery. Don't mistake the master for the attendant, who merely brings what is wanted and leads you to the places of learning."

Then, heedless of them, Sekenre got out his pens and brushes and began writing on opposite pages the tales of Vandibar Nasha and of Lord Radaces, both sorcerers of great renown. But when he reached a certain point, he stopped, because he didn't know how either story was to end.

Vandibar and Radaces stood by the edge of the empty pool. They wept, naming their wives and children long gone. They comforted each other as best they could, and then they looked into one another's eyes, and each clenched his dagger firmly.

"It is death between us, old friend," said Vandibar Nasha.

IN THE STREET OF THE WITCHES

> *Tsarag Vin was fourteen years old when he first came to the Street of the Witches. But he never returned from it. Someone did, who looked like him, who remembered what he remembered and shared his longings; but this was someone else, for truly it is said that whosoever dwells among the Witches, even for a single night, is irrevocably changed.*
>
> *I know this to be true, for I have dwelt there a long time.*
>
> *I am your host, the storyteller, one of the characters in the story, whose identity will be clear enough in time.*
>
> *Be patient then. The Street of the Witches weaves through the back alleys and shadows of every city in the world, every city which ever was and ever will be.*
>
> *It is a path through the labyrinth. It is the labyrinth.*

I

TSARAG'S TRANSFORMATION began subtly, as his teacher, the learned Meras, was telling a story about the Street of Witches, as warning and edification and entertainment; something about a mighty hero of old who ventured there to gain the remedy to a great peril, knowing full well that he must sacrifice himself in the winning of it. But the honor of the Nine Gods or the safety of his city . . . or something high-sounding and terribly important . . . would not be denied.

The boy's attention wandered. He gazed out the window, to where workmen were loading huge bales onto sledges for winter transport. Even when the White River was frozen, the merchants of House Vin were always busy.

"Am I boring you, Lord?" said the teacher.

But Tsarag wasn't even paying attention to the men loading the sledges. He gazed beyond the wooden wall of the Vin compound, to the outer city beyond. He didn't answer.

Tsarag's ten-year-old brother Amasdag made a face. "He's thinking about his *girl*friend . . . He wants to get *married* . . ."

The teacher said sternly, "That is quite ridiculous. The heir to House Vin will marry the bride selected for him by his father, for the good of all." Then he smiled toward Tsarag and added, "Besides, that won't be for a few years yet."

"I'm sorry," said the elder brother. "I don't feel well. Go on with the story."

He left Meras to edify Amasdag. Amasdag stuck out his tongue after

his departing brother. Outside in the corridor, Tsarag Vin wept and slammed his fist into the wall and demanded of the Winter Gods how they could be so cruel.

He wasn't the same after that. He wasn't ever the same.

> For in fact Tsarag Vin was secretly in love with the beautiful Azrekia of House Zavas, the great rival of House Vin. Only one trading family could occupy the inner citadel of White Nevasderat. That one family was Vin. Vin barges plied the river in summer, all the way down to the Crescent Sea. Vin horsemen patrolled the banks. House Zevas was an upstart, a mediocrity, its master consumed with envy.
>
> Yet the heir to Vin had clandestinely met and fallen in love with the daughter of his father's enemy. It was an impossible, ridiculous situation —
> And it is not entirely the story I wish to tell.

IN THE night, Tsarag Vin awoke from terrible dreams. He sat up, drenched in sweat, shivering in the silence, the dream fading even as he sat there, until he could recall only screams and a burning mask which hovered in the air and inexorably settled over his own face, smothering him.

Amasdag stirred under the furs beside him, but did not wake. Meras slept on in his chair by the fireplace.

A spark popped among the embers.

Tsarag slipped out of bed, listening to the faint creaking of the rafters overhead, certain he could hear the snow itself as it fell.

A sudden gust of wind buffeted the shutters. The embers stirred and glowed.

Tsarag shivered, pulling a heavy woolen tunic over himself, then padded barefoot across the wooden floor.

His faithful dog lay by the fire, whimpering and snorting in its sleep. He knelt down to comfort the animal, which raised its head lazily and stared at him.

"Quiet. I have to go."

The dog made to get to its feet, but Tsarag pushed it down gently.

"No. Stay here. They need you to protect them."

And as he spoke, he made a sign, to invoke the protection of Vohg-Zemad, foremost among the Winter Gods, who had always shown favor to House Vin. The boy needed protection and he was afraid, but he knew also that he must go alone, like the hero in Meras's jumbled story, without even the company of a dog, though he did not know why he had to go, or exactly where . . . it was something about the dream, and the burning mask —

> *For a Destiny or a geas or a weird, or whatever you want to call it was upon him; and perhaps he had never awakened at all, but passed from layer to layer of his dream, into true and prophetic vision, even as the soul journeys from* Leshé, *which is dream, into* Tashé *which is death, and beyond, like a sailor on an endless, unknowable sea —*
> *He was compelled. He went. The burning mask spoke his name, summoning him.*
> *Like the hero in the story, he set forth, and did not question.*

HE DRESSED himself stealthily and made his way out into a corridor, past his parents' bedroom, past sleeping servants, and across the great hall, where retainers and guests lay snoring on the tables and benches. On the walls all around hung the shields and trophies of House Vin, even the stuffed head of a fabulous beast some ancestor had slain. In the darkness the jumble of them suggested a tangle for thorn-bushes at a forest's edge.

It was quite an undertaking for the eldest son of the Lord of Vin to sneak out by himself on a winter's night. Servants could be beaten for allowing such a thing to happen. But there had been a great feast that night and they were all drunk. And the boy was small, and silent afoot. He knew the way through hidden doors, a secret stair, a tunnel.

He went out into the night, very much afraid, yet unafraid, as one is in a dream. The air, laden with snow, stung his face. The cold seemed to reach through his thick boots to grab his ankles with frigid, iron-hard fingers.

He was no giant like his father — or the hero in Meras's story today — but he was a native of this land and accustomed to dark and cold. Many a foreigner could get lost in wooden the maze that was Nevasderat, a city of concentric rings of stockades and log houses, rippling out from the citadel and House Vin. There was even a word for such unfortunates, who perished just trying to cross the street or find the privy — *tagheri*, which meant "dancing statue," since the frozen corpse always seemed to be in some absurd position when found, as if interrupted in a revel.

But Tsarag Vin was Nevasderati himself, and would therefore never be *tagheri*.

He went on. A sudden howling wind send an avalanche of snow sliding down from a rooftop onto him. He fell to his knees, then caught hold of a barrel and pulled himself up.

In the dream, which he remembered, in the seeming dream which never ended, the burning mask was before him, like a lantern gleaming through the snow and darkness. Again it spoke his name, and again he felt that compulsion which only makes sense in dreams, which holds the dreamer in place when he would flee, or drives him on without any recourse or mercy or explanation.

The boy replied, "Azit Azim," invoking the Horned One, who watches over travelers.

The mask vanished. Tsarag clung to the edge of the barrel for a second, then shook the snow off himself.

It was then that he heard the screaming, like no sound he had ever heard from a human throat before, something more intense, more horrible, as if all the despair and all the world's pain were summed up in that single cry —

And the voice was a young one.

It was nearby.

It was at his feet.

He crouched down and cleared away the snow from a little window, then watched, appalled and sickened but unable to turn away from the scene in the cellar down below: a boy about his own age bound naked onto a wooden table, while hideous women in scarlet cloaks gathered around him, burning him with white-hot irons, slashing him with knives, while the boy screamed all the more and so struggled against his bonds that his wrists and his feet were bloody. The witches — for Tsarag did not doubt that was who they were — tore away the boy's flesh. They opened him like a bag. They tossed aside what must have been internal organs like so much garbage.

(*He has to be dead now*, Tsarag told himself. *This is impossible. It should have stopped. It can't go on.*)

Yet the screaming went on, that hopeless, sub-animal scream, as two of the witches, wearing thick gloves to protect their hands, carried a steaming vessel to the table and poured molten metal into the boy's open belly.

(*Dying. Dead. Impossible!*)

The screaming stopped. The witches cut the boy's bonds. He sat up on the table, his face now filled with more than human fury.

Then it was Tsarag Vin who cried out, as the boy on the table glared directly at him. Their eyes met. It seemed that the other wore his own face, as if he were looking into a mirror.

"Behold, you will become as I," the naked boy seemed to be saying, but only it was a dream-voice, more remembered than actually heard.

Tsarag screamed and fell back from the window and could only lie there, waiting for death; but the light in the snow winked out as one of the witches curtly pulled down a blind, and there was only silence and darkness and cold.

Tsarag put his hands to his face, to make sure it was still there.

He rose. He went on. He knew that he had come to the Street of the Witches, because it was his time to arrive there, like the hero in his teacher's tale. The Street only revealed itself out of whim, out of mystery —

Once, as the snow whirled in front of his face, he saw a silver carriage drift by, borne aloft by naked, winged men, whose flesh was all the color of ice. Their wings made a hushed, steady sound, like snow and wind buffeting fastened shutters.

A curtain rippled. A lady leaned out from the carriage. She wore a scarlet robe and a silver crown.

She held up the burning mask, which now gleamed like white-hot metal. She heaved it into the air, and then she was gone, and the mask was gone, and the snow was blinding.

When Tsarag could see again, he had come out of an alley into a street lined with brightly-lit shops. Lanterns swayed in the wind, snow swirling around them.

The street was empty, yet he heard, carried on the wind, fragments of incomprehensible conversation, laughter, music, a single voice shouting, a murmur of many voices. He turned and turned again as people in fantastic costumes flickered in the periphery of his vision: a king in tattered yellow and red, wearing a crown the color of bone; and another king, all in black, his face black as the night, his eyes like fire, black dogs licking his hands. Here was a yellow-faced woman all in black silk, her bare arms covered with glowing tattoos; and, again, a barbarian all in furs, with an axe over his shoulder; and a man who seemed half machine, whirring, lurching, making clicking sounds as he walked, his robe like a patch cut out of a clear night sky, filled with stars.

And there was one who had no face at all, whose upraised hood was hollow as a cave, but for a single candle within. This one held the burning mask in pale hands, and called out the name of Tsarag Vin.

The boy stepped sideways, into a shop filled from floor to ceiling with wooden puppets, all of them intricately carven and painted, swaying on their strings in the draught as if alive.

They too called out the name of Tsarag Vin.

But Tsarag Vin was close to tears now. He wanted this dream to end. He wanted to go home. He pleaded. But the puppets laughed at him, and something huge and wooden rose from behind a counter within the shop and a painted face spoke, saying, "Tsarag Vin, this is your home now. You have no other."

He screamed and ran out into the night, and all but collided with the burning mask yet again.

Now someone was wearing it, someone who was very small and thin, and old woman perhaps, or a child, clad only in a very loose, thin white robe that streamed in the wind and didn't seem at all adequate for a Nevasderati winter.

This person took hold of Tsarag's hand, and the touch was solid and warm. It was a young hand, firm. Tsarag allowed himself to be led through deep drifts, along the Street of Witches. Now women in red cloaks emerged from every doorway, regarding him. Then, by some transition he could not follow, he wasn't outdoors anymore, but in a dark corridor. The burning mask had faded to a sullen red glow. It did not light the way. But as he and his companion passed, pale hands, floating in the darkness, uncurled themselves, revealing white flames flickering from the upraised palms.

By this faint light he gained a better impression of his companion: slender, somewhat shorter than he, with very long, black hair that trailed behind on the air, even as the white robe trailed. Impossibly, the stranger was barefoot, and did not seem to feel the cold.

Perhaps it was a corpse that had borne him away, he thought, but corpses are not warm to the touch, nor do they smell faintly of sweat.

Then there was another transition he could not follow, as if a curtain had parted before him, and the light was somehow different. Snow still swirled around him, but through it he saw some other place which was not Nevasderat, but a city of squat, black stone buildings interspersed with the occasional tower, and, impossibly, palm trees.

The other bade him sit, and they squatted down in a courtyard amid carven stone crocodiles. Still the snow fell, and Tsarag Vin felt the frigid night air; certainly the snow on his boots and fur trousers did not begin to melt; but the masked other did not shiver. That gown was thin as spider-silk; through it a bare thigh flashed, then narrow shoulders. The front was open and he could make out faintly luminous scars criss-crossing the bare chest, but there was something indefinable here, something about the light and the way the other moved, and the shadows, so that he could not tell if this was a boy or a girl, even when the other removed the mask.

The light of the mask went out utterly. It was a delicate thing, like a dead, autumn leaf. The stranger crushed it into nothingness, then opened dark hands, and white flames danced from scarred palms; and Tsarag Vin could make out a round, soft, olive-colored face, and dark, dark eyes he could look into forever.

The other wore a lot of jewelry. Silver bands rattled on both wrists and ankles.

"Do not be afraid," said the other. The voice, like everything else, was soft, ambiguous, and strangely accented.

Tsarag Vin thought of the hero in his teacher's story. It was just a story, but it reminded him to be brave.

"I am Tsarag Vin. My father is the greatest prince of Nevasderat. He will reward you richly if you take me home." Already Tsarag Vin was convinced that tonight's adventure, if it were other than just a dream, was a disaster, to be escaped if he could. The best he could hope for was making it back home before his absence was discovered.

But the other laughed and said, "Have you considered that a name can be a weapon? Now you have revealed your secret to me."

"You give me your name now. We'll bargain."

The other shrugged and held up burning hands, "But you have already paid me, without asking for anything in return. What kind of bargain is that? But I did not bring you here to haggle over names. I have many. I contain multitudes. One of my names is Julna of Kadisphon."

Tsarag swallowed hard and tried to contain his surprise, lest it grow into fear. *Kadisphon* was proverbial. *As far as Kadisphon* was to say *to the end of the Earth*. Julna, he supposed, was a girl's name in some barbarous tongue.

Tsarag spoke. "I want to ask —"

"Why?" said Julna of Kadisphon.

"I want to —"

"In the Street of the Witches?"

"Why am I here?" said Tsarag.

"Because you came."

"But —"

"Because we brought you here. Is that more satisfactory?"

"Who —?"

"Because it served our purpose."

Now Julna of Kadisphon held fire in one hand and a bowl in the other. She — and yet Tsarag wasn't entirely sure this was a *she*, as if Julna of Kadisphon were a shadow-thing, too indeterminate for the eye to define — offered the bowl and said, "Drink."

Tsarag Vin knew his stories.

"If I drink, I'll remain here forever. Everybody knows that."

"You are already here forever. If you don't drink, you will never even seem to leave. Go on. It is merely water."

Reluctantly, Tsarag drank. The water was warm. It was just water.

"Now take the bowl with you and go."

"What?"

"Just go. There are no bargains —"

"I want to know —"

"No explanations."

II

> There are no explanations. There can be no explanations. Even the witches do not understand, though they have delved deeper into the shadows than anyone, though they have learned and heard the speech of the Shadow Titans, of whom even the gods are afraid. Their art is like a storm, like a tide; it flows through them toward its own ends.
>
> No answers. Only mystery.

TSARAG VIN awoke, but not in his bed. He sat up in a snowdrift by a barrel and a log wall. He still held the bowl in his hand. He stuffed it into his pocket and got to his feet. He knew after taking but a few steps that he must be in some shabby, outer district of Nevasderat.

He began to run, from fear of more immediately comprehensible things. He had been out all night. His teacher, Meras, would be blamed, possibly even put to death, for the wrath of the Lord of Vin could be terrible and there was no law restraining him, only custom, and the custom was that the occupant of the citadel was not restrained.

Surely everyone would be frantic. There must be house-guards out looking for him, turning the whole city upside down.

He knew where he was now. He ran from the Black Circle, where foreigners and no-accounts dwelt; then crossing the Brown Circle, where stood the shops of free craftsmen who were not associated with any house; and the Red, the place of the lesser trading houses, including House Zevas; and on through Silver Nevasderat, where rose the towers of the nobles, where visiting kings might rest; and finally he plunged through the gate into the White Citadel, home of House Vin.

There a guard caught him by the hood of his coat, laughing, and swung him around.

"And where do you think *you* are going, my bold young sir?"

For a moment, Tsarag couldn't reply. It was an impossible thing, as if a wooden statue had not merely spoken, but squandered its miraculous ability on something completely stupid.

He squirmed, then said, "Let me go. I have to get inside."

"Not here you don't. Only family and servants." The guard scrutinized him up and down. "And you don't seem to be either."

He scrutinized the guard, and it was then that he became more and more alarmed. Something wasn't right. These guards wore *tazams*, loose, sleeveless garments over their furs, on which were displayed the emblem and colors of the reigning house. Of course they did, but the Vin emblem was a fiery eagle, and the Vin colors were yellow and white. These men wore blue and green, with the emblem of a coiled snake.

He had seen those colors and that snake before, but never here.

He could have apologized for coming to the wrong house, but he knew it *wasn't* the wrong house. There was only one White Citadel. He looked past the gathering company of curious guards — all of whom wore blue and green, with snakes — and *of course* he recognized the courtyard where he and his brother had raced their dogs, and the shed where the sledges were stored, and his mother's window, surrounded by white-painted, wooden lilies.

There was no mistake.

These men wore the colors of House Zevas. He had seen them many times, when he had come, disguised, to visit his beloved Azrekia.

That was impossible. If somehow the Zevas warriors had stormed House Vin during the night and won an equally impossible victory, the yard would be heaped with corpses and still swarming with armed men and captives. There'd be broken doors, burnt roofs, much destruction, because the men of House Vin would not give up easily.

No.

He struggled. The guards laughed. He threatened. He told them he was the son of the lord of this place, if they had somehow forgotten, and still they laughed.

Then a sledge pulled up and a man got out. The guards stood at attention. Someone said, "My Lord!" and rattled off an explanation.

It was Lord Duraine Zevas, Azrekia's father. He wore a peaked cap and a coat embroidered with serpent signs. He looked into Tsarag's face and spoke in a kindly voice, as if, somehow, he had no idea who this boy was and had never heard of House Vin. All he said was, "You mustn't make this disturbance, child. You don't belong here. You know that."

Tsarag at fourteen didn't like being called a child. But that was nothing. It was nothing too, that Lord Zevas somehow didn't recognize him. In fact that was fortunate, if somehow House Zevas *had* supplanted House Vin during the night.

But then there was a girl beside him. It was Azrekia, Tsarag's own beloved. *She* didn't know him either. Of course she couldn't have said anything, but he saw it in her eyes. She was first bemused, then puzzled, then a little afraid. He made the secret sign they had between them and she did not recognize it.

All *she* said, to her father, was, "If this boy is hungry, maybe we should let him go around to the kitchen —"

There was a dog beside her. It was — or had been — *his* dog. It whined, and almost seemed to sense something strange or strangely familiar, but Azrekia put her hand on its head and the beast was still.

Tsarag broke free of the guards and ran away from the White Gate, back into the outer city, tears streaming down his face. He ran until his breath came in painful gasps, until the cold air tore at his lungs and he could run now more. Then he stopped, and leaned against a wall in the snow, and tried to puzzle out what had happened. He prayed to the Winter Gods, asking their forgiveness, if this were all some punishment they'd set upon him for whatever sin. No, he didn't think it was that. No, he didn't think this was a dream either. Somehow, somewhere, between last night and now, he had indeed awakened, but not into quite the same city, quite the same world. He stopped people on the street and demanded to know of House Vin, and no one knew what he was talking about. When he claimed to be the son of the greatest prince in all White Nevasderat, they made signs against him, to ward off bad luck, because they took him to be mad.

He spent much of the day in a furious rage, trying to find the Street of the Witches, determined to kill Julna of Kadisphon.

Of course he did not find it.

Once, in his desperation, he went into a shop and asked a metalsmith if he knew the way to the Street of the Witches, and the man was silent for several minutes, then came toward Tsarag with a silver knife, making signs in the air with the tip of it as he did.

"Just let me cut your throat," he said, "and you shall go to the Witches soon enough."

Tsarag escaped, but his quest went nowhere. He swore terrible revenge, as the son of a great lord (or a hero in a story) might be expected to do, but nothing came of that either, and nightfall found him exhausted, unable to convince anyone that he was a person of any account. There was no place for him to sleep other than a derelict barn, now inhabited by beggars. There he was accepted with some suspicion, and even ladled a little soup out of the common pot, which he drank from the bowl the witch Julna had given him.

As he sat there, someone reached over and fondled his fine coat, but he was too weary, too despairing to care.

In the morning he woke up outside in the snow, with blood on his face and a lump on his head. His coat was gone, and his heavy woolen tunic, and his boots, and even his socks.

He wandered, barefoot, shivering in his undershirt, begging from house to house, from shop to shop for someone who would help him restore House Vin to its rightful place. He promised many rewards. People laughed and threw snow at him. Someone came up from behind and wrapped bright ribbons around his neck, the mark of a lunatic. A kindly woman gave him rags to tie around his bleeding feet.

When he tried to sell the bowl he had received from the witches, a shopkeeper merely shrugged and said, "It's cheap southern ware. From the Delta." He waved at his own shelves, which were full of such bowls. "And, look, yours is chipped."

He sat on a barrel at a streetcorner with the bowl in his lap, to beg, and while the sun was high, he could stand it, and he gathered a few coins, but as the sun set, the cold was too much, and he knew he would become *tagheri,* one of those grotesque, dancing, frozen corpses before another dawn arrived.

It was dark by the time he reached the White Citadel again. This time he avoided the main gate, but went to a humbler entrance. His feet were bleeding again and his hands were numb.

He pounded on the door kitchen door for what seemed forever. When it finally opened, the blast of warm air nearly knocked him over. He held up his bowl to beg, but the doorway was swaying crazily and he couldn't make sense of the babbling voices around him, and he fell forward.

III

 No explanations. Mystery. Next, Tsarag Vin grew into manhood, in a mere blinking of the eye of eternity.
 But it is never as simple as that.

PLANNING HIS REVENGE, although unsure exactly what or against whom, Tsarag Vin bided his time. The servants at the kitchen door lifted him up, laid him a warm bed, and later gave him hot broth. He soon recovered and was made one of them. It didn't make any difference that he told them who he really was, for none had heard of House Vin, much less considered it a threat to House Zevas.

No, the Lord of Zevas was by all accounts a kindly man, charitable to the unfortunate, a man who, despite his high position, had no enemies. He was a master at pleasing everyone. He was even, incredibly enough in the rough-and-tumble world of Nevasderati commerce, honest.

So Tsarag Vin became the least of the many servants in House Zevas. He scrubbed pots. He carried out the stinks. He spread new rushes over the floor of the great hall. His tasks brought him, like a ghost, to places he had known all his life, and no one recognized him. He could not enter the master bedroom — where his parents had slept — because he was not allowed.

He wondered if his parents were alive, somewhere else, or if they had merely ceased to exist.

He even regretted the loss of his younger brother, Amasdag.

Once he saw a familiar toy on a shelf, a wooden horse, with wheels. One of the wheels was half gone. He remembered how it had gotten that way, when he was eight and Amasdag four, and Amasdag had flung the horse, which was *his,* Tsarag's, down a flight of stairs. How he'd pummelled his brother then, until Meras pulled them apart.

Now he looked at the toy, and dared not touch it, and wept for Amasdag.

He grew. A year passed, two, three. He was rarely close to the Zevas princes, for he was the least among the servants, usually left in the kitchen or the stables during great events. He saw the master, most of the time, only from a distance.

He watched Azrekia from afar. He might as well have been on the Moon.

But once he met her in a corridor, and he could hardly bear to look on her, but he managed to say, "Do you not know me?" Again he made the secret sign they had between them.

She looked at him oddly. "Should I?"

He made the sign again.

She smiled, and said, "Yes, you were the boy at the gate —"

But before she could say anything more he seized her in his arms and kissed her as hard and as passionately as he could, remembering all their secret meetings, their fears, their shared dangers, how they had planned, desperately, impossibly, to marry in secret, then run away together —

She pushed him away and slapped him across the face.

"How *dare* you? You forget yourself! How *dare* you?"

He couldn't explain. He couldn't find the words. He felt like a helpless, stuttering fool.

"Very well then," she said, suddenly more amused than angry, "I shall assume that you were briefly driven mad by my beauty. It has been known to do that. I, being a great lady, forgive you. But you must not come near me again. You must not forget who I am and who you are. Is that understood?"

All he could do was look down at his feet and mutter, "Yes, Lady."

And, laughing, she swept along the corridor and was gone.

She was gone from his life. He was without hope.

But he did not forget who she was and who he was, and that transformed him. He brooded by himself. He cursed the air. He cried out in his sleep, amid terrible dreams. At an age when most of the servants married others of their class, he took no interest, refused all offers, and gradually came to neglect his appearance and his manner, until he was seldom let out of the cellars or the kitchen, and he did not come close to Lady Azrekia. Lord Zevas heard of the change that had come over him, but did not choose to turn him out. He ordered Tsarag closely watched, and those who watched him could only report that their quarry was elusive. Sometimes, at night especially, he seemed to vanish into thin air.

Though he was no longer a prince here, he still knew the secret ways, the trapdoors, the secret stair, the tunnel that led under the wall into a warehouse in Red Nevasderat.

Tsarag, in his rage, stole away from the house every night. He didn't seem to need to sleep. Fury and pain filled him. He was always dreaming now, almost useless for work. Somehow he was fed. Most of the time, no one knew where he was.

> He was tempted three times:
> Julna of Kadisphon came to him, walking in a dream, darkness trailing behind like a cloak.
> "Curse the Winter Gods," said Julna of Kadisphon, "for they have sent you only ill-fortune."
> "I will curse them," said Tsarag Vin.
> "Spare not your enemies, nor ever forgive them, for they will neither spare nor forgive you."
> "I shall be revenged on them," said Tsarag Vin.
> "Take evil as your good," said Julna of Kadisphon, "for this is pleasing to the Titans of Shadow, who alone can aid you. Despair then, of all else."
> "I curse, I shall be revenged. I despair."

HE WAS seeking the Street of the Witches. He knew from the tales that those who seek such a place, those who deserve to find it, who *do* find it, are the most depraved of human beings. Those who are abducted there, or who find it by seeming accident, may be almost otherwise — but never entirely innocent, or else they wouldn't have been of any interest to the witches, who find that dark door within the soul and pry it open, so that the Titans — those opposite and equal shadows of the gods, of whom even the gods are afraid — may be made manifest and chaos speak to the world like a ravening wind.

So it was in the stories. Now it was more than florid rhetoric.

He sought the witches through his own evil.

He seldom returned to House Zevas at all anymore, and when he did it was only to haunt the place, to cause fear. He dwelt in the city, disguised among the beggars, then in dark houses, among secret guilds. He became a robber, then a murderer, then the terror of much of Nevasderat. He became a black magician, someone who tore up newly-dug graves and arranged the corpses in ridiculous positions, as *tagheri,* and bound the souls of those departed into the corpses, so that he could force secrets out of them, not secrets which would advance his cause, but merely those which would cause pain.

He felt that he was on fire. He loathed himself. He could not look at himself in a mirror, and smashed all mirrors he encountered.

But he went on, for he was the son of a great lord, someone from whom a tremendous, dramatic revenge is to be expected.

Ghosts followed him, howling in the streets.

Heroes came from afar to slay him, so great and terrible was his reputation, but none could find the tomb in which he dwelt by day, and he killed the heroes, one by one, and devoured their hearts.

Still he sought the Street of the Witches in every part of the city. He searched every night. Sometimes he glimpsed it from afar, and ran toward it, but it was never there when he should have reached it.

He killed those he encountered by chance in the night, offering up their souls to the witches and to the Shadow Titans, that he might become evil enough.

He did not hate Julna of Kadisphon anymore. No, he wanted to become like her, to be devious and terrible, to jerk people around, like puppets on strings, to ruin their lives for the pure sport of doing so.

For thus the world is filled with darkness and ruin. Thus are the Shadow Titans nourished.

IV

He never found the Street of the Witches. Instead, he built it afresh within his soul.

AND JULNA of Kadisphon came to him in the darkness, as he slept in a coffin, among the absurd, dancing, frozen dead in a secret tomb. She crawled to his side. He felt her filmy, spider-silk garment brush over him, her jewelry scrape against him as she caressed him gently. He felt her warmth as she whispered in his ear that he had done well, that she was very pleased. Her long hair fell against his face.

He knew that he loved her now. He hated Azrekia. He desired only Julna, the witch of Kadisphon, who had directed his whole life, who had shown him how to be happy.

She told him as much.

She told him what he had to do, to consummate all her desires, and his.

She pressed a bronze dagger into his hand.

When he reached for her with his other hand, she was gone.

He awoke then, covered with sweat, from a long and terrible dream. For a moment he was afraid, unable to understand how he had come to dwell in a pit among defiled corpses, and he remembered all his crimes, but he remembered, too, what he had been before he had committed them, and he wept, trying to figure out if he was a madman dreaming he was sane, or a sane man dreaming he was mad.

It was all a story, he told himself, and he was the hero.

It was all a story, and it wasn't true. No, not really.

He dreamed that he was a boy who wandered out into the city streets one wintry night and nearly froze to death, and everything that happened afterward was no more than delirium as he lay there, dying, or else as he lay in his bed slowly nursed back to health by those who loved him. But he awoke once more in a pit full of corpses and no one loved him except the witch of Kadisphon, and Kadisphon was at the end of the Earth; and the Shadow Titans loved him because he had despaired and cursed the gods, and he was dreaming, a madman who dreamed he was sane, a sane man who dreamed he was mad, good and evil all swirling together like paint stirred in a pot.

He couldn't see the pattern anymore.

Therefore he washed himself and put on clean clothing (beneath which he concealed the knife) and walked through Nevasderat, drawing little notice. He wasn't a ragged boy anymore, but a tall, broad-shouldered man with a jet-black beard. Only his eyes were strange. Anyone who looked into his face turned quickly away.

All the while he heard Julna of Kadisphon whispering inside his mind. She was telling him a story.

And in this story, he came to White Nevasderat, to the citadel of House Zevas. He waited until nightfall, knowing the hour at which the lord and lady and their guests took supper, and when they retired, and when the servants, too, would likely be in bed.

Late, then, he tapped gently but insistently on the kitchen door. At last an old woman came.

"I have a message for the lord of this house."

The woman looked at him, befuddled, half asleep, and finally said, "Well take it around to the front gate. Can't it wait?"

He grabbed her hair and slit her throat.

"No, it cannot."

The knife hummed and trembled in his hand, for it was a witch-knife, forged in some unfathomable darkness between the stars, where only the Titans of Shadow look on.

He entered into the house, silently, knowing the secret ways.

There was only one light burning. He drew near and saw the old teacher, Meras, up late in his study, paging through a book.

Meras looked up when Tsarag stood in the doorway.

"Yes?"

"Teacher, do you know me?"

"No. Should I?"

"Probably not. But you can help me. I am writing a story."

"Splendid! Will you recite it before the house?"

"I will perform it."

"A masque, then?"

"Something like that. But I am not sure how it should end." And Tsarag briefly related all his adventures and deeds.

Meras shuddered and was silent for a time, then said. "The ending must be a tragedy, for this Tsarag has sought the Street of the Witches, and whether he found it or not, he is surely damned. Your matter is perhaps too dark for a popular tale — for the happy ending is always more pleasing — but perhaps if you end with a strong moral, you can perhaps bring it off."

"Thank you," said Tsarag Vin softly. Then he cut off the old man's head with the bronze knife and placed the head on the teacher's desk next to the book. He dipped a pen in the murdered man's blood and spent an hour writing out an account of the tragedy of his life on the volume's endpapers.

But even then the thought came to him, like a whispered temptation: what if the tragedy did not end? What if it merely stopped? He had done so much evil thus far, and it could not be undone, but what if, at this point, he merely walked away? What if he simply did no more?

That was the boy, Tsarag Vin, talking, he who was almost innocent.

But the man, Tsarag Vin, he who was damned, knew better. He gazed into the dead eyes of his old teacher and Meras seemed to agree. There had to be an ending.

Therefore he rose and took the witch-knife in his hand, and made his way stealthily to bedchamber the master of the house and of the master's lady. With that knife he cut out the hearts of Lord and Lady Zevas as they slept, and did it so cunningly, by hideous arts he had learned, that they did not exactly die, but passed from nightmare into something which was neither life nor death, even as the soul passes from *Leshé*, dream, into *Tashé*, death, and beyond, into the unknowable —

With his hideous art he caused their hearts to burn as he held them in that cheap, chipped Deltan bowl he had once brought back from the Street of the Witches. And Lord and Lady Zevas screamed in their dreams, beyond death, while flames crackled out of the gaping holes in their chests and their bodies lit up like huge paper lanterns. They rose from their beds and drifted about the house like spirits of the dancing, ridiculous dead, causing terror wherever they came.

The outcry awakened Azrekia. Her maid, who slept beside her, screamed as she looked up at the bearded stranger looming over them. A single stroke of the knife silenced the maid, and another beheaded her; and Tsarag Vin stood over Azrekia, holding up the bloody head as if it were an offering, and he said softly, "I loved you once, dearest Azrekia."

But Azrekia only struggled and tried to get away. He wrestled with her on the bed and he cut out her heart with the witch-knife, somewhat more sloppily, so that she actually died before he had finished. But he imprisoned her spirit there in the burning corpse and heard her moans and her pleadings come out through her dead, open mouth.

Then Tsarag withdrew from the room slowly, like one walking in a dream, and he made his way to the great hall, which was deserted but for the burning corpse of Lady Zevas, who had blundered among some benches and gotten tangled there. She bumped against a pillar again and again, like a confused moth.

Tsarag ignored her. He sat down in the chair at the head of the great table, the place reserved for the lord of the house, and he spoke in a loud voice, to no one in particular, "Behold, I welcome you to House Vin, for I am the lord of this place and I have restored my family's name and honor."

V

Enough of this. It is too horrible. I have to bring it to an end.
I have to clean up the mess.

TSARAG VIN heard a soft footstep and looked to one side. He saw that Julna of Kadisphon had come to him, as he had always seen her, in her almost translucent gown of spider-silk, her long hair flowing behind her in some imperceptible, magical wind, the jewelry on her wrists and ankles clinking softly as she moved.

Her eyes were so dark. He gazed into them and it seemed that he looked beyond the Earth itself, beyond *Leshé,* which is dream, and *Tashé,* which is death, beyond the belly of the great god Surat-Kemad who devours all things at the end of time; that god whose teeth are the stars, whose mouth is the night sky. He beheld, then, the night sky and the stars rippled, like a curtain stirred by a wind, and the black sky parted like a curtain, and out of the deeper darkness which the eye cannot fathom, he saw, rising up like leviathans drawn to the light of the Moon from out of a midnight sea, the very Shadow Titans themselves, their faces so vast and terrible that even the gods cannot look upon them; and he knew their names and their aspects and their titles: the Titans of Desolation and Wrath and Earthquakes; and Sedengul, bringer of storms to the soul; and Arvadas, Lord of Lust; and Vedatis, the wildest of all, sender of dark dreams.

He prayed to Vedatis, most especially.

Drawn to these, his soul and his mind utterly subsumed into darkness, Tsarag Vin took Julna of Kadisphon in his arms and kissed her passionately, begging to be one with her forever.

"I have done as you told me," he said. "I have despaired of any love but yours."

But something happened. Suddenly the Titans vanished and Julna of Kadisphon was gone, as abruptly as if a door had been slammed in his face.

He could see nothing at all in those dark eyes: just eyes now. Someone else was there.

The one he held in his arms moved differently.

The slender hands pushed him away and, unresisting, he let go, but the spider-silk gown tore and came away in his hands. He stood holding it, gaping stupidly at the impossible, at the ridiculous.

Only a *tagheri* corpse could have laughed, though.

For one thing, the person naked before him was a boy.

For another, that boy, his dark flesh criss-crossed with faintly luminous scars, held a glowing mask in his hands. He put it on his face and the mask came alive in fire, and the features were those of Tsarag Vin as he had once been, only screaming now, in infinite despair.

And the boy reached out his hand and uncurled his fingers, and a white flame danced on his palm. A wind blew, inside that great hall, the air swirling around and around, as motes of light gathered, as those motes resolved themselves into the silently screaming ghosts of all those people Tsarag Vin had murdered and would not allow to rest.

Then boy said, "Know that I am not Julna of Kadisphon, although such a one is within me. I have many names, for I contain multitudes. But foremost I am Sekenre the sorcerer, and I have come to make an ending."

And this is the ending I made. It was only the best I can do. I weep at its inadequacies.

And is it not often claimed that a sorcerer cannot weep?

Is it not said that no sorcerer can ever atone?

I took Tsarag Vin by the hand and led him outside, into the Street of the Witches, which was all about, for he had created it in his mind. The snow was deep and drifting. I know the wind bit at his flesh, but I was naked and felt only the cool night air of the otherwise hot and dusty City of the Delta far to the south. It was one of the many miracles of the Street of the Witches that Tsarag Vin and I met, though he was on the other side the Crescent Sea in some icy land I had never seen.

Such are the least of the miracles, in the Street of the Witches.

He and I walked past the shop where the wooden puppets laughed and called out his name.

Women in red gowns emerged from every doorway, gazing hungrily, their eyes filled with terrible darkness. Even I could not look on them.

"Why are you here?" Tsarag Vin demanded of me. "You are not one of their number."

I explained to him that a witch serves the darkness of her own will. She has made a pact. Her soul is all the more corrupted because she is not compelled. She is wholly consumed. But sorcery is a contagion, like a cancer. The sorcerer contains multitudes. Whosoever kills a sorcerer becomes that sor-

cerer, joining together within himself the soul and mind of that sorcerer and all the others that sorcerer has murdered. The physical body does not age. It is preserved, by sorcery, like a dead thing in a bottle, although it is alive and may be slain. The one who killed and swallowed the sorcerer is still, in some small sense, himself. Thus, three hundred years ago, a fifteen-year-old boy called Sekenre was made to kill his father, a sorcerer, and the boy became his father, who was called Vashtem, and he became Balredon, and Tannivar, and Talno and so many others, whom his father had already murdered, and more, whom he had to murder in the course of his subsequent adventures. Among the great riot of voices within him was Julna of Kadisphon, who was also a member of the Witches in good standing and therefore an abomination. But Sekenre, struggling to remain Sekenre, is, although unclean, at least capable of greater moral complexity.

"All this was her doing, not mine," I said. "I can only begin to comprehend what her purpose was, and I fear I cannot undo what she has done."

"How did she do it?"

"Somehow, when I was asleep, she seized the body and did these things. I saw them only as one in a dream. Now I have awakened, and shut her away again inside myself. In time, I will pry her secrets out of her."

And he said to me, "Sekenre, how may I be redeemed?"

I led him by the hand.

The witches gathered around us. I too put on a red gown and moved among them, and they took me for Julna of Kadisphon and were not alarmed, though they hated and feared Sekenre.

In a cellar room, we bound Tsarag Vin naked to a wooden table. We stripped away his years, and he was a child again. We burned his flesh with iron and cut him with our witch-knives. We opened him like a sack and poured molten silver into his gut and sewed him up.

His screaming stopped then. He looked up, at the window. I saw someone peering in and pulled down the shade.

"It is over," I whispered into his ear.

I took off the burning mask, and let its ashes float away on the air.

NOW THE tale is of Sekenre and is set in the hot and dusty Delta, beyond the Crescent Sea, where few Nevasderati ever venture.

There Sekenre walked into the great, silent temple of Bel-Hemad, the god of spring and renewal, and of forgiveness. He moved like a ghost, his bare feet silent on the marble floor. He wore, in the fashion of the Delta in that time, a brilliantly dyed, loose-sleeved shirt that reached to mid-thigh, and baggy, white trousers torn off at the knees, his long hair tied behind in a braid; and he wore no jewelry. He might have been taken for a common street youth of that place. It suited him to appear as such.

But the god knew otherwise. The god could see that the sorcerer is unclean.

No god will listen to a sorcerer's prayers.

For the sorcerer cannot pray any more than he can weep.

That's what they say, anyway.

Therefore, to atone, Sekenre could only place the heart of Tsarag Vin (which he had stolen from the Witches) in the chipped, earthen bowl and place it at the feet of Bel-Hemad.

He left, as an offering, the toy horse with the broken wheel.

He could only hope that the god would understand, and that on some night, either in a year or a hundred years, there would be a ghost waiting in the temple of Bel-Hemad, and it would be the ghost of that young boy who went into the Street of the Witches in what might have been a dream, and never returned.

The monster, who came back, had ceased to exist.

But the god could grant this much, even to a sorcerer, that Sekenre might lead the ghost of the boy Tsarag to the shore of the Black River, into the Land of the Dead, where he might join with his parents, with his brother Amasdag, with his teacher Meras and with Azrekia who truly loved him, and dwell in the great House of Vin (which is a dream) forever.

THE LANTERN OF THE SUPREME MOMENT

> The supreme moment is one in which absolutely nothing happens. That is how you recognize it.
> — Orkanre the Eremite, *Shouting into Silence*

WHEN HE was twelve, Tsamais was suddenly visited by his father the King. That the King came at all was extraordinary enough, because boy was the second son of a later wife and unlikely to inherit anything. That he came in the night like a secret messenger or a thief was amazing beyond all comprehension, an occasion for terror, for King Zhamon was a fierce and silent man who had slain many enemies; and he came like a shadowy, miraculous apparition.

But Riverland is filled with apparitions and miracles in some seasons, the City of the Delta especially, and the shadows conceal the secret comings and goings of the gods, or of Death, who is the greatest god of all.

The King came alone in the night, beneath the brilliant stars, his bald head gleaming faintly, his black robe billowing, his sandals crunching on gravel.

Tsamais sat up suddenly in the tumbledown pavilion in the remote corner of the palace gardens where, because he was no one of any particular importance, he was allowed to sleep on hot nights.

And the King was there. His face seemed to glow softly. It may have been a trick of the light.

Tsamais dropped to his knees on the gravel, then reached for his robe to cover himself.

His father grabbed him by the bare arm and yanked him to his feet, saying, "Never mind that. Come with me. Now."

And as if in a dream, Prince Tsamais followed, almost naked but streaming sweat in the stifling night. Yet this was not a dream. The gravel hurt his bare feet. His father's touch was hard, dry, and almost cold.

They went deep into the gardens, among the half-ruined mazes, where vines crept over walls and draped the statues of long forgotten dynasts; where apparitions lurked.

Tsamais saw many things, like half-glimpsed images from dreams:

A king, all of bone, black as polished iron, his eyes aglow with some inner fire, his finery trailing glittering dust as he rose from his throne, and lunged forward, his mouth gaping, his teeth like nails.

King Zhamon raised his hand and spoke a word, and something like a bundle of sticks bound together tumbled or shuffled away, whispering.

A flock of perfectly white, luminous birds rose out of the dark water of a stagnant pool, circling higher and higher in utter silence, as if they were creatures of glowing smoke. Then the light suddenly went out of them and they blotted out all the stars in the sky but for a very few, pale and spread far apart, which Tsamais did not recognize.

His father dragged him on. Tsamais glanced back to the stagnant pool and saw someone else crouched by the water's edge, a boy only slightly older than himself, clad in ragged clothes, pushing a toy boat out into the water with a stick. The other boy looked directly at Tsamais and Tsamais was frightened by him, in a way he had no time to define. He saw only a pale round face, and very dark eyes.

Then the strange boy turned back to the toy boat and breathed wind into its sails, and his breath was like white fire.

"Come!" said King Zhamon, hurrying Tsamais along.

Now the great and dreadful Zhamon kicked off his royal sandals and walked barefoot on the surface of black water, no longer in the gardens at all, but on the Great River, among reeds; but the water was black as oil and smooth and cold as marble underfoot when Tsamais, too, walked upon it. In the back of his mind Tsamais understood that this was deep magic, in which *flesh must touch* for the magic to be true.

Something like a crocodile stood up out of the water and spoke to King Zhamon in familiar terms. The thing had a crocodile's head, but the pale, naked body of a man, like a drowned corpse. It was one of the *evatim*, the sacred messengers of Death, who is Surat-Hemad, most powerful of the gods, whose mouth is the night sky, whose teeth are the stars.

(So Tsamais recited piously under his breath, to avoid screaming. Then he bit his hand, hard, for silence.)

More and more of the *evatim* showed themselves. The reeds rattled and swayed at the movement of many bodies. The dead ones closed around King Zhamon and his son, but again the King raised his hand and spoke a word of command, which caused them to pause.

Then he addressed them, familiarly again, but in a speech Tsamais could not understand. This terrified him all the more, for he knew his father was speaking that special language of the Underworld, which only the greatest of sorcerers know while alive, and which comes to others when they are about to die, when Surat-Hemad has touched them.

Zhamon whispered to his son, "They bid me despair and die. But not yet. Not yet."

Tsamais wanted to say something, if only, "What do we do now?" but he dared not, fearing his father as much as the *evatim*.

Therefore he only watched as the King plucked a reed and breathed on it. The reed burst silently into white flame. The King drew a small lantern out from beneath his robe. This Tsamais saw clearly: cylindrical, polished metal, small enough to hold in the palm of the hand, with a tiny door to be opened with a metal ring. But the King did not open the door. He slid the burning reed in through a hole in the side, touching the wick.

The King gave the lantern to his son to hold, and Tsamais held it, marveling now at the intricate carvings in the side of the lantern, each cut through the metal shell so that light shone out, projecting countless shapes onto the rippling black water like luminous, wriggling fishes.

The *evatim* retreated. It seemed to Tsamais that the shapes on the water were more than just wriggling blobs. They came together, like the tiles in a mosaic. They tricked the senses, and seemed to show him that he stood on the threshold of a whole country of fire — the kind one might imagine staring into a fireplace while half asleep, as the logs burn low — where forests rose in delicate traceries of light.

As he watched, as his eyes adjusted to the increasing glare, he thought he saw something moving among the trees; then lords and ladies of that country emerged out of the forest, all of them clad in brilliant light, their faces too bright to look upon.

King Zhamon shook him, and he turned away, into the darkness. He was blind for a moment, his eyes dazzled.

"It is as right," the King said. "You saw them —"

Tsamais interrupted.

"But, Father, didn't you —?"

"I saw only the light, nothing more. That is why, I suppose, I was commanded to give you this thing."

Tsamais was amazed. He wanted to ask who would command his father to do anything. But he did not. King Zhamon continued.

"This is the Lantern of the *Supreme Moment*, my son. That is my one legacy to you. It was fashioned, I suppose, by a god. You may use it only once. Only once may you pass into the country of fire. Choose that moment wisely and well, and it will be for a purpose. Choose it foolishly, and you will be consumed, and the light wasted."

Tsamais made to speak. He wasn't sure what he was going to say. Probably something stupid like, "The supreme moment of *what?*"

But then his father was gone and a chill breeze blew and the light flickered and went out. Tsamais stood alone beneath the unfamiliar stars, and it came to him, then, with deepening dread, that these must be the stars of *Leshé*, that realm where Dream and Death flow into one another like dark waters.

The *evatim* circled around him, slowly, hissing; their voice was the night wind. The waters no longer held him up. He fell, splashing, for an instant terrified beyond all reason that he had lost the lantern. He thrashed about desperately for it in shoulder-deep water until he realized he still held it in his hand. Perhaps for that reason the *evatim* parted momentarily and let him pass.

Something cold and hard and massive, like a sunken log come to life, brushed against him and nearly knocked his legs out from under him. Struggling, half swimming, gasping for air, too breathless to scream, he fought his way through reeds. He waded waist-deep in mud. Thorns tore at him. Still he clutched the lantern and burst through some hedges and suddenly found himself in the garden by the pool where the ragged boy still crouched, watching the toy boat drift.

Now Tsamais saw that the boat was a funeral boat, and a king lay upon it.

The other boy said to him only, "You have to hurry back now."

And Tsamais found himself back at the pavilion as dawn broke, shivering while one of his eunuch tutors made *tsk*ing and clucking sounds, shaking him as if to awaken him from a dream.

But it hadn't been a dream because Tsamais was muddy and cut with thorns and he still clutched the lantern, which he quickly hid under a pillow, then placed it behind a loose stone when the eunuch's back was turned.

On that day he attended his father's funeral, and the body of the dead king — who had died in his sleep of a disease, or been poisoned, or strangled, or merely touched directly by the hand of Surat-Hemad — was placed in a boat and set adrift on the Great River where it floated upstream, against the living current, until it disappeared into a darkness like a shadow cast by nothing, which defied even the sunlight of the bright day.

BECAUSE HE was merely a leftover prince and unlikely to inherit, Tsamais was allowed to grow up. The eldest of his many brothers, Tekam, became king. He reigned for a year, then died, it was said, of a fall from his horse. Zhaemre succeeded him, a great warrior, who fought many battles, each of them a little closer to home than the last.

Tsamais spent his youth in enforced idleness, in the palace, among the gardens when he could get away; in an endless round of fêtes and ceremonies and hunts. He spent many summer weeks with the court, sailing up the river to the broad marshes near the border of Reedland, where the best hunting was, and he and the other young men would ride in flat boats poled by slaves and strike down game birds with forked spears.

Then the borders of Reedland were no longer safe, and Tsamais retreated into books, sitting as long as he chose in his pavilion in the gardens with a scroll or a codex open in his lap, reading, first, stories of adventures and escapes and magic; then more serious history and the legends of the gods. Once he leaned back against a stone, felt it shift, and drew out the almost forgotten Lantern of the Supreme Moment. He looked at it now in sunlight. It seemed like a tawdry thing, like one you could get in a shop for a few coppers.

But he remembered how he had acquired this thing, and he did not dismiss that memory as a dream, and he pondered.

He tried to discover what god had fashioned it.

So in the evening of a certain day in his nineteenth year, he sat in the pavilion, watching the shadows lengthen as the sun set. Here the gardens were truly fallen into ruin. A long-legged bird waded in a nearby pool.

Hesitantly, looking around to make sure he was alone, Tsamais got out the lantern and placed it on a stone railing. He lit a piece of reed by ordinary means — stirring the coals in the brazier where he'd prepared his own supper — and slid the burning reed in through the round hole in the side of the lantern until he touched the wick.

At once the shapes cut into the shell of the lantern came to life, and it seemed that the bright folk from out of the forest were walking around him now. He felt the heat of their nearness, but it was a gentle, pleasant burning, which did not hurt him.

And a bright king stood before him, wearing a beehive-shaped crown like a king of Riverland, clad in gleaming scales and jewelry. His bare arms and his face were almost too brilliant to look upon. His sandals crunched the gravel.

This one bade Tsamais open the door of the lantern, and Tsamais opened it, and gazed into the Country Behind the Fire, and it seemed he could see for miles to where a golden palace arose behind forested hills.

"This waits for you," the bright king said.

Tsamais might have stepped through in that instant, but suddenly another hand snapped the metal door shut and the bright people drew away and vanished, and there was only ordinary light now, such as any lantern might cast. But Tsamais's eyes were still dazzled, and for a time he could see nothing at all. He covered his eyes, and still a thousand suns burned behind his eyelids, only slowly fading, while a voice spoke to him, deep and commanding and oddly accented, like the voice of a foreign king, he thought, a fierce man angered and barely able to hold back his anger.

"This is not the supreme moment."

But when Tsamais could see again, he beheld only that ragged boy he'd seen before, the one by the pool pushing the boat, hardly a commanding presence, thin and frail as a reed, barefoot and splattered with mud. Tsamais could see now that the other was considerably younger than himself, maybe thirteen or fourteen, or just undersized, a starveling. It must have been a trick of the light that he'd ever seemed otherwise.

But there was something about the boy's dark eyes in his round, pale face, something about the way he spoke, now with an entirely different, softer voice, still accented, but only with the rustic tones of several hundred miles upriver near the border of Reedland; *something* made Prince Tsamais heed and even feel a little afraid when the stranger shook his head gently and whispered, "Do not waste the gift you have been given."

Then the boy raised the lantern to his face and put his lips to the place where Tsamais had slipped the burning reed in; and the boy sucked the fire out of the lantern, inhaling it all, so that darkness closed around the two of them like a curtain, and the only light was from beneath that ragged boy's clothing, traceries and jagged lines across his chest and down his legs which seemed to resemble old scars, outlined in fire.

A moment later the lantern rested on the stone railing again, and Tsamais was alone, but for the long-legged bird wading in the pool nearby.

The bird looked at him once, shook its head, and spread its wings, then rose into the night sky as silently as burning smoke.

WHEN TSAMAIS was twenty-two, his brother, the warrior-king Zhaemre, died suddenly, of a fall from his horse it was alleged. But had someone cut the horse's tendon with a razor? That was whispered.

Two more brothers, Anedis and Horek, contended for the throne. A cousin, with (or assuming) the ancient royal name of Wenamon, opposed them both. Now the satrapies fell away, and the countries of the Great River no longer paid tribute to the City of the Delta. The quays were empty. Few ships came, even from across the Crescent Sea. Sometimes, in the evening, Tsamais could walk the walls of the city and note smudges on the horizon, from distant cities burning, or the dust of battles.

The skies were filled with portents.

And it happened that Wenamon allied himself with certain rebels and overcame Anedis first, then Horek. In the midst of a great storm, propelled by howling winds and astonishing, driving rain the likes of which had not been seen in centuries, he approached the almost defenseless capital. His ships filled the Great River like a flock of enormous birds swimming, their sails billowing or flapping or ragged like fluttering wings.

His trumpets blasted above the voice of the tempest.

Fearfully, those atop the walls watched as the usurper drew near, standing in the prow of the foremost galley, clad all in gold and white, holding aloft a spear and a hooked staff, the emblems of the ancient dynasties, while his barbarian wizards chanted and rattled gourds and clanged upon metal drums and cymbals.

Someone standing behind Wenamon raised up the beehive-shaped crown of the great kings of the Delta.

Suddenly the wizards were silent, and the oarsmen of the galley stopped rowing, and in that instant of drifting silence, in the rain, the crown descended into place on the head of Wenamon the False; and Tsamais, who was watching, saw something so absurd that he was certain no one else could see it at all, that it was a vision intended for himself alone, or else he was merely going mad: the one who crowned Wenamon was not a priest or some minister of state, but that ragged, barefoot boy from the garden, standing on an upended crate behind Wenamon so he could reach high enough.

No one else seemed to remark on this.

And Prince Tsamais thought to himself, *Surely this is the supreme moment, and I am undone, and will soon die.* Of course the usurper would have to kill him. He didn't have the lantern with him. He wasn't sure what he would have done if he had.

But even Tsamais had only a second to observe or think, because the sky split apart and a lightning-bolt blasted the usurper to cinders, his head, trunk, and limbs flying in all directions, trailing smoke, splashing into the water, as the galley itself began to break apart and settle to the bottom.

Now all was a chaos of shouting, struggling men, of ships drawing near or struggling to get away, their oars and rigging clashing, tangled amid raging wind and pouring rain.

Those on the walls bowed down and covered their eyes, or fled. But Tsamais stood upright, and watched the ships scattering. The storm stopped, as suddenly as if a door were closed to shut out the wind and rain.

Later that same night, Tsamais went to his pavilion in the garden and got out the Lantern of the Supreme Moment and merely stared at it. He made no attempt to light it, or to open the door, or to summon forth the folk from the Country of Fire, for he knew this was not the supreme moment at all, but one of a crisis that had passed as mysteriously and arbitrarily as it had arisen.

And the boy was there with him. This was not a surprise. "It is not the supreme moment," he said.

"I know," said Tsamais, merely holding the lantern and looking at it.

"But it will come."

The boy had an odor about him, like that of a wood fire doused by rain. Tsamais saw that his clothing was charred and torn away. His chest and shoulders looked red. His old scars glowed softly.

Suddenly forgetting that this was an apparition, some terrible agent of mystery, Tsamais merely asked, "Are you hurt?"

"Deeply and profoundly and long ago," the boy said, "and at times, I fear, beyond all hope of healing. But all things may change, when the supreme moment arrives."

"I too hope for that much," said Tsamais.

Then he was alone.

*   *   *

TSAMAIS WAS seldom alone after that, for he was running out of brothers, and was therefore an important person, courted by lords, flattered, cajoled, vaguely threatened, while eunuchs and slaves fluttered about him like flocks of silly pigeons, and he spent his days on display, in grand robes, waiting and waited upon, expectant.

But actually Ptaneoc was king, second son of old Zhamon's third wife, and for once no once challenged him. Ptaneoc reigned for a surprisingly long time, almost fifteen years walled up within the palace, lost in amusements, in debauchery, in attempts at magic. There was silence in the City then, as much of the population trickled away, and those who remained whispered of things far away, events in the now unreachable territories where, Tsamais, in his youth, had hunted birds along the River. New kingdoms were rising up, it was said. There were even new gods. But so far no conqueror or god had descended on the Delta itself, and some poet more daring than most compared the State to a stagnant pool.

At least King Ptaneoc renovated the gardens. That much was credited to him.

He died there, miserably, surrounded by jeweled catamites, having overindulged, it was said, in candied eels, a delicacy of which he was particularly fond.

And it was in the night that someone came into the chamber of Prince Tsamais, barefoot and smelling of wet ash, and placed the Lantern of the Supreme Moment at his bedside. The room seemed to be filled with a miasma. Not even the servants who waited on him and slept at the foot of his bed like dogs seemed to notice. But Tsamais sat up and beheld that same pale, dark-eyed boy, almost naked and covered with glowing scars. The boy had not aged at all since he had first seen him. Now Tsamais had gray in his beard. It came to him, as the result of his many researches, that this boy lived outside of the flow of time, as some great sorcerers were reputed to do, and that he too was stagnant, caught in the instant just *before* the Supreme Moment of which he spoke, always waiting, but never arriving at his goal.

That was just a surmise, but when the boy stood before him in the night it all seemed absolutely clear.

It seemed pointless to demand of him who he was and what he was and what he was doing, for understanding, like an apparition, appeared when it would.

Perhaps it was precisely because he had not asked, that the boy whispered to him, "I am called Sekenre."

Sekenre. That was a name from the times of the ancient dynasties, a legend of a wanderer who was always a child but never a child, a sorcerer who could not age or change or be healed or even truly die, for when a sorcerer is killed he comes to life again inside the mind of the murderer, so that a successful sorcerer, who has slain many, is a composite being, one of whom might be a centuries-old child named Sekenre who contained multitudes, even as the cover of a book contains many pages; but the cover and the pages together make up the book; and the words in the book are written with pain and sorrow and longing, in a babble of voices.

Sekenre. Possibly he was the last of his kind, who had thus devoured and now contained every other sorcerer in the world.

Sekenre. Perhaps only a child who was somewhat disfigured and a little bit mad.

For Tsamais to explicate this riddle and thus arrive at the Supreme Moment, more was necessary.

It was necessary for him to exert himself and know love, taking to his side a certain lady called Amherefti, who had been his mistress, and without permission or public ceremony, in secret and by ancient rite, in the pavilion in the garden, he made her his wife.

It was necessary that Azdegerd, son of Ptaneoc, become king for a short while, then die without issue, so that, at last, silently in the night, the eunuchs came to awaken Tsamais where he slept in the garden beside Amherefti and placed crowns on both of them and proclaimed them King and Queen of the Delta and (by implication, though not in actuality) of Riverland all the way up to the black mountains where the River is born in unmapped gorges, where eagles and winged gods soar above the spray of the waterfalls.

And it was necessary that Tsamais put to death all the partisans of Azdegerd. When one of the nobles tried to run him through with a spear, it was necessary that many more die, slowly and hideously and noisily, in the great forum of the city, before the temples, while the grim, stained, and often crumbling statues of gods and heroes on the rooftops looked down.

It was necessary to become cruel.

It was necessary, also, to wage war, to push back the barbarians from the walls of the city even as one might attempt to push back an incoming tide; even as it was hopeless, even as most of the money put aside for arms was pillaged by corrupt officials; even as the most vigorous effort gained only a little more time and everyone knew it.

And it was necessary to sorrow, when Queen Amherefti died in childbirth and Tsamais had no heir.

It was necessary to get out the Lantern of the Supreme Moment and stare at it, and even to light the wick and let the room be filled with shapes projected in light into the walls, but to know that the moment had not arrived and the lights were only lights.

It was necessary to listen for Sekenre, and to command all servants, even slaves, to wear shoes with wooden or studded soles, so that if he heard a very soft footstep, Tsamais would know who it was.

It was necessary to wait. To grow old. To be regarded as a senile fool not worth deposing, to be known as the last, the very last, in whose person, with whose final breath history comes to an end.

It was necessary for these things to be true, for Tsamais to sometimes forget that he was Tsamais the king and remember a twelve-year old boy who was dragged into a garden at midnight; to fall back into dreams and memories as the two flowed together and were one and the same; to cease to care; to ask no more questions, put aside all researches, all speculations, and merely wait.

In the end it was necessary to become, in his mind and soul, as still and stagnant as a black pool.

Then Sekenre came to him, unaged and unchanged, nearly naked, smelling of mud and ash. He looked as if he'd been hurt, deeply and profoundly and a long time ago. Tsamais mumbled something. The boy did not answer. He put his arm behind the old king's shoulders and raised him up out of his bed. It was a humid, breezeless night. The king lay in the pavilion, in the garden, a favorite spot.

No one challenged them as they walked into the garden; as if time had stopped, and the servants who slept at the king's feet like dogs and the guards on watch all remained suspended between one breath and the next.

The *evatim*, messengers of Surat-Hemad, the Lord of Death, rose up out of stagnant water and spoke in familiar tones, but Sekenre answered them and they parted and let the old man and the boy pass unmolested.

The reeds stood absolutely motionless all around them.

And the King kicked off his royal sandals and walked with Sekenre upon the black water of the River, beneath the few and faint stars of *Leshé*, where Dream touches the borderlands of Death. There Sekenre placed the Lantern of the Supreme Moment upon the surface of the water and breathed into it with fiery breath, until the black water and the night sky were filled with glowing shapes projected through the holes cut in the shell of the lantern. And these shapes were of mountains and forests and cities, of men and women and fabulous beasts, of armies on the march, of great argosies.

And King Tsamais said, "I don't care," and was beyond all caring, for he saw his whole life as a dream which he might as well go on dreaming in stagnant idleness. He sought nothing. He required nothing. He was empty.

Sekenre bade him crouch down and gaze into the lantern. "It is time. Open the door. You must do it. I cannot."

Tsamais opened it, and the two of them tumbled through, or perhaps the fire came out and swallowed them.

There was an instant of pain, and Tsamais thought that his body had been burned away, so effortless did his movements become, as if he were a thing of smoke, drifting. But he looked down and saw that he was returned to the vigor of his youth, and naked, suffused with light, so that his very flesh glowed with holy fire.

He knew somehow that it *was* holy, that thus the gods reach out and touch the lives of men.

Sekenre grabbed hold of his arm and whispered, almost weeping, "Lead me on. I cannot see."

Sekenre was still muddy and smelling of ash, but fires danced all over him, and he seemed in great pain. His eyes were closed. Blood and tears streamed over his face.

"Help me to go on," said, "A sorcerer is unclean and may not see the holy things, or travel into holy lands, without such help."

After a while Tsamais had to carry him in his arms. The boy-sorcerer weighed almost nothing. He felt like a bundle of sticks. And he spoke, telling Tsamais how he was indeed that Sekenre who had become a sorcerer in ancient times by murdering his father, Vashtem, who was also a sorcerer of great power, and who arranged his own murder, that he might live on in the mind and body of his son; but this did not lessen the stain of the crime, which was sorcery itself and filled Sekenre with a babble of voices, until his mind was like a cave of angry winds, and sometimes he could not hear himself shouting among them. It was true, too, that a sorcerer lives outside of time, and may move back and forth between tomorrow and yesterday, yesterday and tomorrow, as one might walk on a gravel path.

Now Tsamais carried him into the Country of Fire, through the burning forests, across the molten mountains, and though Sekenre felt the pain of the burning, he was not burned; and Tsamais understood that even a sorcerer is of a mixed nature, not entirely evil, and it was Sekenre's hope to be made clean, to be smelted like ore and have the dross cast away, to be healed.

The lords and ladies of that country gathered around, and their faces were too bright to look upon. They followed Tsamais in solemn procession singing hymns in the language of the gods, while birds of fire rose up on every side and filled the sky with the thunder of their wings.

Here, in this country, only the stars were dark, black orbs fixed in the sky, few and far between, in no constellations Tsamais had ever seen before.

They came to a great palace of sculpted flame, and passed beneath its high arches, while liquid fire poured down splashing into the floor; and sometimes Tsamais waded through such fire up to his knees, holding Sekenre high above it out of harm's way, while the boy now only whimpered and babbled like a sufferer lost in the delirium of fever. Long corridors twisted, turned, and folded in upon themselves in ways senses could not follow, but at the very last emptied into a central, sunken chamber like the bubbling mouth of a volcano.

Flesh must touch, so that magic may be true. Tsamais walked barefoot and unharmed across the surface of bubbling lava to where a huge coffin-boat drifted amid swirling fire. Therein lay a giant, ten times the height of a man, clad in burning robes, but serene and infinitely powerful, his face almost too beautiful to behold.

This was a god, not dead, but waiting to be born. This much Tsamais understood, either because Sekenre said so amidst his delirium, or because the fire roaring in his ears began to speak with its own voice.

For the Earth is young, and still spits up gods every once in a while, as volcanos spit up stones.

Sekenre reached out blindly, and touched the face of the god. It burned him. Tsamais heard him cry out, and he heard the burnt flesh hissing. But Sekenre found the god's eyes, first one, then the other, opening them; and the god came alive; and Sekenre touched its mouth, and the mouth spoke the word "*Chakaz,*" and thus did *Chakaz-Hemad* name himself and rise up out of his coffin boat and direct Tsamais to set Sekenre down on the surface of the boiling lava.

This burned, and Sekenre cried out, but he did not sink. The sorcerer and the god both crouched down, and both of them fashioned molten metal with their hands, and with desperate, delicate care, Sekenre carved countless intricate shapes into the shell of the Lantern of the Supreme Moment.

The door of the lantern was open. Within, in the heart of the Country of Fire, another Sekenre and another *Chakaz-Hemad* fashioned the Lantern of the Supreme Moment, within which the boy and the god fashioned the lantern, while Tsamais, purpose of his entire life and existence now served, stood aside and merely watched.

Then Sekenre closed the door of the Lantern of the Supreme Moment, and the darkness was so blinding, so profound, that Tsamais felt that he was falling forever into nothingness.

INSTEAD HE found himself in the night, beneath familiar stars, among the reeds on the bank of the Great River. Nearby, a heron waded. It glanced at him, shook its head, and leapt flapping into the sky.

Sekenre groaned. Tsamais lowered him gently into a shallow pool to ease the pain of his burns. For a long time the two of them conversed, Sekenre at first merely babbling, speaking in many voices at once, then slowly returning to himself.

His burnt flesh glowed beneath the water, softly, as if his whole body were a paper lantern.

He opened his eyes.

"Many sorcerers," he said, "are wholly consumed and mutilated by their sorcery. I am comparatively fortunate."

"Are you the last?" asked Tsamais. "Have you devoured all the others?"

"No. I think there are a few more."

Then the sun rose, in the face of it, too bright to look upon, was the face of *Chakaz-Hemad*, a god of beautiful yet terrible aspect, of swift and merciless judgments, who is as indifferent to mankind as are fire, the wind, or the storm. Yet he is called the god of justice, and worshipped by men; and Tsamais, whose youth was restored in the Country of Fire, looked into the face of Chakaz-Hemad and was not blinded; and he is known to the ages as the herald and prophet of Chakaz-Hemad, for he lived out an entirely different life, and loved for a time, and married, and had sons, but was called away again by the god, and ravished by the fire of Chakaz-Hemad until he had completely forgotten his own history. He died a martyr, somewhere in the East.

That history was written down by Sekenre, who got up out of the shallow pool, whole but not cleansed or healed of his sorcery — for the wind does not heal, nor does the storm, nor the fire, though all of them will drive men on to their destinies. He took the Lantern of the Supreme Moment which he had helped fashion back into Yesterday, turning through time as one might on a gravel path, to give it to King Zhamon, that fierce and silent man, who, himself, finally understood that he could never reach the supreme moment because he could not cease striving for it.

Sekenre wrote. He sat in the pavilion in the ruins of the palace garden, clad in a purple shirt embroidered with golden thread, which once King Tsamais had worn, but now fit Sekenre like a gown, so he could belt it with a robe and draw it to his knees to hide some of his scars.

Throughout many a stifling day he sat, by a stagnant pool, writing the history into a book in delicate script, illuminating the images until they seemed alive, resting his various pens between his ink-stained toes.

The supreme moment is not a moment, he wrote, b*ut an absence, a void of time, which swallows up kings, prophets, and even gods.*

But not, perhaps, sorcerers. He did not write that. He closed the book.

FROM OUT OF THE CROCODILE'S MOUTH

I shall draw forth my precious treasure from out of the crocodile's mouth. I reclaim what he has devoured.
— *The Book of Returning*
(sometimes attributed to Sekenre the Illuminator)

I

THE BIRDS HIGH above might have noticed him, but he was not prey, and so they continued circling in the evening air, over the marshland, where great reeds stirred in the chill breeze and open water rolled gently, black in the shadows, gleaming orange and gold in the rapidly vanishing sunset.

Insects sang in the sighing wind. With a splash, a startled heron took to the air, its wings flashing orange, then golden as it vanished.

But the short, slight figure kept on walking. He wore a loose tunic several sizes too large for him, belted at the waist, and loose trousers rolled up to the knees. A leather bag hung from one shoulder. His bare feet sank into the mud until his legs were splattered with it, but when he walked upon the open water there were only spreading ripples, for he walked *on* the surface of the water, as weightless as a ghost or a passing mist.

He might have been a boy in his mid-teens. He had a boy's face, soft and beardless beneath a tangle of dark hair; but he held a living flame cupped in his outstretched, scarred right hand. This tiny fire flickered in the darkening air, burning nothing; and by these signs the wild creatures knew this was no ordinary child of mankind. The night hawks and owls, circling above him, gathered like a storm, but kept their distance. Croco-diles, drifting like sullen logs, did not stir as he passed.

He held out the fire to light his way. He walked upon the sunlit waters and the dark; and the night descended suddenly, and the sky filled with brilliant stars around the crescent of a day-old moon, low in the west. The moon sank. For an instant more, the waters gleamed, golden, pale white.

Then, by subtle changes, the stars faded and were fewer, no longer the stars of Earth at all, but stars of *Leshé*, which is Dream, and has its own strange constellations. *Leshé* likewise faded as the traveler moved deeper into mystery, to the frontier marches of *Tashé*, which is the country of the

Dead.

Here on the cold, black water, as whispering, pleading, jabbering ghosts gathered around him, he waited for a time, until he saw a dark, lumbering shape rise up a shallow pool. The thing crashed through reeds. It reared up, and he saw clearly the crocodile face and human body — naked, pale, like that of a drowned man — of one of the *evatim*, the dread messengers of Surat-Kemad, Lord of Death, who was king of this land.

Anyone who beholds one of the *evatim* face to face knows that he is about to die, and may, perhaps, have time to breathe a brief prayer.

Except sorcerers, who do not pray, and who, at times, traffic with the *evatim* and treat even with Surat-Kemad, the Devouring God, whose mouth is the night sky, whose teeth are all the inescapable stars of Earth, *Leshé,* and *Tashé* put together.

The boy waited, fire in his hand, while the crocodile thing crouched down before him and, somewhat to his surprise, removed its head, which proved a mask. The face underneath was flabby, hairless, and pale, indeed like a man long drowned, but the eyes were alive. They gleamed with reflected light, like those of a dog when it nears a campfire. The body, as far as he could tell, was gross, distorted, and moved clumsily. Perhaps it had a tail. It was not something he needed to know, only that sorcerers are ultimately disfigured beyond all recognition by their sorcery, and that this other was one of his own kind, a sorcerer, and therefore his enemy.

The two of them circled one another on the surface of the black water, warily, like two scorpions in a jar, the boy walking slowly, the other half-crawling.

The other held out a clawed hand, as if in friendship. The boy drew back.

It spoke in a voice more like the wind in the reeds than anything human. "We have been allies in the past —"

"We have had common interests, against others," said the boy.

"And now?"

There was no need to explain that all sorcerers, ageless, pursue one another through the centuries, seeking to devour one another; for whosoever kills a sorcerer *becomes* that sorcerer, and contains within himself the soul and mind of his victim, and all the others that one has likewise slain, so that each sorcerer is a composite being, with many souls and voices, whatever his exterior visage; and each sorcerer aspires to be the *last*, incorporating all the others, the sole survivor at the end of time, who will confront the gods.

This much was written in books. Both of them had read such texts, or composed them.

They circled.

"I name you," the boy said. "I call you He Who Swims Among the Dead. Thus I gain power over you."

"I name you Sekenre, son of Vashtem."

That made him miss a step. Even now, as they tested one another, feinting, it almost caught him off guard. He steeled himself. The other knew his real name, which his mother had given him more than three hundred years ago. But at least he didn't seem to know his *secret* name, which arises from sorcery; knowledge of which in the hands of an enemy would have been more serious.

"Sekenre, don't you remember? We were friends once, long in the past, when you really were a child —"

Sekenre searched his many minds for any memory of this person and found nothing. He did not ask who he was or had been or what he had become. If ever the two were united in death, one or the other would know.

"I have what you require," said the other.

"What price?"

"A token. For old times' sake."

"I don't believe that."

"Small matter. I have what you want. One day, you will have what I want. Here is the thing. Take it."

The other tossed something into the air. Sekenre caught it with his free hand. The other put his mask back on and sank back into the dark water. Sekenre stood alone, a necklace of crocodile teeth dangling from his left hand.

II

AND HE KNEW, of course, that he held in his hand exactly what he *did* need, a very great treasure indeed, for these were no ordinary crocodile teeth, but the very teeth of the Surat-Kemad himself, the Eater of Days.

How, or through what terrible crime the other had obtained this thing, he did not care to ask. If they two ever met again, and fought, and one slew the other, the victor would know everything. It could wait.

But here was Time itself Reclaimed, in his hand.

Were it possible for a sorcerer to pray, he might have breathed a brief thanksgiving. Were it possible for him to believe in such things, or disbelieve in them, he might have thanked or disbelieved his luck.

But for a sorcerer, such things merely *are*. They fit into some greater pattern, like a handful of tiles from a larger mosaic he can but dimly make out.

He knew exactly what do to. He walked into the darkness, on the water, among the reeds, through the mist, into the Deadlands. The *evatim* parted before him, the black water rippling silently, for they knew that the power of their own master was about him.

He came to a place, a little rising of land, dry and flat behind the barrier of reeds at the water's edge, which has perhaps been somehow prepared. There he crouched down and drew in the dirt with his finger. He broke off one of the teeth from the necklace. He unintentionally cut his finger in the act of doing so, shook his finger, sucked on it, then patted the front of his tunic several times to make the bleeding stop.

But that was a small thing. More carefully, he broke the tooth again, and buried one of the pieces in the dirt. The other he put in his mouth, holding it under his tongue.

He spoke certain words and breathed cold fire upon the earth; and then all around him, as if shadows had somehow gathered and become solid, a house of reeds and wood shaped itself, like a blossom rapidly opening.

He tried to get up, but hit his head on the underside of the porch. He crawled on hands and knees to get clear, then stood and gaped, open-mouthed with wonder, feeling emotions he had not experienced in a very long time.

This place had been home, on Earth, in real time, long ago. Of course he knew it had ceased to exist in real time, but here, by the magic of Surat-Kemad's tooth, it was reclaimed.

He bounded up onto the porch, running his hand along the very solid-feeling railing. He opened a shutter and leaned in, then didn't even bother finding the door and clambered in.

Then he wept, for memory and joy (though it is written that sorcerers cannot weep, any more than they can pray or believe in luck). He found himself in a room he knew so very well. He had lived here, in this house, not in his childhood, but in what might have counted as his adulthood by ordinary standards, when he was twenty, thirty, fifty, seventy. All his familiar things were about him. A wooden, articulated serpent hung from the ceiling, a *hevat* such as his mother once made, a thing which could seemingly come alive when filled with wind.

For old times' sake, for memory, he had managed to preserve one. He had not seen it in a very long time. Here it was.

He found his old books on the shelves. His old blanket draped over a chair, the shoes he never wore in a box under the bed.

On the nightstand was a carven heron, a toy, something he had saved from his actual childhood.

But those were small things. In this place he had dwelt once, in some semblance of happiness which is seldom afforded to sorcerers, with *her*, with Kanratica, his beloved.

Now all he had to do was wait. He lay down on the bed. He thought ruefully that she might scold him for getting his muddy feet on the covers.

He waited, knowing if that he could reclaim one thing from out of the crocodile's mouth, he could reclaim another, as long as he didn't run out of teeth. He put the necklace on, over his head, and ran his hand over the teeth, reassured by the great number of them.

He knew that he had, literally, all the time he needed.

Therefore he lay back, in that simulacrum of a house on an island in the Land of the Dead, and dreamed a mighty dream, and in it someone walked on the porch of the house, and that someone stood over him where he lay. For an instant he thought it was some other, but he willed it to be his beloved, and in his dream it was she. In his dream, too, he awoke seven times, had his meals, studied from his books and sat at his familiar desk, writing into the one book he always carried with him in his leather bag.

Each night, in his dream, she drew nearer. By some dream-given sight he saw her moving through the darkness like the light of a distant ship, drifting slowly nearer.

He dreamed that he heard her voice, that, as he lay dreaming, she sat down beside the bed and combed his hair with a silver comb, pulling at the tangles, complaining humorously that even after so many centuries, he had never learned to keep himself neat.

He dreamed that she sat beside him in the shadows and sang a most ancient and mysterious song predating all human languages, a song which can call back the setting sun and bid it rise again; and he dreamed that the sun rose in the west, out of the blackness of *Tashé*, illuminating also *Leshé*, and then he truly *awoke*, in that room, in broad daylight, the blue sky of Earth itself visible through the window.

And the silver comb was on the nightstand beside the toy heron.

And *she* was with him in the room.

He got up. She stood before him, as a young girl, his own apparent age or perhaps a little older, framed in soft sunlight streaming through the window, clad in the crown and almost diaphanous robes of a princess of the Delta, a daughter of the Great King, though she was not the daughter of a king.

Her feet were bare and the edges of her gown were damp. She had walked a long way upon the River, and up out of its depths.

He drew her in his arms, yet her eyes were still closed. She stood like one in a trance, or walking in sleep. He kissed her very gently on the cheek and whispered, "Kanratica, open your eyes."

She opened them.

He smiled and said, "It's me."

"Sekenre?"

"It's been a long time," he said.

"For me the days are as a single twilight, and I do not count them."

"For me they are as a single morning, filled with expectancy . . ."

He lost the train of thought. Perhaps they were both quoting some ancient poet. Now he felt very relieved and very tired. His days and nights *had* been as one, filled with the pain, fear, strugglings, and conjurations which allow the sorcerer no rest.

Yet now, with her, he could rest. He held onto her hands, and she became more substantial to his touch. He led her out of the room, onto the porch, where they overlooked the sunlit Great River.

"Tica," he said, "I have called you back out of love, because I want us to be as we were before, forever."

"We lived one lifetime already," she said. "Is that not enough?"

"You know it is not."

She made to say something more, perhaps, but he hushed her with a finger — leaving a drop of blood on her lip — and then with a kiss, again, gently, warmly. For a time they sat on the porch dangling their feet over the edge into the water, and they both spoke and remembered the time when he had been truly young, before sorcery swept him away like a leaf in a torrent.

For an instant, then, it seemed that he had truly reclaimed Time from out of the Crocodile's mouth, and all the things that had happened these past three hundred years and more were as naught.

But even as they sat there the sun faded, and the sky grew dark. When stars appeared, they were not those which shine upon Riverland, but the stars of the Death Country.

Something else was on the porch with them in the darkness. It moved heavily, like a sack being dragged.

Tica turned to him in alarm.

"It's all right," he said, and again he broke one of the teeth off the necklace. Again he cut a finger, accidentally.

The Moon rose. The porch was empty but for the two of them. He clutched the front of his tunic with bleeding fingers.

"It's nothing," he whispered. "I'm fine. Let's just sit here a while."

It was a release, to be here, as if he were letting go of so many burdens, as if he were sliding down a slope into cool, refreshing waters. All those other selves within him, the sorcerers he had variously conquered and murdered over the years, and *their* victims and their victims' victims, all the souls accumulated within his crowded, shadowed mind, seemed to fade away. Another image came to him: of a serpent shedding its skin over and over, until all that was left was delicate and tiny and made of light.

It was so seductive to go on like that forever.

And it seemed that when he broke yet another of Surat-Kemad's teeth from the necklace, he cut the palm of his hand, but there was no pain; and he arose with Kanratica and they two lived again through a perfect and quite ordinary day from their past life together. Nothing of particular note happened. She sang in the morning. She washed the sheets from the bed, chiding him for getting his muddy feet on them. He sat and wrote in his book, arranging his memories as a hoarder stacks coins, because they please him *just so*.

The miracle was simply that they had this day, that at the end of it they lay down together as lovers, that they did in fact love one another with timeless ardor; that in the end, when they drifted off to sleep after lingering, pleasant reminiscences, he again dreamed.

But there the miracle stopped. He dreamed that he was being devoured by crocodiles, right here in the bedroom, while she stood beside him, screamed, and could do nothing.

There was someone else in the room, a huge and heavy figure with a long, inhuman face.

III

WHEN HE awoke, it was to the twilight and grey stars of the Deadlands. There was no roof overhead. The house was a ruin, much of its walls gone. The bed was damp and soggy and had collapsed in on itself.

Kanratica helped him to his feet. He felt light-headed, a little weak, dizzy. But her grip was strong, steadying. He looked up into her face and saw that she was not a young girl anymore, but a woman, perhaps forty. A stranger might have taken her for his mother.

But he had known her at forty too, and loved her then; for though sorcery preserved his body from age, he had passed through those years with her.

Her expression was grave.

"Sekenre. Don't do this."

He broke free and stood, for a moment unsteadily. He waved her away.

"No, no, I know — all will be well in the end."

"Will it?" She gazed at him.

He looked where she looked and saw that his clothing was torn and sticky with blood in places.

"I'll — we'll —" He looked at the ruined house and said, "but we will have to go someplace else."

He would take no argument from her. He, because he loved her, could not be angry. She, because she loved him, would not leave his side. Together they dismantled part of the house and built a reed boat. Then he took what little he could carry, his leather bag with the book he had been writing in, and the toy heron, and some stores and an extra blanket; and they two set out in the boat upon the River as the current carried them.

But this was the Black River, which flows into the mouth of Surat-Kemad, on which the funeral boats of the dead are placed.

Therefore Sekenre stood up in the bow of their reed boat while Tica held steady at the tiller; and he broke two more of the teeth of Surat-

Kemad from the necklace and cast them into the air, commanding, first, the Moon of Earth to rise above the river and the marshlands — and it rose; and night-birds whirled overheard, shrieking — and then the Sun; and they drifted downstream in the full light of day, on the *Great River*, which flows through the waking world, and reaches the Delta and the City of the Delta and the Crescent Sea beyond.

More than once, they passed ships on the water, even a war vessel of the Great King, sent upriver to enforce his will upon the Satraps.

Throughout the long, hot, lazy day they drifted.

"We'll just go on forever like this," he said.

She shook her head sadly. There was wisdom in her eyes. She bandaged the cuts on his hands.

"It's all right," he said. "I'm a mighty sorcerer, remember?"

"I thought," she said slowly, "that was exactly what we were trying not to remember."

"Well, I —"

And he broke another of Surat-Kemad's teeth, and another, and another; and he commanded the sun and moon to flit about the sky like birds; and he called up all the days he and Kanratica had shared together, examining each as a hoarder lovingly examines each golden coin in his hoard. He wrote the stories of those days into his book, and the script, it seemed, curved forever in on itself like an infinite maze, and the pages, too, were infinite, so that he could turn them and turn back, and never find the same one twice. He lived all those days again, with her, suspended in time on the River, sometimes beneath the skies of Earth, sometimes in Dream, drifting again, backwards on the Black River, into Death.

And he was drenched with blood. And he hurt. And he was very tired.

And someone, huge and hunched with a long face walked on the water beside the boat, whispering in a voice that was scarcely a voice, "That's right, Sekenre. Remember. Love. Remember. Enjoy every last minute of it. Let go of all else. Soon you shall be with her forever. Think of that and nothing more."

He awoke once and looked up through fevered eyes, too weak to rise, and he beheld Kanratica as an old woman, almost seventy; but he had known her during those years and loved her then, though to strangers he claimed to be her grandson, and their love was, indeed, very strange by then.

"I know what I'm doing," he said. "We'll be fine. I know what we have to do."

"I know what we have to do," she said.

IV

IN THE DARKNESS, beneath the stars of Dream, the reed boat bumped against a wharf in the City of the Delta. The old woman didn't bother to tie it up. She merely lifted her burden in her arms and climbed into the streets, straining at the effort.

But she climbed. She walked. Sekenre, in her arms, lay dreaming.

In the darkness, ghosts gathered around them like mist. Once they encountered an actual dreamer, a woman's soul abroad from her body on some quest in a dream, and she alone seemed solid to them. Kanratica and this other conversed in the secret language of dreams, and Kanratica whispered of the wishes of the dead, and the other spoke of one who was neither quite dead nor alive, who swam among the *evatim* disguised as one of them, though he wore but a mask.

This one, said the dreamer, was close at hand, and close to the completion of some project long labored upon.

Kanratica thanked the dreamer and moved on.

The *evatim* followed them through the streets, at a distance, but closer than before, as if they sensed that the power and protection of their master about these two was still present, but had diminished.

Soon, perhaps, there would be feasting.

Sekenre was awake now, in Kanratica's arms. He reached up to the necklace he still wore, and broke a crocodile tooth, one, then another.

They entered into the vast palace of black stone, where dwelt and dreamt the Great King of the Delta with all his court, and, moving among the dreams of the King and the courtesans and soldiers, drifting between squat pillars like shadows cast by flickering lanterns, they came to the throne room itself in the Hall of Audience.

Clad now in dreams, halfway between waking and death, Sekenre and Kanratica wore the ornate garments and beehive-shaped crowns of a king and queen of the Delta.

He wrote the history of their long, joint reign into his book.

But he was bleeding so much. Blood poured down his legs, over his feet.

He understood, dimly, that all the old wounds of his sorceries, which had been healed by sorcery, had opened up, as if someone had discovered the secret keys to each of them and unlocked the elements of his mortality, one by one.

Kanratica, now very old, said to him, "Sekenre, you've had enough."

"No," he said. "We'll be fine. I love you —"

"But no sorcerer," she said, sorrowing, "may ever love. He dare not. It is too dangerous. He needs his strength to go on, so he might be the last and face down the gods at the end of time."

"With you beside me," he said, "sure, I could do that."

"Sekenre, enough," she said. And she said another word, "Kazat."

He was unable to stop her as she snatched the necklace from him, breaking the string. Crocodile teeth scattered down the marble steps before their thrones.

Sekenre screamed. For an instant he saw Kanratica standing before him, wrapped as a mummy, her hands crossed upon her breast. Her eyes were open. She spoke inside his mind.

"Kazat," she said. "You have fallen victim to a kazat."

"What?"

"You know perfectly well what. You lived in Reedland far longer than I."

He did know that there was a species of water-lizard called a kazat, which had the unique property of breathing dreams into the water to daze its prey, so that a small fish would just drift, dreaming ecstatic fishy dreams and feeling no fear, even as the kazat devoured it. The blood of the kazat was used in medicine, to take away pain.

It was some struggle to focus his mind, to figure out what this odd lecture in natural history meant, why it was relevant now.

He heard the teeth of Surat-Kemad trickling down the marble steps like pebbles.

And the thought did come to him: *What if in the midst of the dream, the dreamer awoke?*

And he thought he heard Tica's reply, "Then he would lose the dream, but lose it he must. Therefore, awake!"

"Won't the kazat be surprised?"

"Yes, he will."

V

TICA WAS GONE. The palace was gone. Sekenre, returning to himself, lay among reeds, beneath a black sky filled with the grey stars of *Leshé*, the country of dreams, which faded into the fainter and stranger constellations of *Tashé*, Death.

Someone great and heavy leaned over him. This other stank of mud and of the river. He leaned down and touched Sekenre with his great claws, tearing away the front of his tunic, tracing the ancient wounds which had now begun to bleed again.

He took off his crocodile mask and leaned close to whisper, "Sekenre, son of Vashtem, now is the day when you offer what I want, which is your soul, and the souls of all those captive within you."

Sekenre, like one in a fever, but who has just come out of a delirium, lay still and began to recite in a faint voice.

"The sorcerer cannot pray, nor can he weep, nor has he any friends, nor knows he joy, nor can he love —"

The other leaned lower to hear, then whispered, laughing softly, "Well, you and I have had some experience, and we know that it's a little more complicated than that."

"*Kazat,*" said Sekenre.

The other ignored him and went on. "How lucky we've been able to have this little chat —"

"*Kazat. The sorcerer cannot afford to believe in luck,*" said Sekenre as, with the last of his strength, he drove the long, thin knife he always carried upward into his enemy's heart.

For that instant, Tica was with him, helping him push the knife up, up, up. For ghosts do return, particularly if one breaks and scatters the teeth of Surat-Kemad.

"*Kazat,*" she whispered. "*Awaken! The sorcerer cannot afford to dream. Kazat!*"

Together, they found the enemy's life, and took it.

And then there was no need or possibility of explaining anything, as the heavy body fell upon Sekenre, and blood poured over him; and the soul of the slain sorcerer poured into him; and among the multitudes imprisoned within the enemy and now transferred into Sekenre's mind was a certain *Regash* from the land of Thain, which lies beyond the Crescent Sea; and this *Regash*, whose secret name was *Avedamas*, which means

"The Serpent Who Drinks" contained within him the minds and souls of a thousand other sorcerers, and the echoes of all the sorcerers *those* had ever murdered, echoing unto nightmare infinity.

Somewhere from those depths had come the suggestion that this Sekenre, who had retained far more humanity than was common for sorcerers, could be despoiled by the illusion or memories of love — even as the *kazat* lulls its victims with beautiful dreams — and therefore this *Regash* had labored for many years to gain the teeth of Surat-Kemad, casting down thrones and kingdoms, massacring countless innocents, paying such great tribute to Death Himself that such a thing became possible.

And now Regash and Sekenre were one, and their crimes were one, and their thousand souls were one; and rage, memory, fear all flowed together, like a swollen torrent, bearing that which was still Sekenre like a fallen leaf, farther and farther away from Kanratica, whom he loved.

He tried to reach to her, to feel the warmth of her touch, but he felt only the cold mud and the weight of his enemy's corpse upon him.

All he could do was crawl out from under that corpse, which he saw now was barely half-human and did indeed have a crocodile's tail. He lay down in the mud beside it for a day and a night, healing himself once more with sorcery, making himself that much more dependent on sorcery, that much less mortal and human, less able to turn aside from the path which must lead him to the end of time and a confrontation with the gods.

IN THE NIGHT, beneath the stars of Death, then of Dream, then merely of Earth, his wounds glowed like pale fire. While he lay there, he searched deep within himself for the enemy's identity, that one who had claimed to have been a friend from the old days, from Sekenre's own childhood . . . but that person was like a name in a palimpsest, erased and written over so many times that the original was completely lost.

Therefore he thought about Tica, and could bring her name and her face and her voice into memory, but only as a memory.

A vision came to him, not a mere dream now, such as any boy might have who is lonely and longs to be somewhere else, but something more, as if a shiny tile had fallen out of some vast mosaic he could not see; and here it was, a part of the larger whole, gleaming before him.

He seemed to be running in the darkness. He was naked, but his flesh was hard as metal. There was no warmth to him, no softness. His hands were stiff, entirely covered with scars. He was terribly hungry, though he had devoured all others of his kind and his belly was filled with blood, and the souls of every sorcerer who ever lived were contained within him. Yet he could not be satisfied.

He ran toward a rising sun that gave no warmth, across black, gleaming, featureless water.

And as the sun rose, he saw something else in the sky, shapes like clouds, but not clouds at all: faces human or nearly so, or else the faces of animals; here the heron, there the crocodile, again, the jackal.

The very gods. He ran to confront the very gods, with hunger and anger and sorrow in his heart.

Many voices spoke within him. As the vision faded, he was still trying to sort them out.

At the very end, he thought that Tica would know what to do. He turned to ask her, but she was not there.

WHEN HE HAD the strength, he got up and found his satchel with his book in it by the water's edge. As the sun rose, he sat on a grassy islet, turning the pages, drying them out, searching in vain for the pages in which he had written in such detail of his stolen days together with Tica.

These, he could not find.

But he did find, marked with the broken string which had been the necklace, where she had written an account of all that had happened between them, and concluded:

The sorcerer cannot afford to love. But he can be loved. Farewell.

DREAMS OF THE STONE KING'S DAUGHTER

ON WHAT should have been the last night of his life, the Exile sought out the Stone People. It was a crazy thing to do, as dangerous as death itself. He didn't care. Perhaps that was why he did it.

He was a tall, dignified man of middle years, with a neatly-groomed beard going to grey, an incongruous figure to be climbing a mountain slope in the brilliant moonlight, while the frigid wind whipped his cloak around him like a flag and numbed his ears. He belonged in a more sedate setting, among gentlefolk (not the half-barbarians in the town below).

But here he was. He climbed. Pebbles rattled from where his numb fingers caught hold, slipped.

Above him, unreachable, loomed five columns of black, glass-like stone, sculpted by the wind, called (variously) the Towers, the Five Peaks, or the Upturned Hand, where (so the townspeople had told him) Death roosted; not Surat-Hemad of the Lowlands, the Crocodile Who Walks Like a Man, whose mouth is the night sky, whose teeth are the number-less stars; but some other: black-skinned like that stone, eagle-headed and eagle-winged, with stone-strong arms.

He could almost believe it. But death waited for him in the town too, though it be the most remote (from the perspective of the royal court at the Delta, at least) in all the world. Even now a messenger from the Great King slept in a gaudy pavilion erected in the courtyard of the tavern (for it was beneath the dignity even of the King's messenger to set foot in so mean an establishment).

On the morrow the messenger's servant would knock on the tavern door and deliver the message. The Exile would not have to read it know that the game was now up, that the months of writing exquisite, over-long, and slightly self-pitying poems repenting his Error (which could never be named, as a condition of his banishment) and begging to be readmitted into the Eternal Light of the King of Splendor who is brother to the Sun and beloved of the Nine Righteous Gods (et cetera, et cetera) had ceased to amuse and now he was ordered to die. Opening veins would suffice. Something more imaginative, up to and including hurling himself into one of those mist-filled gorges where the Great River vom-ited forth from the Mouth of the World (or was it the Mouth of Surat-Hemad?) would be looked on with favor. The messenger's job, dignity be damned, was to make sure the order was carried out.

Yet the Exile was the most distinguished person the people of remote Kadisphon would *ever* see. He would become legend. They would tell their grandchildren about him. So they warned him. They showed him another way out of town.

And the Exile took it, not because he was afraid to die. Often, during the exquisite boredom of his sojourn here, he would have welcomed death. (He'd put that into the poems.) No, it was because, having dwelt among these people for so long, having listened to their myths, their stories, he had come to believe that here, at the edge of the world, the miraculous might yet linger. Surely he, after all his suffering, deserved, on the last night of his life, some epiphany —

He climbed. The wind blew. The Moon was dazzling, almost as bright as the Sun.

It was one more of the stories people told in the town, how, on such nights as this (while decent folk huddled behind shutters) the Stone People are manifested. In a another time, he might use such material in a better poem than the ones he had been writing lately.

Older even than the gods, the Stone People were dreams of the Earth-Mind; they were of the Earth which is (paradoxically) mindless, yet dreams, like a wind of stone or waves of stone cast up by that wind (a better image). They were prefigurements of living things, shapes moving on such a vast time-scale that only visionaries could see them, so the story went, only prophets, poets, and the mad (or perhaps the dead). Only the utterly silent could hear their voices (or music), those who had achieved perfect silence within themselves (as might prophets, poets, the mad, the dead), for the sighing of the Stone People was the slow grinding of mountains as they rose and fell. The voice of the Stone People was indescribable. Perhaps, in all the time Mankind had so far existed, no word in the Stone Speech had yet been uttered. There had only been an intake of breath among these tricksters, who danced on mountaintops on moonlit nights and delighted luring mortals into their own world and time, where it might take ten thousand years of wind and erosion for one of them to lower a hand or blink an eye.

All very pretty. The Exile cast his own long, fluttering shadow before him and climbed, straining, the cold stabbing his lungs, his breath coming in gasping puffs.

HE HAD been still capable of innocence when he first came to the capital, decades before. Old Wenamon was king. Into his court the future Exile was admitted, and there he prospered in a modest way, and if the old man sometimes nodded off at recitals, his beehive-shaped crown of the Delta and the River sometimes leaning precariously forward as he did so, that hardly mattered. The glittering nobles and, more importantly, the Princes in their peacock-plumed helmets could be had as patrons. Gold flowed one way, flattery the other, a steady commerce. Sometimes he still aspired, as a poet might, to beauty. Sometimes he even achieved it. More gold flowed. The king nodded off, ailing. If the old man's heart was ripped out one night in an explosion of blood — the circumstances were obscure, albeit dramatic — that hardly mattered either.

Nor did it matter that there had been a sorcerer at court for a time, a grotesquely malformed fellow named Moon whose forehead and chin did indeed extend like the points of a crescent moon, whose face truly did give off light, in certain darkened rooms at least, by which glow some of the nobles and even Princes died.

If war came and went like a tide, and if something even odder happened to the sorcerer than had even befallen the king, the poet tried to tell himself that while this might inform the sensibility of his work, otherwise he was apart from it. He thought of himself as a man walking late at night by the shore of the Crescent Sea. He can feel the spray in the darkness, but if he knows his way and is careful, his robe does not get wet.

When a prince called Vahranes, more vigorous than the rest, managed to kill off his rivals and seize the beehive-crown, that could only be a good thing. The slow decline of the realm was reversed. The satraps bent their knees to the Delta once more, and the Great King's hand reached all the way to the mountain towns. If a dark, corrupt heart beat beneath the gleaming breastplate of power, it was easy to be dazzled by the gleam. Under such circumstances a poet might do serious work.

No, he had not truly lost his innocence until that night when the eunuchs fetched him from his chamber in his nightgown.

"I have to dress," he said.

"You don't need to wear anything," they said.

With some trepidation he let them lead him along, until soldiers swung wide bronze doors and he found himself in the lamplit suite of the King himself. The place was strewn with golden pillows and hung with golden cloth. Amid half-clad courtiers, who seemed to writhe over one another in the shadows like worms, King Vahranes sat, wholly naked but for emblems of his power, a necklace of golden plates across his chest, a band on his arm. He was unashamed, for what can a king be ashamed of before common men? He picked up a limp, pale girl (the bruises on her neck were evident even in this light) and flung her into the poet's arms.

She felt cold, heavy.

"But, Sublime Majesty, she is dead."

"Not entirely," said the King, laughing. He opened a little jeweled box, within which a flame flickered in the shape of this girl, like a tiny, animate, luminous sculpture of indescribable delicacy.

He blew the flame out.

"Now make love to her and write about it."

The thing in his arms moaned.

That had not been his offense. The King had been pleased with the results of *that*.

NOW THE Exile saw something completely incongruous.

He had come to a broad plateau beneath the unscalable Five Peaks. Clouds scudded below him, out over the world, hiding, then revealing, then concealing again the darkened plains of the Lowlands, where the Great River wound like a vast, gleaming serpent in the moonlight to seek the distant City of the Delta and the court, now as inaccessible to him as those Five Peaks or the abode of the gods.

His own shadow danced across bare stone in the brilliant light, yet someone else was waiting for him, who didn't belong in the Exile's visionary experience at all, like a dirty thumbprint in the middle of an exquisite painting: a scruffy-looking boy who could have been a beggar on the streets of the (remote, and steaming) capital, maybe an undersized fifteen, with an unkempt mop of dark hair; pale, soft face, and owlish eyes; barefoot (quite impossible for climbing), and clad only in flimsy trousers torn off at the knees and a sleeveless tunic of the same gauzy material, which the wind had already shredded, leaving him nearly naked (he should have been freezing; he should have been dead).

The Exile stood there, his own cloak flapping, snapping, loud.

"Are you?" he shouted. "One of —?"

But the boy only held up a finger to his lips for silence, then cupped his hands together, and opened them, revealing a flame burning there, steadily, without flickering at all despite the fierce wind, and the flame took the form of an exquisite maiden, dancing.

ONCE THE Great King Vahranes conducted the soon-to-be Exile *alone* down a secret stair, into a vast vault beneath the City of the Delta, a place which stank of mud and corruption, where the whole world seemed to be held up by squat, black pillars as wide as mountains.

"Come. I want you to see this," said the King, walking, his boots making sucking sounds in the mud.

The poet followed, draping his robe over his arm to keep the hem clean.

They walked for what may have been hours, or forever, in a dream, a nightmare; for surely kings did not go off with anyone *alone*, except perhaps to kill them, for secret pleasure or to fulfill some obscure vow.

Therefore the poet was very much afraid, but still he followed, for he had been commanded; and they walked, with no sense of time or distance. The only light was from the King's hand. Perhaps he held a taper. Perhaps his flesh was burning. It was hard to tell. The dream that was not a dream brought them to a vast chamber where stone mummy cases stood in long rows. Their original carven faces had been chipped away and refashioned recently. The cut stone gleamed, brighter-colored than the old. Now the face of each dead man was made ridiculous with clownish noses, drooping eyes, or, even once, an elephant's trunk; and each dead man cried out (silently) in the utmost outrage and despair.

The Great King explained how the very wicked or the very powerful were sometimes not sent into Death's Country on funeral boats, as was immemorial custom. They did not ride the black current into the belly of Surat-Hemad, the great crocodile, whose mouth is the vaunted night; but instead resided here, for all eternity.

"But why?" the poet dared to ask.

"So I can torment them," said the King.

And the King led him farther, past innumerable such mummy cases, vast shadows flickering by the light of the King's hand, until they came to one case which was open and empty, its lid swung wide. The face of this one too had been recently altered, but in a far less crude fashion, to suggest the features of the King as he was now, in life at the height of his power.

The King stepped inside, crossed his arms in the position of a dead man and said, "Well, what do you think?"

"I don't understand, Lord of Eternal Glory."

"It's for *me*. I can come here any time I want. For am I not lord of both the living and the dead?"

The poet couldn't think of what to say. He feared that the King was mad, on top of all else.

Vahranes only explained, in a very odd tone of voice, a mixture of sarcasm and perhaps a trace of sorrow, that he'd brought him here just to inform his sensibilities. "I want you to know. Let it inspire you. Plumb the mysteries for me."

Then he closed his hands together and the fire went out, and the two of them were back in the royal chambers as if they had never left.

Only the soon-to-be-exiled poet's robe was filthy, for in his distraction he had let it fall from his hands and drag in the mud.

NOW, ON THE PLATEAU, in the moonlight, the boy leaned down and placed the flame-girl on the ground. The fire went out, but her shadow was there with nothing to cast it, dancing, flickering, whirling across lichen-encrusted stone.

The boy pointed that the Exile should follow her with his gaze. This was unnecessary. How could he do otherwise?

The Exile watched and saw that there were eagles in the sky now, as if the Upturned Hand had released them, their silhouettes passing across the Moon, their shadows huge, joining in the dance. He saw that over the aeons the wind had wrought strange carvings on nearby stones. Where the ground folded slightly, and rose around a massive boulder, there seemed to be an old woman huddled, sleeping. But as he watched, as the shadow-girl caressed her, the old woman awoke and sat up, her hair streaming in the wind. (Yet she was still made of stone.)

The old woman seemed very knowing, very wise. She turned to the Exile and to the boy and laughed.

Now, there, *there*, the girl-shadow grew very large, by some trick of light and cloud (and swirling eagles); and a great, broad-shouldered warrior stood near her, embedded in a cliff face (but it was more as if he stood, alert, spear in hand, behind a gauzy curtain). His beard was the heaped talus below a ledge. He seemed to open his eyes (or did the wind merely polish stone with impossible swiftness?) and step forward. A sharp, broken bit of ledge nearby was the tip of his spear.

And, at last, *there*, for an instant the whole sky flickered — dark, light, dark, light — as if individual nights and days went by in fractions of seconds; then there was only steady moonlight again (for the Stone People are only visible for the duration of moonlit nights over countless centuries, which are to them one continuous night) and all the mountaintops around him had acquired faces, male and female, old and young; and the Peaks were as the spikes of crowns. At last the Exile beheld what he took to be the King and Queen of the Stone People, seated on thrones above the great mass of their courtiers and servants. Some of these spread their wings, like eagles. Some crouched, half-formed between men and beasts. And he saw that the dancing shadow was cast by the Stone King's Daughter, of whom travelers spoke cautionary tales, she who dreamed the dreams of all the Stone People, who gazed (mystically, paradoxically) into Time in both directions at once and saw the beginnings and endings of all things. She was the greatest trickster of them all.

Now she had ceased dancing, and sat by her father's knee.

Cold wind and swirling dust blew across the stone faces.

They opened their eyes. They stirred and raised (or lowered) their hands; and the Exile knew that he, at last, beheld the Stone People.

And the Stone People gazed down on him — and on that incongruous, scruffy boy who sat on a rock now, shivering and clasping his knees.

Not knowing what else to do, perhaps (or out of vanity?), the Exile spread his arms wide, as he might before the Great King and the court, and began to declaim.

Instantly there was darkness, as if he'd been hit over the head with a club.

HE OPENED his eyes in darkness, and his vision adjusted, and he saw the inside of a familiar, shuttered room with rough stone walls, in the upper storey of a tavern in the town.

A faint light, a gleaming pinprick, resolved into a candle.

He had been seated at a rude table, writing by candlelight, as he often did.

Some kind of hallucination? A dream? *No!* He trembled in his rage. *No!*

A vision at the very least, some kind of prophecy or visitation, fraught with meaning —

The tavern keeper came in, gathering wooden cups onto a tray. "We're closing, sir."

"I need a little more time."

The tavern keeper shrugged and spoke as he never really would have been so bold to. "I don't think you have any more time, sir."

Therefore the Exile took heart, knowing by this one incongruity that his vision continued.

The tavern keeper left and there was something else: a shadow, flickering over walls and ceiling, cast by nothing, furious like a huge, fluttering moth. It had been there for seven nights now. No one else could see it. Now he saw that it was a girl's shadow, dancing.

Was it laughing at him?

The door opened. Ordinarily that door led to a landing, then a rickety flight of stairs down into the dark belly of the tavern's common room; but now moonlight streamed in, dazzling him.

The ragged boy entered, holding a flame in his hand. The air was cold. He could see the boy's breath, and goosebumps on his bare, bony chest.

With some awe, certainly with expectation (bordering on demand) the Exile asked, "Are you one of them? Are you one of the Stone People?"

"No, but she —" The boy held out his hand, whereon danced the tiny, exquisite flame-figure (was that fire, or was it moonlight?) of the Stone King's Daughter. "She fell in love with me as she beheld me struggling through Time, and I, foolish as you, was beguiled and came to rest in her arms, and so fell among the Stone People, as you have."

The boy sat down on the bench beside the Exile, and the shadow of the Stone King's Daughter danced upon the walls and ceiling.

The Exile caught hold of the boy's shoulder.

"You are not made of stone, certainly, but you're cold —"

"I was near the Delta when she came to me, in the desert, amid some old, dry tombs, looking up at the Moon when I heard her voice in the perfect silence — I didn't have a chance to prepare for my journey. The departure was very sudden —"

This close, the boy smelled of sweat, as one might from shivering too much.

"Who are you?"

"A sorcerer, called Sekenre."

"I knew a sorcerer once," said the Exile, describing Moon and, such as he understood, what happened to him.

"I met him one time only," said Sekenre, "and I slew him, and his soul has dwelt within my own this past hundred and more years."

"No, that was only twenty years ago, but too far back for you to have been there." For an instant the Exile wondered if the boy too, like the King, might be mad. There were a lot of crazy people running around loose these days, not all of them visionaries.

The boy closed his hands together, extinguishing the flame he held. He placed his hands palm-down on the tabletop. Now the only light was from the candle, which burned steadily, while the Stone King's Daughter's shadow flickered wildly on the walls. Those pale hands gleamed in the candlelight, as did sweat-slicked forearms. The boy's narrow body, in shadow, revealed itself criss-crossed with jagged, glowing scars which bespoke wounds that should have killed him several times over had he been an ordinary child; but the Exile accepted, now, that this boy was not.

"Know you not that a sorcerer moves through time quite differently than do other folk? For the sorcerer, years, even centuries, are as a series of dreams, not necessarily in the same order that you perceive them. His way is hard. It is filled with pain. But it is very difficult to end it. When he is hurt, he heals himself with magic, until his body is like an old garment so often repaired that it is more patches than original cloth. Even when he dies, he goes on, as my father, who was very ancient, goes on in me. I slew this one you call Moon a hundred years ago. He is in my soul, a small part of the composite which is Sekenre, for I am Many, Devourer of Many, in a small way like unto Death, which devours all; and a sorcerer does not age, not in the body. He ages by taking more and more of his kind inside himself, until his original identity is diluted and perhaps gone; but someone, *something* remaining of him, the last sorcerer in the world, will exist until the end of Time, when he must confront the gods and demand redress for their cruelties and for the very act of creation itself — and that, my friend, is a sufficient span for even the Stone People to notice. Therefore the Stone King's Daughter fell in love with me and beguiled me."

"Can a sorcerer love?"

"They say no sorcerer can ever weep."

"Can one love?"

"The boy Sekenre, who is the mask concealing the sorcerer, can indeed love, at least when he stops and thinks back and remembers a boy named Sekenre who became a sorcerer once — rather against his will, but that is another story — and I think he can weep. But never mind that. What you have to do is make the Stone People weep."

"Make them? Why?"

"Otherwise they will never release either of us. They'll keep us for all eternity, which for them is about as much time as it takes to speak a single word."

Sekenre got up. He handed the Exile something, then was gone out the door. Moonlight dazzled for an instant. The door closed.

When the Exile's eyes had adjusted in the darkness once more, he saw by candlelight that Sekenre had given him a folded parchment, sealed with the royal seal of King Vahranes of the Delta and the River.

He tapped the message on the edge of the table nervously, but did not open it. Instead he gathered pen, stoppered ink-bottle, and the manuscript of his latest pleading effusion into his case, but left the case and the unopened message on the tabletop and went to the door.

No flickering shadow danced in the room now. He was alone.

He hesitated, his eyes closed, thinking, *No, not a dream. More. I deserve as much.* He tried to think of what might make the Stone People weep, odd as that might seem.

He opened his eyes and the door and saw, for just long enough to blink, the common room of the tavern below. The royal messenger's gaudily-liveried servant looked up at him from the bottom of the stairs, bored, then walked across the crowded common room to order a drink.

Again moonlight dazzled the Exile's eyes, and he was climbing in the cold wind. Sekenre climbed with him, a little above, at least until Sekenre slipped and fell down into the Exile's arms. The older (was he really?) man caught him. The boy (could he still be called a boy?) trembled, frigid to the touch. The Exile wrapped him in his cloak and the two climbed together, until they came before the Stone People once again (who shifted as they watched, in some slow, stately procession the eye could hardly follow).

Black eagles circled overhead, crossing the Moon, casting huge shadows over the land.

Sekenre sat apart from him in the fierce wind and moonlight, huddled with his hands clasped over his knees, his feet dirty and cut from climbing. He looked, the Exile thought, deceptively frail at first, then more like a stick-figure carved of ageless iron, destined to endure for a very long time.

As she danced, Stone King's Daughter reached down and caressed the boy on the cheek. He, astonishingly, wept. She did not.

With great deliberation then, using every rhetorical trick he knew, the Exile spoke (nay, shouted, into the wind, unable to hear himself over the whistling crags and his own wind-beaten clothing) of the Great King's wickedness, his many cruelties, monstrous crimes, blasphemies against the gods, against nature itself and against men; he spoke of the King's glory, which was a terrible thing, which surely threatened gods, nature, and men. He spoke with real passion, with pent-up feeling he had not dared release since he was very young, naive and innocent himself; but he spoke with a certain arrogance, as if to say, *Look, I, who seek beauty and often achieve it despite even this, must put up with such things and know the peril of them. Isn't that enough to make even stone weep? Don't I deserve better?*

Those were not his actual words, but that was what he really said, and even he knew it.

He thought, at the very last, of the old courtier's joke, *Be sincere, whether you mean it or not.*

The darkness was like a club to the head.

IN THE tavern room, the shadow of the Stone King's Daughter fluttered over the walls and ceiling like a dark moth.

The tavernkeeper came in, rattling his tray of cups.

"Sir —?"

"I need a little more time."

"Perhaps you would care to stay all night? On a night such as this, with the bright moon, it might be advisable —"

The Exile tapped the sealed parchment against the table's edge impatiently. The tavernkeeper left.

And Sekenre was there. The Exile hadn't noticed the door opening this time. Instead, the room filled with a cold, damp breeze that stank of mud and corruption.

Sekenre held up fire in his cupped hand.

The Stone King's Daughter's shadow flickered on ahead of them, over squat stone pillars that seemed to hold up the world. Mud and slime dripped out of the darkness above. Somewhere nearby, a river flowed, stinking of death.

The boy took the Exile's hand in his free hand, holding up the flame in the other. His hand felt cold and hard, but not of stone. They walked through endless, dark mud until both of them were splattered with it, often sinking almost to their knees.

They came to a great, dank hall filled with grotesquely defaced mummy cases, where powerful men of the past were refashioned into drooling, babbling, screaming idiots and clowns.

They beheld the Great King Vahranes standing with his arms crossed upon his chest, within his own mummy case, a smirk on his face.

"Well, Poet, what do you think?" the King said.

The Exile looked at the King, then at Sekenre. He hesitated, even if he was, nevertheless, beginning to understand.

Therefore it was the boy who strained, one-handed (for he held the fire in the other) to heave the heavy lid of the mummy-case shut.

The Great King screamed, in outrage and despair.

The lid slammed shut with finality, like the Door to Eternity.

AMONG THE moonlit peaks, thunder echoed.

"KINGS ARE as dayflies," Sekenre said. "They won't impress the Stone People."

"Dayflies?"

"Little insects you find in the marshes. They live only one day, which is the entirety of their lives, during which they fly, mate, intrigue, fight for such power and glory as insects fight for, and perhaps, in their own way, seek such beauty as they are able to seek. They sing their histories, hoping to be remembered, and, to themselves, they have lived a long and storied time, but still it's a single day in the spring, and to human beings they're just something that buzzes around your ears."

THE EXILE stood before the Stone People while the King's Daughter danced.

His words came of their own accord. He swelled up, as if to burst, a tide within him, a huge wave of words and memories, legend and glorious song. He tried to relate the entire tragic history of the world, all the calamities of mankind from the beginning of time —

He got about two sentences into it before the darkness hit him over the head, thundering.

★   ★   ★

"WILL YOU be staying, sir? I would recommend it, on a night like tonight." said the tavern keeper. "Perhaps you would care to avail yourself of the bread and cheese in the box under the counter. Help yourself —"

"I will not be staying long —" said the Exile, testily, tapping first his
pen, then the sealed message on the edge of the table.

He went to the door, and in the moonlight, as they climbed, Sekenre
said to him, "Tell them about your Error, your Crime, your Sin, whatever.
You must tell them about that."

"I can't. I gave my word."

"Very good. That's it —"

"I cannot —"

"Precisely."

He stood silent before the Stone People.

The darkness came. In the tavern room, the keeper rattled his tray of
cups. The shadow danced. The keeper said he'd leave the door unlocked
and joked about their being nothing to steal except these worthless cups.
Besides, who would be abroad on a night such as this?

The keeper went out.

Sekenre tapped the sealed parchment on the tabletop, not impatiently, but as if keeping time with something the Exile could not hear.

A shadow flickered.

The Exile wept, saying, "My Error, my Sin, my Crime — and I asked
myself then how one could commit a crime when among such criminals
— but now I ask myself how I could possibly think it mattered, or how
my word of honor to those who had no honor ever mattered — and so my
Error was a kind of pride. The Great King led me aside, among the tombs,
down below the city, where he reigned over the tormented dead, and he
said to me, 'I see in you the possibility of innocence, despite my best
efforts to corrupt you. It burns like a candle-flame, far away in the darkness, but it burns steadily and I cannot extinguish it. Therefore it is an
unforgivable affront. Get out of my sight! I banish you to the ends of the
Earth! Go!' For he believed in his heart of hearts that all men were utterly
corrupt, that evil was the natural darkness, which the light of human
virtue (or innocence, or beauty) could only briefly disperse (casting enormous shadows, which are Death, as the feared Shadow Titans are the cast
shadows and ultimately the deaths of the gods). This was the whole basis
of the King's own magic, his source of strength and tyranny. Seeing light
within the heart of his courtier-poet, he was afraid, and sent him into
exile; and the Exile's true sin was one of prideful lying: the Exile could not
admit, even to himself, that he had lost sight of that light long ago, if,

indeed, he had ever seen it."

"You speak as if of someone else," Sekenre said.

"It is someone else. I am nothing. I have nothing to say which could make the Stone People weep or anybody else give a damn."

"Then you will not be able to escape them."

"I don't even care to escape them. It doesn't matter. I have nothing to say."

"Then stand before them and say nothing."

"I tried that already."

"No," said Sekenre, tapping the parchment a little more slowly now. "That prideful silence spoke volumes. It was anything but empty. Empty, now, stand before the Stone People and be filled with their tears."

"Why?"

"I cannot explain. Does there need to be a reason?"

"No," said the Exile.

They went to the door. Brilliant moonlight flooded the room. Then there was no room, and as they were climbing over the hard stones in the frigid wind, in the moonlight, great black eagles cast long shadows upon them, then swooped down and took them both up in their claws, seizing the Exile by his hair and his cloak and his thick clothing; seizing Sekenre by his shoulders, the claws piercing him until blood streamed down his back and sides. The eagles bore them up to the very tops of the mountains, which were alive as the Stone People danced their stately dance. The eagles let go. The Exile and the sorcerer fell. The Stone King's Daughter reached out and caught them both in her cupped hands, which were filled with moonlight like flames. She whispered to them. She spoke that single, secret word, which for the Stone People takes all of eternity to utter and is the entirety of their speech, which not even the gods have ever heard (but to the Exile, who did not care, it was just a word); and she bore them in her hands, walking upon the clouds or upon the earth or perhaps dancing from mountaintop to mountaintop until she set them down on a kind of shore, where stars sparkled like foam in whispering surf, where untold eons passed in a few instants, and where the mountains of the world rose and fell and lapped at their feet like waves in the ocean.

And there, to some music the Exile and Sekenre but faintly heard, she danced and laughed, up to her tricks.

The wind blew. It was very cold.

There the Exile had visions of the gods themselves, swimming like children among the stone waves, splashing and laughing like children, then emerging, growing somber, taking counsel among themselves as they walked along the shore; and they battled with the Titans, and lusted among themselves, and feasted, and grew old, and died, and were buried in the earth while the Stone People looked on.

The Exile understood that the gods themselves were dayflies, even as men, even as insects.

But he had a further vision: of a pale, moon-gleaming, very familiar, absurdly slender figure, nearly naked, bleeding from grievous wounds, bearing a silver sword way too large for him to wield effectively, running barefoot across a muddy plain into the gaping jaws of Death, which is Surat-Hemad, the crocodile god who is more than a god (who devours the gods), whose mouth is the night sky, whose teeth are the numberless stars; the boy running even as those stars at the end of Time faded into darkness and Death became invisible; a son with his long-dead father's sword upraised, seeking the monster's heart, which beat like a slow, solemn drum.

THEN THE vision ended, and Sekenre groped to touch the Exile. The boy's eyes were dazzled; for was it not rumored or written somewhere (or had Sekenre possibly told him in one of their discourses together) that the sorcerer, being unholy, cannot see the gods even under such circumstances as these?

Very tenderly, then, the Exile wrapped his cloak around Sekenre as he sat trembling on a rock, and held on to him so that he would not fall, and related to him, falteringly, groping about for the words, all that he had seen and learned.

"Through you, I *have* seen them," said Sekenre. "It's the best I shall ever do. It will have to be enough."

Then the Exile wept, and the Stone King's Daughter wept, having heard all of this; her tears filled her cupped hands and burned like fire. Sekenre and the Exile (who had been a poet, whose forgotten name was Vael Nacenas) tumbled into that fire and were consumed by it, knowing as they did a kind of death and rebirth over an infinity of time.

★   ★   ★

THE TAVERN keeper knocked and entered. He gathered wooden cups onto a tray.

"Are you finished your poem now, sir?" he asked.

The Exile put down his pen.

"Yes, quite finished." (He did not add that it would be the last he ever wrote.)

"We're closing, sir —" He started, rattling the cups on his tray (but not dropping any). "Oh, I see you have a . . . guest?" The man hurried out.

The Exile laughed softly. Sekenre admittedly looked more like an apparition (bloody, glowing) than a guest.

He held up his hand to the boy's face.

"Can you see?"

"Only as you do. Five fingers."

WHAT THEN? What then? Sekenre wrote the rest in a book in which he had been writing such things for centuries, in tiny and ornate script sometimes so dense that certain pages looked solid black until one found the key. Other pages were from the future. Sometimes, when he was bold or a little bit mad, or when he was in despair, he would read some of those pages, but even then (perhaps his fingers could not find them, perhaps it was like sifting through sand) he did not turn to the last, where the book ended.

He wrote this much: the Exile picked up the sealed parchment from the King and would have burned it unopened, but instead Sekenre bade him open it and read.

It was an order, not to die, but to return to the Delta.

"I don't know of what use I shall be there," the Exile said.

Sekenre wrote this: that the Exile came down from the upper room with a strange boy wrapped in his cloak. People stared, as they might. He didn't care. The two of them spent a couple of archaic copper coins at the public baths, which in this town consisted of little more than a room with a stone oven, a bucket of water, and a drain in the floor.

They went into the public market and outfitted the boy with such clothing and provisions as he might need for a journey in the mountains (including heavy climbing boots). People talked about that (they told their grandchildren) when they saw the terrible wounds the boy had suf-fered (though he did not seem to be actually injured — and was it true that the marks on him glowed faintly in the dark?).

The two parted with few words, perhaps with some actual regret.

The Exile returned by caravan to the Delta, over the course of several months, where a mystery awaited him and he became, himself, a notable enigma; for his parchment and its seal were unquestionably authentic (there were similar ones in the archives), but more than a hundred years old. Yet, rather than dismiss him as a madman who had perhaps stolen the document from a tomb, the new king, Wenamon XXIV, still young, but already called the Philosopher (he who was also to be named the final glory of the City of the Delta, the Sunset King) was intrigued, and bade his servants treat the Exile kindly.

The King watched him as they both aged, the King standing in the doorway to the Exile's chamber, while the Exile sat, holding pen above paper, never writing a word, while a wild shadow from no apparent source flickered upon the walls.

Sekenre wrote also: That the sorcerer climbed up, toward the unscalable Peaks (the Towers, the Upturned Hand of Death). The way was difficult, even for him. He sought not the Stone People (travelling only by day, or on cloudy nights, huddled in his tent or in caves when the Moon shone bright) but the eagles, hoping to converse with them, to learn the answer to the mystery that would not let him rest: *what not even the Stone People knew, that he who had been loved by the Stone King's Daughter loved her, incomprehensibly, in return, and begot a child on her, which would be delivered of her at the end of time. Then, in the final vision, who was that running across the plain, into the Crocodile's mouth, waving an antique sword?*

SEEKING THE GIFTS OF THE QUEEN OF VENGEANCE

WHAT DO you want, little man?

Sekenre the sorcerer asks you this. I really want to know.

What?

What do you want among the mysteries of time and fate, and the babble of the gods? In such a context we are all little men. We might as well admit it.

Let me tell a story, speaking it aloud as I write it in my book, fabricating as I make it true.

Let me tell of that late and decadent time, when Wenamon the Twenty-Seventh ruled in the Delta, and the galleys of the Great Kings no longer ranged the length of Riverland nor crossed the Crescent Sea. Instead, they rotted in the mud. Barbarians grew bold, the satraps arrogant, and the nobles gave themselves over entirely to pleasure.

Perhaps it is true that this Wenamon was old and weak and stupid, that he sat in the gathering darkness with dotard courtiers and a handful of priests as decrepit as himself. They peered into a black glass, desirous of knowing the future, though it was a future beyond the reach of any of them.

Why?

Surely the gods did not say. Surely the oracles did not tell, though by then the land was so filled with gods and oracles that the divine voices were like the buzzing of locusts.

Let us say only that Wenamon the Twenty-Second had two sons. The eldest, Valtho, was to be king hereafter. Wenamon's queen had died in the birthing of the other, Prince Leonas, which was a waste, the old king thought, since he had loved his queen, and of his second son little was expected except an early death.

Such a waste. But the old king did not know if he wished it otherwise. He'd always had great difficulty making up his mind.

He knew only that the end-time had come.

Therefore he gazed into his darkened glass. He saw something rising up out of it, a speck of light, growing brighter.

He heard a buzzing sound.

⋆   ⋆   ⋆

THE PUFFY-FACED eunuch said to Prince Leonas, "Do not be melancholy, Lord. Enjoy the pleasant night. Come and be with the others."

The eunuch was absurdly made up, in so much finery and feathers — and his trembling manner added to the impression — that he could well have been an enormous chicken.

What this creature did not say was, *Your brother, who will be king, com-*

mands it. He wants to keep an eye on you.

"Cluck-cluck," said Prince Leonas. He closed the door in the eunuch's face.

"Wh-what was th-that, Lord?"

"Cluck."

"I don't understand."

"Give me a minute. I'll be right with you."

Leonas hurried to make ready. He *robed himself,* eccentric behavior in a prince under most circumstances, but now essential, lest tattling servants observe the thing he had made ready, or reported that Prince Leonas wore a shirt of mail under his gold-brocaded, formal court garb.

The eunuch fretted outside.

For an instant, Prince Leonas trembled with a murderous rage he could barely control. It frightened even himself, though he knew his cause was just. Now was the time to be bold. At twenty-three he was already old enough to feel useless, and he knew that his end was upon him. An oracle had told him as much, in several thousand words of flowery amphigory.

Dare. Now. Be avenged for the thousand little insults he had suffered from his brother.

Save the State.

His rage masked a terrible fear. He waited until it passed.

"Lord Prince!" Your brother is waiting."

"I am sure he is."

Leonas allowed himself to be led through the vaulting, black-stone palace, amid the massive, drum-shaped pillars, past effigies of former kings the size of houses, and further, where shadowed side-corridors opened onto infinities, revealing whole suites of rooms no one had used or even explored in generations. He imagined that there could be an entire other kingdom there, as unknown and invisible to him as he to they. He imagined he could flee there, if his plans went awry, and live out his life amid the shadows.

But he did not want to.

The eunuch led him outside, turning to make *tsk*ing sounds when he tarried.

They came to the White Garden, where statues, railings, benches, and the enormous, crouching idols of the gods were of white marble, where white trees and blossoms shone faintly in the moonlight.

Paper lanterns lighted the way along a certain path.

Something, like a bundle of sticks come alive, trailed white rags across that path and disappeared.

The eunuch didn't seem to notice.

Below the White Garden was the Black Garden, where everything was replicated in black stone, and black flowers opened to the night sky. There, an owlish-faced, barefoot boy in a scruffy robe sat on one of the benches. He held something glowing in his cupped hands, which gave off a buzzing sound.

A cloud crossed the moon for an instant, and the boy was gone.

Next came the Red Garden, where even the moon seemed swimming in blood. Much of the Red Garden was in ruins.

Prince Leonas felt a peculiar humor come over him. This, too, like the apparitions he had seen, was a portent. He would figure out what it actually meant later.

Now he waved his hand and said to the eunuch, "Do you suppose we could clear all this rubbish away, and make a training ground for soldiers?"

"The Lord Prince your brother has enough soldiers. They train elsewhere."

"We could graze cattle here."

"You speak strangely, Lord Leonas."

Ah, not Lord Prince Leonas. More likely Lord Food-for-Vultures Leonas. Is that it?

"I know," said Leonas. "Don't bother to say that my brother has enough cattle and they graze elsewhere."

"Even so."

"We could always build a few temples for extra gods. Send our mighty fleets out to capture a few."

The eunuch did not reply. There were already thousands of gods in the Delta. Kings had been accumulating them for centuries.

"My brother already has enough gods. I know. I know."

The eunuch did not laugh at this little joke.

But they heard laughter soon enough, in where the land cupped to form an amphitheater. They were below the gardens now. Leonas could smell the river. Mosquitoes whined in his ears. In a pillared pavilion surrounded by rearing stone horses, Prince Valtho and his sycophants had gathered to celebrate some festival, the meaning of which had long since been forgotten.

Everyone wore masks, plumes, wings, clownish costumes. Among them, Leonas was a severity, an intrusion. He intended as much.

"The Lord Prince Leonas greets his brother!" a herald cried. Everyone bowed and swept, exaggerating so much they could barely contain their hilarity.

"And the Lord Prince Valtho greets him in return," said Prince Valtho, stepping down from the pavilion onto the path, smiling his terrible smile. Leonas noted, unsurprised, that his brother already sported the beehive-shaped crown of the Great Kings of the Delta, though their father was still alive.

Leonas masked all his feelings, as a prince must.

"I greet my brother," he said.

"I greet —" said Valtho, putting his arm around Leonas in an unwelcome embrace, seizing Leonas by the neck in his massive hand. Valtho was a giant, more than a head taller than Leonas. He could have snapped his younger brother's neck right then, gracefully, and bowed to the applause of the ground.

"And how is our dear mother?" Valtho whispered.

"She is as before."

"Give her my regards when you see her. Soon."

To the crowd, Valtho smiled broadly and waved his free hand. Music and laughter rose up, like an incoming tide.

Firmly and not all that gently, Valtho led Leonas into a side alcove amid some hedges and halted before a statue of a man being crushed to death by a winged serpent.

"This must be your favorite," said Valtho. "Tell me the story again. I know it is your favorite."

"The hero is the serpent," said Leonas evenly. "He is Prince Agracas. His brother Ptamenes enchanted him into serpent form, then summoned an eagle to carry him far out into the desert. The distance was too great for a serpent ever to crawl back. But King Neoc, god of Justice, gave Agracas wings —"

Valtho squeezed so hard that Leonas choked. Bystanders turned away discreetly.

"What you must remember, brother mine," said Valtho, "is that nobody is going to give you a set of wings."

He let go.

Leonas, acting as if nothing happened, spoke loud enough to be overheard. "Brother, yes, as a sign of our love for one another, it *is* time we drank from the double cup!"

So the cry went out and the double cup was fetched on a platter before Valtho could respond. This vessel was actually two golden cups which King Wenamon had ordered joined together on the birth of his second son. Now the princes demonstrated their affection for one another, each pouring the portion the other was to drink, then raising the cup together, carefully, so neither spilled a drop.

Valtho smiled.

They drank.

It had been a simple matter for Leonas to flick open the secret compartment in one of his rings and drop poison into his brother's drink.

They drained the double cup.

Everyone was laughing. Suddenly Leonas didn't know what they were laughing about. All around him, people were taking off their masks, revealing corpse faces, or bare skulls, or nothing at all. He heard a buzzing sound. Incongruous among the glittering lords and ladies, the barefoot, ragged boy stared up at him with dark, dark eyes that could swallow one's soul. A speck of light rose out of the darkness, buzzing.

Prince Valtho was laughing loudest of all. He stuck out his tongue. It was blue, which, of course, meant that he had taken an antidote to any possible poison.

"Have you considered, dear brother, that you're not actually very good at this?"

No! This was all wrong. Leonas struggled as if chains were upon him. He fell into darkness.

The dark-eyed boy's face glowed like a paper lantern. "Is this what you want?" he said. He held something on a silver platter.

> *What do you want? You want the story to end some other way, like a nightmare you try to revise just before waking, to force a happy ending. You want to rend and tear the narrative, shattering all continuity, forcing it into another shape.*
>
> *Is this what you want?*
>
> *It isn't the boy who offers the platter. It is the Goddess Malevendra, Queen of Vengeance, with her hair wild, her mouth frozen in the rictus of a scream, her spiked crown bloody, as she is always depicted in art. Indeed there is so much blood that it pours down out of the Red Garden until it forms a sea, and the pavilion and the courtiers are covered up and drowned; and the*

moon rises like a burning coal out of that sea of blood; and the Goddess Malevendra walks upon the waters, barefoot, her ragged gown trailing behind her. She is as gaunt as a bundle of sticks, but strong enough to snap a prince's head right off, which is perhaps what she has done.

Delicately, she approaches Prince Leonas, offering him, on the silver platter, awash in blood, nothing less than the severed head of Prince Valtho.

"Is this what you want?"

"Yes, but maybe with an apple in his mouth."

The goddess doesn't get the joke. Instead, Prince Valtho's dead lips ripple as if he is going to laugh. A faintly luminous, blue scarab beetle crawls out of his mouth and fills the night with the sound of its buzzing.

Perhaps you would prefer the story this way, Lord Prince:

PRINCE LEONAS sat on the cold, hard sand before the campfire. Somewhere behind him, a camel snorted. Certainly he could smell it. Certainly, too, he knew how he had come to be here, though the details were fading now, as if he had awakened from a dream.

On the other side of the fire, the owlish boy reached up his hand and caught the glowing scarab beetle. He pressed the insect gently to his chest and allowed it to crawl into his loose, ragged garment. Leonas knew that the scarab was a messenger of Surat-Hemad, the crocodile-headed Lord of Death, Who lies in the mud at the center of the universe, He Whose teeth are the stars, Whose mouth is the night sky, out of Whose belly the Great River flows and into which it and all things inevitably return.

Leonas looked up. To the east, there was a faint glow. It was almost dawn.

He saw that they had camped in a ruin, to get out of the wind. Sand whistled among the stones, buzzing.

"I am the sorcerer Sekenre," said the boy.

Leonas would have taken him for a beggar. He judged him about fourteen, slender, beardless, with those dark eyes that held one. He could not look away. He said nothing.

"I know what you want," said the boy, "for I have lived for many lifetimes and I contain lifetimes within me; for the sorcerer does not age, and he who slays a sorcerer becomes a sorcerer; and we are many." His voice shifted then, once, twice, many times, a babble of accents and tones and languages, speaking of names and places Prince Leonas knew only from history, and especially of a King Wenamon, fourth of that name, who died under bizarre circumstances *centuries* ago.

Leonas tried, but could not convince himself that he was in the presence of a mere lunatic.

Yet the boy sat as a child sits, legs flat on the ground in front of him. Adults are seldom that limber, and sit cross-legged.

"So, you know what I want?"

"Yes, and I can give it to you, if you truly desire it."

> *What? What? It doesn't fit!*
> *Revise again. Enter an unexpected element.*

"YOU! SHUT UP! Who are you talking to?"

A chain rattled and the boy was yanked around to one side. Leonas was astonished to see that there was a shackle around the sorcerer Sekenre's left ankle. The ankle looked swollen and bloody, too. The chain therefrom snaked in among the stones, where the camel rested.

A gigantic man crawled into the firelight, holding the other end of the chain, a pale-bearded, uncouth barbarian clad in a ridiculous mixture of fine cloth, gaudy jewelry, war-gear, and animal skins. His face and bare arms were almost luminous in the firelight. Leonas had seen such men before, mercenaries or prisoners from beyond the Crescent Sea.

"I *said*, who are you talking to?"

"No one, Master."

The barbarian caught Sekenre by the hair and held a knife against his throat.

"Do not betray me. If you're making a spell against me, know that I can slit you apart like an apple."

"I warned you what would happen if you did."

"Maybe it would suit me to become a sorcerer, even a little one."

"Maybe it would suit me to become a barbarian, even a big, strong one."

The barbarian spat. He looked around. He didn't seem to see Prince Leonas.

"Just shut up. Go to sleep. Do sorcerers ever sleep?"

"When it pleases them."

The barbarian shook himself like a huge dog shaking off dust, then crawled away and lay down among the stones.

"Just shut up," he muttered.

Over the huge man's snores, Sekenre whispered, "Actually, I do not wish to become a barbarian. That part of me which was a boy named Sekenre in Reedland long ago wants to retain the form and shape and memory of who he is, so I humor this uncouth fellow, who thinks I am his slave."

"But are you?"

"I am one, like you, like he, who seeks the goddess of Vengeance, who is Malevendra. I do so for my own purposes, which you are not to understand. *You* are the one who is to lead us to her. For this reason I have summoned you. You will be rewarded richly of her treasures, which are pain and fear and the deaths of enemies; and she will give them to you freely, or else in exchange for a terrible price; but she will give them, if this is what you desire."

"It is what I want," said the prince.

"Shut up . . ." said the barbarian, without really waking.

Now, now, imagine again. It doesn't fit. Leonas actually dreams of pleasant things, of a time when he was a child and sailed paper boats in a fountain in the White Garden, of a particularly delightful troupe of clowns who once performed at court; of quiet afternoons when he sat alone beneath the blue sky, ignored by the courtiers as he tried to compose properly classical verse on a blank tablet before him, the sort princes write and flatterers praise and subsequent generations forget. He couldn't find the words, but he didn't care.

Leonas dreams that he can just get up and leave his life as he has lived it thus far. He removes his face as if it's a mask and places it, vaguely glowing, on the bench beside his empty tablet, and he goes away, into another land, or perhaps in another time, as if he's walked into one of those dark, unexplored corridors in the palace and emerged into a different world entirely. There he has adventures, marries, has children, then grandchildren, and grows old. There he cannot be sure if he is an old man dreaming he was once a prince, or a prince dreaming he is an old man.

Leonas tears and tries to re-thread the dream, but it comes apart, like a tapestry burst apart by a sudden wind. Think Queen Balsinoe in the story, whose husband, sons, and warriors had all been slain by magic. But, by magic, she kept them alive, and sent them forth to conquer her enemies. She could keep them alive as long as she continued weaving the tapestry of their adventures. She couldn't stop, even for an instant. She dared not sleep. By drugs and magic and pain, she kept herself awake, for days, weeks, even years. But at the very last she inevitably nodded off, for just a second, and when she awoke it was too late.

The wind had blown the tapestry apart. The threads, delicate as spider silk, were drifting all around the room. She could not catch them.

Likewise, Leonas cannot catch the fragments of his dream. Parts of it that flash by like pictures in a book whose pages are flipped by that same, destroying wind:

Leonas, Sekenre, and the barbarian on a long journey into the desert, away from the River, across the blue-white, trackless sands. A journey of pain. The barbarian holds the boy's chain in one hand and the camel's leash in the other. He hoards their water. After a while Sekenre is limping so badly that he has to be allowed to ride. But the barbarian won't let him drink.

They travel only by night. Leonas leads the way where there is no apparent path. He, in turn, follows the flight of Sekenre's glowing scarab beetle.

The barbarian, whose name is Vaggakodissa, chatters endlessly of his name and his deeds and the vile crimes of his enemies, elaborating both his ambitions and his and hatred, composing his own epic and chanting it to the expressionless moon and the night sky.

"THIS IS THE place," said Prince Leonas.

"This is the place," said Sekenre, to Vaggakodissa, who came to a halt and caused the camel to kneel.

"Huh?"

It seemed a stretch of desert like any other. Here the dunes had given way to bare, cracked earth and scattered stones. The land sloped downward slightly. In the distance, mountains rose, black against the evening sky.

"I charge you," said Sekenre, again to Vaggakodissa, "to be true to your word."

The boy climbed down from the camel. The barbarian viciously yanked him off his feet, then crouched down over him, got out a key, and undid the shackle. Sekenre rose unsteadily to his feet and limped a short distance away.

"You weren't thinking of running . . . ?"

"No, Master."

To Leonas, the boy said, "Are you certain?"

"Can't you see?"

"I see the moon rising."

"This is the place."

"Who the *hell* are you talking too?" demanded Vaggakodissa.

The scarab beetle circled about, lit on Sekenre's chest and crawled under his clothing.

Therefore Sekenre walked forward a few more paces. Blood poured out of his wounded ankle, far more blood than any human body could possibly contain, great rushing torrents, which filled the desert and made it into a sea. Vaggakodissa watched this impassively. Leonas was amazed and afraid, as the moon rose like a burning coal out of the red sea, as the face of the moon screamed at him, frozen in the rictus shout of madness so often depicted in portraits of the goddess Malevendra.

Then Sekenre removed his clothes and stood naked by the edge of the bloody sea, and Leonas could see that the boy was covered with terrible scars, huge, raised ridges of flesh, many of which burned in the moonlight with reddish, inner fire. Surely no one wounded thus could have survived. Yet Sekenre walked out onto the surface of the blood sea, sending great ripples spreading before him.

After a short distance, the boy turned, and bade Leonas follow after him, instructing him to first remove his shoes, for flesh must touch if magic is to be true.

Leonas saw that the buzzing scarab had embedded itself in Sekenre's chest like an enormous tick, gorging itself.

The prince stepped out onto the surface of the sea. He felt nothing beneath his feet. Oddly, his footsteps created no ripples, as Sekenre's did.

They walked, leaving Vaggakodissa far behind, and spoke of vengeance, and of death, and of the ways of sorcery. Sekenre told how the Malevendra was once a mortal woman, who was hideously wronged, raped by an order of men who had sworn themselves to perfect chivalry. They forgot their oath, and in their wrath killed one another, ever urged on by Malevendra who gave birth, in her pain, to ten thousand monsters, until at last she knew only her pain and her anger. She forgot who she was and could not stop, and still she does not stop.

"This blood is hers," said Sekenre, "and yours, and mine, and the blood of all men."

"Why do you tell me this now?" said Leonas.

But Sekenre did not answer him directly, and went on to tell how sorcery is much the same as vengeance, as each sorcerer distrusts and fears all others, how they make alliances only for short intervals, and fight one another in fantastic wars among the stars. By each act of sorcery, the sorcerer is transformed, transfigured, mutilated. He cannot stop. He is a slave to his passions. He devours his enemies and is devoured by them until all are one in their shared pain.

Only the rarest of sorcerers knows how to stop, to let go.

Leonas regarded the boy's scarred body.

"Ah, I see."

"Do you know what you want?"

"Yes, I do."

"Are you sure?"

The goddess rose before them, terrible in every aspect, blood streaming down her sides. In one hand she held the beehive-crown of the Great Kings of the Delta, in the other, a golden sword.

> But Leonas is not sure. He wants me, the author, to make things come out right for him. Rip this out. Repair that. Make a happy ending.
>
> Oh, friend Leonas, what is written is written. What is done is done. Even I cannot change very much of it.
>
> Leonas tries to think back. The images are flipped by the wind. His brother, laughing, with a blue tongue, all the other courtiers, laughing, their tongues painted blue in imitation.
>
> But there is something more. A creaking, wooden house overlooking a papyrus swamp. Reedland, he somehow knows. Sekenre grew up here, long ago. It is Sekenre who would return there, who has lost something irretrievable, but now it is Leonas who dwells for many years in that house, which creaks with the river's passing, which seems to grow extra rooms from time to time, into which he can wander and find things he thought he had forever lost.
>
> In one of them, he finds all the verses he never managed to write.
>
> In another, he meets his brother, Valtho, who says to him, "Let us forgive and be reconciled."
>
> Sekenre walks in on them as Leonas is screaming and bludgeoning his brother to death with a boat hook.
>
> "The way to stop," the boy says, "is merely to let it go and turn elsewhere."
>
> But Leonas does not stop. His fury terrifies him, but he cannot stop.
>
> That's where the thread of the story breaks. There are only drifting fragments now.

This:

*   *   *

SEKENRE STANDS at the edge of the bloody sea. He gives the golden sword to Vaggakodissa without a word, and turns his back as he dresses himself, all but daring the barbarian to strike him down.

"With that sword you will kill all your enemies," the boy says. "Every time you draw it, someone will die. Every time."

The barbarian spits.

"You have what you want. Now honor our bargain."

The barbarian bounces a purse of coins off the boy's chest, laughs, mounts the camel, and rides away.

Leonas looks on, appalled. "You work for *money?*"

"When it pleases me," says Sekenre. He stoops and takes up the purse. The beetle beneath his clothing buzzes. "Nevertheless, I would gladly give it to you, if you would but turn aside from your intended path."

Leonas holds the crown. "I cannot. I will not. It is my destiny."

Then you know what you want.

This:

In the darkness, Leonas and Sekenre enter the black stone palace of the kings of the Delta. The boy's bare feet are, of course, silent on the smooth floors, but the prince's footfalls are likewise without sound. For a long time they sojourn in that shadow court, among the kingdom of the ghosts, in great halls where mummy cases stand in rows receding into the infinite distance, where the air is thick with the wet, muddy smell of the River of the Dead and the ghosts of dead men rise into those mummy cases and whisper out of the golden masks, and speak of times long past, of great deeds and small sorrows.

Some of them can even remember happiness.

But Leonas refuses to tarry.

And this:

The scarab flies through the vaulted halls. Prince Leonas races after it.

And this:

Sekenre and the goddess Malevendra sit by the edge of the bloody sea, weighing their sorrows. The goddess is almost human in her aspect. The boy has let his robe slide down, until he is naked to the waist. His scars are beginning to fade.

He cups the scarab beetle in his hands, then tosses it into the air and watches it fly away.

To conclude our history:

When King Wenamon the Twenty-Seventh had passed among the Kings That Were, perhaps given a slight nudge in that direction, or so it was rumored, by his son Valtho, the palace was gaily decked out in flowers from the gardens, and the coronation was held in the great hall, where the colossi of the former kings gazed down.

The image of Wenamon XXII was still under construction, and draped.

Everyone painted their tongues blue for the occasion.

In the midst of the ceremony, which is both solemn and somewhat frivolous, after the priests had chanted and the acrobats dressed like birds had begun to tumble in their ridiculous flight, a murmur of consternation spread through those assembled. The news was too incredible. Some laughed it off. Others made signs to ward off evil. There was whispered talk of omens, portents, and the ending of history.

A woman fell down and began to prophesy, but the ushers dragged her off.

One of the acrobats missed the hand of another and fell to the floor with a bloody splash.

There could be no denying, then, what the matter was. The ceremony came to a halt. Everyone stood there, unsure of what to do next.

For the crown itself, the most sacred and ancient symbol of the kings of the Delta, was missing.

Valtho stood bare-headed, glaring at his priests.

But before he could order any executions, a voice rose above all the others, utterly clear.

"Are you looking for this, my brother?"

Leonas entered the hall, holding the crown which the goddess of Vengeance had given him. There were cries of amazement and fear. Ladies turned to flee. Soldiers drew their swords. Valtho swiftly snatched a spear from one of the guards and hurled it at Leonas at close range, but somehow he missed, or the spear passed through, and transfixed a certain lord, who fell dead, his spirit rising up, demanding vengeance.

And Leonas screamed the scream of Malevendra, which is without words, like the roaring of a terrible storm. Those who heard covered their ears, or fell down faint, or died; but for Valtho, who faced his doom bravely, as Prince Leonas rushed upon him and tore Valtho's head from his shoulders. Blood showered upon the crowd.

Then, remembering every insult, every humiliation, now at the very pinnacle of his triumph, Prince Leonas shouted, in that same thundering, incomprehensible voice, "Look! Look! Now I am king in the Delta!"

He tossed his brother's head aside and placed the crown on himself, but it passed through him as if he were made of smoke, and rolled across the floor.

> *I am Sekenre, who has written this in my book. See, there it is. At first the page looks solid black, but then it resolves into tiny script. The entire tale takes up that space, there, about the size of my finger.*
>
> *I cannot repair or revise any further. Endings have a way of working themselves out.*
>
> *Why are you weeping, Leonas?*
>
> *Did you not think, once, ever, to forget about vengeance and turn away?*
>
> *Of course you did. But it was too late for you, I am afraid.*
>
> *I alone understand.*
>
> *Your brother's tongue was blue. He had taken an antidote. He poisoned you. You died that night in the garden, and were buried there, without any rites. It takes a restless ghost to locate Lady Vengeance. That is why I summoned you. I used you as a navigator uses a compass, and for that I ask you to forgive me. I too sought Malevendra, but merely to converse, for my own reasons. She gave me no gift. I asked for none. That is how the part of me which is Sekenre stays afloat in the raging torrent which is sorcery, in the centuries of his many lives. Other sorcerers are grotesquely transformed by their hatreds, by their unending dread. They drown in it. Sekenre knows how to let go.*
>
> *Into this scheme barged Vaggakodissa, not entirely anticipated. I shaped him. I made him part of the larger pattern. I wrote him into my book.*
>
> *Didn't you wonder why the barbarian kept asking who I was talking to? He wasn't very good at seeing ghosts.*
>
> *Leonas, you were dead before the adventure began, but if you had so chosen, you could have lived out a lifetime of peace in a single second, suspended like an insect in amber, timeless, as your dying brain cooled.*
>
> *But you chose otherwise, to kill as only a vengeful ghost can.*
>
> *Let me try to repair things a little bit:*

★   ★   ★

SOME YEARS after the barbarian usurper Vaggakodissa drew his golden sword too many times and slew his sons and then himself, and there were no more kings in Riverland, someone came into the ruined gardens by the old palace. The villagers who dwelt nearby reported that he was short and small, a dwarf, perhaps, or a child. They agreed that he was plainly clad and barefoot. Why he was there, or what he did in that haunted place, they could not say, for no one dared to venture in after him.

I'll tell you.

I gathered the bones of Prince Leonas, which were scattered under the overgrown hedges near the statue of the serpent Agracas and his brother Ptamenes. By the river's edge, I made a vessel out of reeds, and with ancient rite, with tapers lighted on either end of the tiny boat, I waded out into the water until I saw the ghosts which hover like mist at the edge of the River of the Dead, and I felt the black current, which flows into the belly of Surat-Hemad, the crocodile-headed god, Who waits at the end of time to devour all things, that One whose teeth are the numberless stars, Whose mouth is the night sky.

I let the boat go and whispered the name of Leonas for the last time, commending him to Surat-Hemad.

LORD ABERNAEVEN'S TALE

The crocodile closes his mouth. It is finished. It is begun.
— The Litanies of Surat-Hemad

I

I WAS already more than half awake when the dream came to me, already aware that I lay in my stateroom aboard the steamship *Empress Faustina*, completely cognizant of the steady thrumming of the ship's engines through the bulkhead, which had deprived me of sleep on so many other occasions. *Then*, I say, it was *then*, as I slid out of my bunk and began to grope about among my things that the lightbulb overhead seemed to dim steadily — not, some other compartmentalized division of my rational mind noted, as if the power were failing, but as if the room filled with otherwise invisible, black smoke. Then, *then*, I felt the cold, damp, *earthy* breeze wash over me — not salt air from an open porthole, but more like the breath of a vast pit, dug in the heart of a deep forest, somewhere in the far north. The whole stateroom smelled of mud and dead leaves.

And she came to me, walking up, out of that darkness, out of some abyss which was of course entirely impossible in a cramped stateroom aboard the *Empress Faustina*; but she came. In my lucid dream, fully aware that I was dreaming, I beheld the sheeted white form walking up, up, toward me, turning in slow circles as if ascending some spiral staircase I could not see, up out of very core of the Earth, her shroud or robe trailing behind her in some roaring hurricane I could not sense.

Her face glowed, like the rising moon, as exquisite as a perfect sculpture of white marble framed by streaming black hair.

So she had once been. So I had seen her long, long ago, but not now — it could not be —

"*Witch!*" I cried out. "*Leave me!*"

She laughed, in that beautiful voice she'd had, back then, when we both were young. "Quite, quite impossible, my love. You know that we must embrace again, and finish what was begun."

"*Leave me, witch!*"

Again, that laughter, but no beauty in it this time. She came at me like a fury, and swiped at my face with a clawed hand.

"You don't mean that," she said. "You *love* me. Why will you not address me by my name?"

And I wept, clutching a bleeding cheek. I pounded on the steel bulkhead. I knew that it was true, that I hated her, that I feared her, that I fled from her for almost thirty years, and — as I feared most of all — that somehow, in some twisted way, I still loved her. Yet I could not bring myself to say her name: the Lady Eudochina Kias.

My heart would stop before I did that.

So I could only cling to the metal wall, and weep, and pound my fist, with my eyes tightly closed, and after a time it seemed that the temperature within the cabin rose, the air smelled of salt once more, and somebody was knocking on metal somewhere far away.

I opened my eyes. The cabin was bright with electric light. Someone was knocking on my door. I threw a robe around myself and opened it.

Whoever stood outside seemed short and dark and didn't wear the impeccable uniform of the crew. He spoke in a soft voice, in a slight, unidentifiable accent.

"Are you all right, Sir?"

"Yes, yes. I am well. It was just a dream."

He looked at my bloody cheek.

"I must have cut myself shaving," I said quickly.

"Ah."

He turned and went away, swiftly, soundlessly, as if, perhaps, he were walking barefoot on the cold metal deck. That struck me at the time as merely odd, an incongruous detail, but of no particular importance.

THOROUGHLY AWAKE as I now was, and shaken, all I could do was tend to the cut on my cheek, then finish dressing and leave the stateroom. I carefully locked the door behind me. We were approaching a wild, backward country, and there would be thieves as soon as we made port — if not sooner.

I ceremoniously slid the key into my vest pocket.

Yes, attending to every detail, impeccably dressed now, ready to face the world, I made my away along the dim corridor until my hand found a railing and my feet a stairway. I started to climb up, up, up, like the apparition in my dream, out of the darkness of the ship's bowels, to the observation deck topside, in front of the funnels.

It was dark there too, for dawn was still several minutes away, yet the sight of the stars comforted me, for they were familiar, something I had known all my life, unchanging; though hadn't I read once, in some children's version of barbarous myths, that the stars are supposed to be the teeth of some cosmic crocodile, the Lord of Death, who has already devoured us all?

So then you might look at the stars and wonder: if we dwell without the very jaws of Death, were we ever alive?

A silly notion. I shrugged it off.

I saw only the familiar sky. I walked out onto the observation deck. On the horizon, to the southeast, a star brighter than all the others flickered and guttered; and I felt a certain excitement, even dread clutching in my heart, for here was my first glimpse of Riverland, that wild, dark place where people still believed in cosmic crocodiles and the Death that walked like a man.

The light on the horizon, of course, could only have been the bonfire lit atop the squat ruin of the great lighthouse in Delta Port, already familiar from the engraved frontispieces to so many travel books.

I might well imagine that I had already opened, and entered, such a book, that all which was to follow was already written down therein. A fabulous tale. A fable. An impossibility. I felt an odd dislocation, an escape from the real, the rational world where there is pain —

A voice broke in.

"You've come to pray, Sir?"

I turned to confront a large, red-faced man in a flowing golden robe and mirrored, silver medallion: The High Reverend Margos Targeddon, Sun Guardian of the First Order, who had been chaplain on our voyage.

The first faint daylight appeared in the northeast. The stars began to fade. It was indeed time to pray. So here was the Reverend Targeddon, in full clerical garb, a symbol of rational, monotheistic Truth to disperse the darkness of paganism . . . to get rid of the devouring crocodiles . . . not to mention witches . . . but where was the congregation?

"I —"

The clergyman smiled, as if to forgive — it was something he learned to do professionally — as if to say, *Yes, of course, too much drinking last night, the banquet overmuch, everyone else still asleep or seasick; I understand. Oh times, oh morals!*

Of course he didn't understand anything, the fat, blithering, tottering fool — he hadn't developed his sea-legs, and held onto the railing to steady himself — but I joined in, and we two chanted the psalms of Holy Father Sun, which every child learns in school (alongside Riverlandish mythology with its crocodiles) and never manages to forget.

I helped him ease himself to his knees, straining, as he was more than twice my weight. With both hands he held up the Sun medallion he wore — as big as a dinner plate — and we two gazed on it in silent adoration, while the muted thunder of the ship's engines rumbled beneath our knees, and the sky lightened. Gradually the featureless disk (only a Riverlandish idolater would think to put an *image* on it!) filled with the pure and perfect light, and so it was that the world was once more cleansed by Divine Reason, and all nightmares and night-haunters banished.

"Well," gasped Targeddon, as I helped him up onto a bench. "Well . . . I say . . ."

He seemed to take a while to catch his breath and gather his thoughts. I found that comforting, too, to be in the presence of someone more muddled that myself; for I am, I say, I admit, a terribly *nervous* person on account of my experiences and sorrows, and sometimes I lose my way a little. But now the sun was up, and we enjoyed a cool morning breeze, to be treasured in that short interval before the day turned hot as a furnace. By some trick of the atmosphere, the water gleamed blindingly.

And so we sat side-by-side on the bench, two calm and rational men from the Bright Empire, ambassadors of civilization to the wild place that now revealed itself before us. As my companion hemmed and harrumphed and caught his breath, mopping his streaming brown with a copious handkerchief, I sat primly, and beheld Riverland by the light of day, fabulous Riverland which, I could well imagine, had not changed in any essential way in five thousand years. Time vanished here, travelers reported. Some crocodile must have swallowed it. Here were the black, incredibly ancient walls of the City of the Delta, like shaped mountains, fallen into ruin in many places, the battlements and rubble alike bedecked with palm trees. The harbor in the foreground already swarmed with small, sailed craft. A gunboat, steely gray and almost as big as the *Faustina*, edged its way toward the docks.

Beyond the walls were more sights made familiar from the clichèd engravings in travel books: the famous lighthouse, like a squat pyramid with its top sheared off, black smoke drifting upward from the summit; the massive dome of the temple of Bel Hemad, which is still maintained, and even the colonial authorities dare not shut it down. I could make out other temples too, many of them ruins, and the Thousand Statues of the Old Forum, which stood atop pillars and rooftops like a congregation of giants gathered to scrutinize newcomers. Of course there were newer buildings, hotels red-roofed and tiled in the style of the Bright Empire . . . and flags everywhere, of the ancient dynasties of Riverland's kings, of the Empire and the Protectorate, and even (though it doubtless offended the natives) of the Church, the brilliant banner of the Holy Sun, perfectly white on a field of gold . . . which was doubtless where Reverend Margos Targeddon came in.

My companion seemed to have dozed off. I would have left him there, but he stirred as I rose.

"Ah, yes, I appreciated your company, My Lord."

"Not Lord," I said curtly. "Just Sir. A Mister."

He blinked and shook his head as if that some somehow reset the clockwork within his dim brain and make him understand.

"I have business here," I said.

"A man of commerce then? I had taken you for one of the aristocracy. I meant no offense —"

"It is personal business."

"Ah," he said, and I did not like that *Ah*, the kind he learned to utter professionally, the sanctimonious, hypocritical *Ah* of his kind, which pretends to say, *I am a man of the world, like you, and yes, I understand why a great lord like yourself might choose to travel incognito, for some intrigue, for thrills; yes your secret is safe with me, though I caution you, for your own good —*

His presence had become smothering, as if I were soon to be buried in an avalanche of self-righteousness and sweaty flesh, unable to escape while the Sun Guardian of the First Order warned me in his sternest, albeit fatherly manner of the fashionable and dangerous dalliances of the decadent rich, who indulge in so-called pilgrimages of spiritual discovery among the idolatrous ruins of Riverland and all her terrible, false gods. It was as if this poison had a new flavor, so they tried it out for the novelty. Yes, I had heard that sermon before, and could well imagine the *entire discourse* embedded in the Reverend's monosyllabic *Ah*. From the way he raised his eyebrow I knew that he was entirely capable of spewing forth thunderings — as continuous, though less muted than the throbbing of the *Empress Faustina's* engines — against madness, occultism, neo-heathenry, or, worse yet, total apostasy.

I could well imagine. He could imagine nothing. Angry, but perfectly controlled, I took my leave of him.

How could a fool like that understand? He could not! How could he know what it was like, when, after nearly thirty years of respectability and peace, my life changed so horribly — nay, it *ended* with the bloody tread of pestilence within the walls of my estate — for indeed there were scarlet footprints found outside the chambers of the stricken — and *one by one* they died, first my beloved wife, Simonis, then all three of my sons — the eldest almost a man — followed by my two daughters, *one by one* perishing, their sheets found soaked in scarlet, their bodies covered with inexplicable wounds, their *throats* having somehow grown gangrenous under the chin, as if their heads had been all but cut off.

Science, reason itself, the holy light of Blessed Father Sun were all useless then, as the witch went howling through the corridors each night like a baleful spirit to announce that someone else was to die.

How could this blubbery, ridiculous clergyman understand that?

How could he know that, bereft of all joy, all purpose for living, I had become mad for a time, howling as wildly any spirit, but that, in the end, the madness had *heightened* my senses, *clarified* my mind, enabled me, by some means which transcends reason, to *know* what I had to do?

How, I ask you. How?

For that reason, incognito, but beneath a veneer of respectability, I had journeyed to Riverland.

No, I didn't expect him to understand.

Though it was daylight now, I felt as if I stood at the edge of some limitless darkness, and was about to plunge headlong into it.

II

AH RIVERLAND! Fantastic place, where the shadows never fade, where apparitions come by daylight!

The engravings in the travel books don't do it justice.

As soon as you step ashore in Delta Port, you are overwhelmed by the *babel* of the place, not just sounds, though a dozen languages jabber away at once, anywhere, it seems. There waft the odors of exotic spices, of meat cooking on the carts of sidewalk vendors, of sweat and dust and dung; and sometimes, even the odors of the desert itself — for the desert beyond the River has an odor of its own, which I cannot describe as other than *ancientness*. It is never entirely absent.

Then there are dazzling bursts of color. It takes a while for the eye to sort them all out: the sun gleaming off colored glass in the newer buildings, off white-washed walls in startling contrast to the black, ancient stones. But you hardly notice the stones at first, for the surging masses of people everywhere: imperial officials checking one's papers and stamping one's passport (no sanctimonious *Ah*, from any of them; they looked bored), a native in a conical cap shouting and directing the tangled traffic of camels, horses, donkey-carts, and porters with impossibly huge loads on their backs, all befuddled by the occasional modern steam-car. Everyone is dressed in bright tatters, for that is the fashion in Riverland now, after a dozen conquests and the coming of the Bright Empire with its inexpensive, machine-woven cloth and gaudy dyes. Now even the poorest beggar is bedecked in incandescent scarlets, iridescent blues, a green that gleams like gold, yellows, dark purples . . . not necessarily whole, not likely to be clean, but clad brilliantly in combinations that nobody in the civilized lands north of the Crescent Sea seems to have thought of.

The faces themselves, some of them so dark they're almost black, but most of them merely olive-complexioned, like many of our own southern provincials — the faces, whether cajoling, begging, slyly inveighing, obsequious, or stoically indifferent, the faces remain *inscrutable*. I don't think we shall ever understand these people. I don't think we shall ever tame them.

For a moment I felt almost sorry for Reverend Targeddon, who had doubtless come to evangelize, if the heat of his sacred Father Sun didn't kill him first. He wouldn't get far.

But I, of course, had come for another reason entirely.

Where better to shed one's ghosts than in the land of ancient ghosts?

I HAVE mentioned apparitions. What are apparitions by daylight but memories come alive in this immemorial land?

It was only when I stood in the quiet shadows of the temple of Bel-Hemad that the memories returned.

Storied place! I, in my broad-brimmed traveler's hat, with silver-tipped cane in one hand and my single cloth bag in the other, stood in the musty, echoing darkness of that temple, beneath the famous dome, gazing up at the weathered, but still serene, seated idol of the god, on whose shoulders and in whose lap pigeons perennially roost. The top of his head seemed to glow from the sunlight shining through the hole in the center of the dome. His stone eyes gazed down, revealing nothing. This was a god of springtime, of flowers, of forgiveness. I knew him from books. The Reverend Targeddon would doubtless be fuming about heathenry at this point. Let him. The temple was an impressive monument, ten times more so when you considered how old it was.

It was best admired in silence, so I stood well to the back, amid a few natives — old women mostly, sitting silently on the smooth floor, either rapt in worship or just there to get out of the sun. I waited for a tour group to pass, for silence to return, and then I slowly approached the god, and jokingly made a little prayer, the way you toss a penny into a magic fountain, even if you don't believe in its magic.

I made the half-hearted prayer, yes. The melancholy within my heart was a darkness, a void. I had come a long way to . . . unburden myself. Would the god speak to me?

Yes, he spoke, but not aloud, not in words.

A memory arose within my mind as if I were living it again, more intense than any recollection. Perhaps time folded back on itself, and I truly did relive that night when I was fifteen years old, when my brother Armisdas (who would have been nineteen and had just inherited our father's title) awoke me out of an uneasy sleep on a summer's night, and bade me get dressed in silence.

"I want you to see something very special," he said.

I had always thought he held me in contempt. I could not imagine what he wanted to share with me. I was suspicious, afraid of some trick or trap.

He led me out of my room. I looked to right and left. there were no servants. Together we made our way down to the stables. Again, no one was around. In secrecy, beneath the full light of the moon, we both mounted the huge black stallion which had belonged to our father, which only a Lord of Abernaeven could ever master. On this beast then, we rode faster than the wind, overtaking owls and eagles in their flight (or so I remembered, in this waking dream, as the god answered me). Hillside and heather gleamed silver beneath the brilliant moon. We came to a lake, behind some hills, a place I should have known; it could have only been a few miles from home; but it was as strange to me as the far side of the Moon on this night.

There, gliding across the surface of the lake like a ghost, was the most beautiful lady I had ever seen, in a white, trailing gown like mist. As I watched she paused, once, again, and stooped down, then raised up out of the water other ghosts, one by one, taking each by the hand in a gesture of indescribable grace: knights in ancient armor, lords in elaborate robes and diadems, ladies in fine gowns. All attended on her, and bowed, and swayed with her when she began to dance to some music I could not hear.

I was afraid then, knowing this to be some unholy thing.

"Is she a witch?" I whispered.

"Yes," said my brother. "Isn't she *wonderful?*"

I could not speak. I could only agree as he directed our black stallion out onto the glowing surface of the lake. It did not sink. We rode into the midst of those assembled there. We watched them swirling around and around us beneath the moon in that fantastic dance.

And it seemed that the night sky rippled, and the stars drifted like glowing foam to form faces that gazed down on us as the Lady Eudochina Kias greeted each of us by name, and took each of us by the hand as we dismounted.

I felt a thrill of fear that she had known our names, without being told.

For there was no beauty or kindness in her voice now. She spoke to me, I felt, as one might address a morsel, and yet still she was beautiful.

Then, for just an instant, the Moon vanished, and I saw that the faces among the stars were ancient and horribly vile, and that the attendants on the lady were skeletons and drowned corpses. I made to cry out then, but my brother Armisdas clapped his hand over my mouth, held me tightly, and whispered, *"Do not. Upon your life, do not."*

"UPON MY life?" I said aloud, in the temple, coming out of my reverie. "Merely that?"

Then someone was tugging at my bag.

"I'll carry that for you, Sir."

Aha! I thought. A thief, for which countries like this are well-known. I raised my silver-tipped cane to brain him if he didn't let go. I didn't care that we were inside a temple.

"You don't have to do that, Sir."

He held onto the bag. The speaker was a skinny boy. I couldn't guess his age: thirteen, fourteen? I saw a soft, round, olive face, unkempt hair and dark eyes. Almost in defiance of current fashion he wore a loose, long-sleeved shirt of dark material, the color of the night sky. I think it had little stars embroidered into it. Whatever, it was several sizes too large on him and billowed like a tent. I glimpsed ragged pants torn off at the knees and dirty, bare feet.

"And who might you be?" I demanded, almost amused at his persistence.

"Your servant, Sir." He spoke my own language perfectly, with a very slight accent. Then he let go of my bag and made a sweeping bow, almost a dance step, executed with perfect grace in the doubtless centuries-old, practiced manner of ancient Riverland.

"I didn't hire any servant."

"But you need one, and therefore I am here. Lord Abernaeven, your brother, Armisdas sends a message of greeting and bids me be your guide in the country which he has made his own."

OF COURSE it *had been* a trick and a trap, on that night long ago, when my brother led me to the lake.

The Lady Eudochina Kias was a witch, the greatest and most terrible of witches, the kind who was not supposed to exist in our modern age.

But she did exist, and we two came to her night after night, drawn to the brilliant, searing, all-consuming flame of her being.

We traveled the Great Northern Continent with her, throughout all the lands of the Bright Empire. I cannot list all our rites, all our depravities. Suffice it to say that my brother and I learned many things — how to know the future, how to crush a man's life by closing your hand, how to find buried treasure by summoning up the dead and torturing them into telling you where it is.

We moved in the circles of such creatures as herself. We joined many secret societies, which met in crypts, in tombs, or on the estates of the decadent rich. Yes, we defiled holy places, we murdered, we offered and blood to the darkness. *And the darkness answered us,* for we freely and knowingly came to worship the Shadow Titans, who are a myth, in whom no modern theologian will aver belief. In the storybooks the Shadow Titans are equal and opposite to the ancient, pagan gods — the very ones which our Bright Empire has banished by force of Reason. Yet *those* ancient gods beheld the Titans on the first day of the world — *they* saw their own shadows as the Sun rose behind them; and the gods were afraid, and the shadows have dwelt in the darkness ever since, to whisper, to summon, to tempt and seduce sorcerers such as ourselves.

In ancient times we would have been burnt alive for what we had done, and rightly so. Now, we were free, precisely because society had relegated such beliefs to the nursery.

Now we laughed.

Now my brother and I were rivals in crime, as we competed for the favors of the Lady Eudochina Kias and she, laughingly, granted them to both of us.

There was even a time, incredible as it might seem, when I was *grateful* to my brother for what he had led me into, what he had allowed me to become.

But it was a trick and a trap. How stupid of me to allow any goodness in him, even of the most perverse kind.

For I came to understand, through his own offhand remarks, through researches of my own, through secrets extorted from the hapless dead, that I was as a fatted calf, led along a prescribed path, taught such mysteries and evils as would sufficiently *ripen* my soul — and then I was to be the sacrificed, offered up to some design of my brother's, who had played me for a fool, while he and his witch-whore laughed at me.

So I took action so direct, so startling, that it caught them off guard. On a storm-filled night, with lightning screaming around us, with wind howling over the mountaintop where we three had met for our sabbat, as the Shadow Titans manifested themselves in the sky above us and even we did not dare — any more than the gods dare — gaze directly into their eyes, I suddenly drew a saber from beneath my cloak and struck off the Lady Eudochina Kias's head. There was an explosion of blood, but to my amazement, her body vanished utterly, like a burst bubble.

There wasn't much more to be said after that. The storm ended. The Titans drifted away behind the clouds. My brother, stunned, could only let out a wail of despair and flee. He disappeared. It took me months to learn through what contacts I still had in occult circles that he had gone to Riverland, to master its darkest arts, to *find a passageway into the land of the dead,* where he might be again with his precious Eudochina Kias.

Madness, I thought. Fine. Let him go.

In time my brother was declared legally dead and I was the new Lord Abernaeven. *More than twenty years passed,* during which I wrestled with the conundrum of my own corrupted soul. There was *no* way I could atone for my sins. Were I to admit them, I would be shunned forever.

And to what end? The past does not return. Better then to think of the future, to keep silent, to merely *cease doing evil*. It would hardly right the moral balance of the universe — not the sort of thing Reverend Targeddon would ever approve of — but it was the best I could do.

I became a paragon of respectability. I married Simonis, the daughter of a neighboring landowner, more out of a sense of propriety than anything else, had children by her, and in time even began to love her.

So I survived, and did no harm to the world — until the bloody deaths began, and the ghost of Eudochina Kias came howling in the night.

AND AGAIN I felt that thrill of fear in the dim, echoing temple, when the boy spoke my name, and I knew that my doom was sealed, that my visions had all been true, that the purpose for which I had come into this land would never let me go until I had resolved it.

For I'd had a previous message from my brother, a year ago. I still carried it with me, though I had read it a thousand times. The paper was soiled, mud-splattered, and came in an envelope marked all over with barbarous writing I could not read (thought it also bore a provincial stamp of the Bright Empire). But I could read the message itself, sure enough. It said, in handwriting I had not seen in twenty years, only:

> *Brother,*
> *Come at once. SHE is here! All is forgiven.*
> *— Armisdas.*

That from the brother I intended to kill, who had apparently sent this scruffy, barefoot servant to tend to my needs.

III

I LET SEKENRE carry my bag. That was the name my servant told me, a very old name, out of a book of oriental tales. There was a boy named Sekenre once, in the days of the earliest kings of Riverland, who descended into the country of the dead and came back out again. Being a sorcerer, one whose soul was diseased and riddled through with evil, he could not die, for the earth and the Great River would not accept him. But that part of him which was still a boy, which could still remember being human, clung to what he had once been. He didn't wear shoes, because in ancient Riverland a father gave his son shoes the day he declares him a man, and Sekenre's father, also a sorcerer, died under hideous, if uncertain circumstances without performing this essential rite. Indeed, since the sorcery to which he himself was captive would not let him grow any older, Sekenre was frozen forever as he was, an unholy thing struggling to remain a child, morally ambiguous, though capable of kindnesses, a trickster figure, whose "myth" has been the subject of learned tomes by scholars of the past century or so.

All of which is rubbish. If this boy beside me had said, "I am that one," I would have believed him utterly, as, in time, I came to anyway.

It was disconcerting to note, that, for all his elaborate bow had been graceful, there was something wrong with his walk. At first I thought he'd hurt his foot, but it wasn't exactly a limp, more that the rhythm of his movement was just a little off. It was only when I insisted we pause to rest on the surprisingly long walk to my hotel, as I sat down on a bench in the searing heat and he squatted down on the pavement in front of me that I saw that he had an ugly, raised scar all the way around his right leg just below the knee, as if the limb had been actually severed, then re-attached, but not quite correctly.

How could that be? Both of his legs were criss-crossed with other scars, and the palms of his hands seemed to have been seared with burning. Once when he scratched his head I noticed that part of one of his ears was missing.

But I didn't ask directly about any of this. In Riverland there are things one does not ask.

What was I to make of this person my brother had sent to fetch me? Was the boy my enemy, my friend, or something else entirely?

In Riverland, the apparitions and questions come by themselves.

So do answers. One learns to recognize them by subtle signs, as they appear to test and tease us.

I could only follow and see where I was led.

We came to a little square where craftsmen displayed toys for sale, mostly puppets and figures made of wood. But there was also a bank of brightly-colored pinwheels, of lacquered paper, spinning merrily in the breeze, set up high where children could not snatch them.

Sekenre paused, and looked up longingly at the pinwheels, as if fascinated and delighted by the flashing colors.

I wondered how a great and terrible sorcerer, hundreds if not thousands of years old, or even a boy who carried luggage for tourists, could not afford a pinwheel if he should want one. But in the story, some aspect of the trickster-sorcerer was still a child and might even be, conceivably, innocent of the ways of money.

A Mystery of the East, I decided.

I put my hand on his shoulder. "If you serve me faithfully, I'll buy you one. Is it a bargain?"

"A bargain," he said, without smiling.

It was a light moment. There were so few light moments.

That evening, in the hotel, there were more visitations.

When we had approached the place, the porter made to relieve Sekenre of the bag and shoo him away, but when I insisted he was my servant, he was allowed inside, though ordered to sleep in the corridor outside my room.

I looked out on him once, through the keyhole, and saw him crouched down, with living flame cupped in his hands, while over him towered hideous beings, with bodies like flabby, naked men, pale as drowned corpses, and with the heads, claws and tails of crocodiles. These spoke to Sekenre in grunting, hissing speech, and he replied in the same tongue.

I knew them, from my book of tales I'd read as a child. These were the *evatim*, the messengers and servants of Surat-Hemad, the Lord of Death. To see them is to know that one is about to die, unless in the presence of a very great sorcerer.

That must have been part of a dream. It was already beginning. In my dream that night the Lady Eudochina Kias came to me as I had known her, as I had dreamed and obsessed over her in my youth. This time her manner was loving and gentle. She pressed her finger to my lips to hush me, then she drowned me in kisses, and she whispered, "I have found you again and I will have you again, as it was before, as it ever shall be."

And I awoke, spent and sweaty and weeping, hoping impossibly for the forgiveness of the witch-woman I had murdered twenty years before, and cursing my own weakness that I might hope for such a thing.

IV

IN THE morning, Sekenre and I boarded another steamer he had chosen, the incongruously named *Bird of the River,* a high, shabby, hulking thing, like a row of tumble-down houses mounted on a barge, with a smoke-stack among them belching black smoke and sparks and a paddle wheel at the back. If this was any kind of bird, I thought, it was a wobbling, brainless domestic turkey which now attempted to swim.

Yet swim it did, and chugging slowly against the current, we made our way up-river, out of the Delta, where the Great River was so wide you could barely see one bank from the other. All day we passed cultivated fields and tiny, baked-mud villages. Crocodiles sunned themselves on the sandy shore. In a few places, spear-carrying villagers escorted washer-women or herdboys with cattle to the water's edge. Often we saw farmers irrigating fields by hoisting buckets water up out of the river on a beam made of a bent, yet flexible tree.

How quickly, then, civilization fell away, and the land became, again, truly timeless. The noisy, ridiculous *Bird of the River* was the intruder here. I could well have been looking out on a scene of five thousand years ago.

Sekenre sat beside me on the crowded deck. It was a little cooler here than in my cabin, for all the boat was swarming with passengers, natives and tourists, all of them loud, some of them smelly . . . and one very familiar, the Reverend Margos Targeddon, who had dispensed with his clerical garb and now wore a sensible white suit and straw hat.

"Ah, we meet again, Sir! Your business is not in the city."

"No, it is not."

"Nor is mine. I am come to preach the gospel of Light here among the ignorant."

"Ah," I said, with considerable irony.

He started, then noticed Sekenre at my side.

"And who is the little heathen?"

"My servant."

"Ah."

"Ah," said Sekenre, in perfect mockery.

The Reverend made an excuse and hurried off. I didn't know what he thought of us, what he imagined. I didn't care.

It was in the darkness, at the end of the day that Sekenre began to speak freely. We had come to the famous bend in the river where both banks are lined with enormous statues of the gods of Riverland, carven out of the living stone of the cliffs. Outlanders always strive to come upon them at night, for they are more impressive that way, the ravages of time half-concealed by shadows, the human or beast-headed colossi looming over the river like mountains, agleam in the brilliant moonlight. Reputedly, also, the cooling of the stones after the day's heat makes them speak. It is a phenomenon widely reported by travel writers, but best observed, I think, from a sailboat, or a barge, or from the shore. Over the noise of our vessel's engines and paddles, I could hear nothing.

In the darkness, as the stone gods drifted by, Sekenre began to speak, almost in a different voice, now, an older voice, more heavily accented than before, with odd turns of phrasing. He named the gods as we passed them: Neoc-Hemad, with the sun-shield on his arm, whose flaming arrows strike down the unrighteous, no matter where they might hide; Delivendra, the Lady of the Lantern, who counsels peace and forgiveness; Malevendra who seeks eternal vengeance; and Bel-Hemad whom I already knew, god of flowers. Haedos-Hemad was the one with a sparrow's head and, by his side, far more fearsome, sat Regun-Hemad, the eagle that walks like a man and reputedly soars amid the gloomy peaks at the River's source, in the still unexplored interior of the Southern Continent. The Eagle-God is a messenger of Death, who brings the word of Surat-Hemad, the all-devouring Holy Crocodile.

The old gods of Riverland, Sekenre told me, were born from the mud of the River in the beginning of the world. When the sunlight touched them, they leapt up into the sky.

"Now they have turned into stone?"

"Still they leap into the sky."

"Have you seen them leap?"

"Holy men can see them. I am not holy. I cannot see them."

We were both silent for a time. The I said, "I feel that this whole country could swallow me up."

"So it already has. Riverland is merely a little closer to the Crocodile's mouth than the rest of the world. But everywhere, look up." He pointed to the stars. "Those are his teeth. Are they not seen even in your own country?"

He sat with his feet up on the bench, his hands around his knees, his face resting on them. For an instant, it seemed to me, he looked, not like a child, but like a very old man.

That must have been a trick of the light. So too must have been the way that the scars on his legs, and more underneath his dark shirt, seemed to glow softly.

The Crocodile's mouth was open wide. Willingly, I plunged headlong into it.

TWO MORNINGS later we reached Reed Town (called Arnatisphon, the City of Reeds, in ancient times, Sekenre told me). It was a decrepit, ramshackle place, a collection of rotting wooden houses on ancient pilings, and a few stone edifices overgrown with moss. Everything seemed slimy. The place stank of fish and stagnant water.

It was better in ancient times, Sekenre told me. We had a few hours to spare. He took me through the city, touring the ancient wooden temples, the bazaars where, in defiance of any laws of the Bright Empire, craftsmen carved new gods every day and put them up for sale.

These were only little gods, though, not like the stone colossi who leapt into the sky.

We ended up in a cramped temple, little more than a dingy room at the end of an twisted alley.

There wasn't much to be seen, just a barbarous carving hanging on the wall, of a naked boy — about Sekenre's age? — impaled on thorns, their sword-like points plunged all through his body, so that anyone thus wounded should have died; but the expressive face seemed very much alive, the eyes wide, filled with pain and utter bewilderment.

Sekenre gazed on this thing for a long time, until I became impatient to leave.

Then he made a little sign with his hands, and we left.

"That is the Thorn Child," he said, "so ancient that no one can remember his beginnings. They say he was the first sorcerer."

From Reed Town, then we journeyed further, this time in a low, narrow craft rigged with triangular sails. The river had become shallow and swampy, black with mud. Insects buzzed in the air.

Once again we had familiar company, as the Reverend Margos Targeddon, the Sun Guardian heaved and panted his way aboard.

"Your business, Sir, takes you further into the interior?" he said.

"It does. And yours?"

"I go to preach the word in the very heart of this pestilent country!"

"Do you have any idea how far you might have to go?" I said.

He only shrugged and made a sign of holy resignation, tinged with more than a little exasperation.

"Ah," I said.

So we journeyed together yet again, aboard a sailing vessel whose name I did not know, something like *Bar-wul-Yann* in the Reedlandish tongue. The turbanned captain did not speak my own language, or even Deltan, though Sekenre could converse with him and the captain treated the boy with an odd degree of deference.

Reverend Targeddon noted this, and *tsk-tsk*ed about heathenry and sin.

"Ah," I said.

Now if we had passed any stone colossi, we would have heard them speak, but here the banks of the river spread out into endless marshes, filled with motionless reeds. There didn't seem to be any wind or current. Our progress slowed almost to a stop. Flocks of wading birds lined the nearer bank. Here and there crocodiles rested among the reeds, or drifted like old logs.

Once we passed an ancient, ruined tower which rose out of a sand-bank like a broken finger, crooked, about to topple. This was all that remained of a great city, Sekenre told me, which was destroyed by the gods for its wickedness. Now only the dead congregated there, but they did so often.

I thought then that I would be among the dead soon myself, but that I was determined to find my brother Armisdas and send him hurtling into the abyss before me.

"I've come a long way. Are we close to where we're going?" I asked.

"Yes, very close," said Sekenre.

A great melancholy seized me. I could have confessed all my sins to Sekenre, or even to Reverend Targeddon, then and there. Things were almost clear. As I followed, as I waited, questions and teasing half-answers manifested themselves in my mind like shapes of smoke.

I was drowsing beneath the brilliant stars. Sekenre slept with his head in my lap. I had a vision of the Lady Eudochina Kias holding up a light, and I asked her if she had become Delivendra, the Lady of the Lantern, or Malevendra, the Queen of Vengeance.

But she didn't have time to answer either, because the river pirates hit us first. They must have paddled alongside in small boats. That far up the river, where the gunboats never come and the laws and rationality of the Bright Empire are but a rumor, there is no law, and such things happen.

Suddenly everything was shouts and screams and clanging swords. Dark shapes heaved themselves aboard from every direction. A firearm went off, splitting the night with its roar and its flash, but to little effect. I lurched to the railing and looked down. People and goods were plunging into the water. Crocodiles closed in. I saw the Reverend Targeddon, in his clerical robes again, all afire, tumbling into the darkness with splash and a hiss.

"Come! We will go to your brother now," said Sekenre. He took my by the hand, and in his other hand he held living fire, which danced on his outstretched palm, and didn't seem to hurt him, though his palm was very scarred.

He took me by the hand, and he led me out of the drifting vessel. The fighting was over now. Most of the crew were dead or evading crocodiles, the pirates occupied with robbing corpses and heaving luggage overboard, to be towed ashore by confederates.

They didn't bother us. They didn't seem to see us.

Sekenre stepped over the side, into the water, which held him up as if he stood on polished glass.

"Take your shoes off," he told me.

"What?"

"Flesh must touch, for magic to be true."

So I did as he commanded me, and we two walked upon the black water as if on smooth marble, passing the crocodiles as they swam eagerly, and passing, too, the *evatim,* who have the heads of crocodiles and the bodies of drowned men and who approach more slowly, drifting with terrible inevitability. These had come to feast on the souls of the dead, even as the crocodiles had come to feast on the flesh. Yet it was ill luck to behold them, and one could die doing it, unless in the company of a powerful and ancient sorcerer out of some old storybook.

We walked, hand in hand, for hours it seemed, barefoot on the black water, sluggish rippling waves spreading behind us as we passed. We saw luminous, skeletal herons, and ghosts among the reeds. Sekenre explained to me that we were not on the Great River anymore, not the one which flows through the lands of living men, but instead upon the *other water,* as the Riverlanders call it euphemistically, the river of the underworld, which flows in the opposite direction from the living river, and carries the dead into the belly of Surat-Hemad.

I noticed, after a while, that the stars overhead were not the familiar ones, but fewer and more faint and arranged in no constellations I had ever seen before.

"They are the stars of *Leshé*," said Sekenre, "which are of dream, on the border marches of the land of Death, which is called *Tashé*. We are deep into the Crocodile's mouth now. This is your brother's adopted country, where he dwells in high honor, as a lord, and where he wishes to meet you once again."

"Is he alive?"

"After a fashion. He has become a very powerful sorcerer. For that, he has suffered and sacrificed much."

"You are a sorcerer, too, Sekenre. You have suffered."

"And you, Lord Abernaeven?"

"I — I was never more than a dilettante!"

"Let us hope so. Look, we have come to your brother's dwelling."

Now *evatim* by the thousands swarmed up out of the black water, covering a dark beach with their pale bodies, with their vast and terrible heads. Some of them bore corpses or parts of the corpses of the drowned in their jaws. They vomited up mud and blood and dead men's bones, and, as I watched the mass of this debris, and of the *evatim* themselves *grew*. It heaped upon itself and rose up like a wave against the sky, eclipsing the pale stars of the Dreamlands and of the Deathlands which lay immediately nearby.

The thing swelled and splashed, like a excretion of the mud and the river, an eruption, which then froze into place and became the image, the obscene parody of *Abernaeven Castle*, of my ancestral home.

The huge gates swung open. Holding Sekenre's hand, I entered the courtyard, then a vestibule, then the great hall of my house, only the stones around me and the rafters above were not stone and wood at all, but the flesh of the living and the dead, writhing, groaning, oozing blood and black water.

Here were familiar objects about, the family arms on the wall, the banners of our house, the armor our ancestors once wore. We passed from the hall into the great library, up the spiral staircase of rusting, cold metal. Once I reached out for a random volume, but it collapsed into mud at my touch.

And then I heard the lady Eudochina Kias's howling laughter.

And I heard my brother calling me.

We proceeded, then, into the upper reaches of the house, into the great, canopied bedroom, where my children had been begotten, where my wife had died, where modern science and reason and the Righteous Light of Holy Father Sun had failed me utterly.

Now my brother was there.

I confronted him.

Sekenre opened his free hand, and a blue flame leapt from it. By this I could see the darkened room, the mud and water dripping from the ceiling and from the rotting canopy over the bed.

A wind blew suddenly, and made the flame dance. Something I took for a huge tapestry billowed heavily.

"Greetings, at last, my beloved brother," said Armisdas.

It took a minute for what I saw to register. He was there, but no longer even remotely as he had been. He had become *part* of the vast wall-hanging. His flesh and bones and veins had been softened and stretched and interwoven with the darkness itself into the tapestry which was, in its perverse way, a complete record of all our depravities, the outlines of figures and scenes glowing like luminous wounds. Yet, flayed as he was, he was still alive, the strands of his flesh joined with some *other,* and with living fibers out of the air, which receded above and away into the unfathomable distance. The whole mass breathed and heaved and sighed.

Only his face was recognizable, floating amid it all, glowing slightly like a moon lost among dark clouds. His face was still *young,* as he had appeared when he was twenty, when he had been, as few males can ever be accurately described, *beautiful,* blond and pale and perfectly formed, the ideal counterpart to his witch lover.

I, by contrast, had aged so much, becoming haggard beyond my years, my slenderness more suggestive of a cadaver than of youth.

My brother's expression was one I knew all too well, of wholly deceptive, *compassion,* as if he were, in an act of supreme generosity, about to confide everything he knew to me.

"Still whole and sound, brother? Hale and hearty? You always were the dabbler. Sorcerers, as I think you know, must suffer a lot of pain to get what they want. Both the pain and the rewards are . . . indescribable. But you never had the stamina. Nor does your companion, Sekenre. A character from an old nursery-tale, I understand. He is nothing. A lackey. I sent him to fetch you. I don't need him anymore. Kill him for me, will you, as a reconciliation gift?"

I looked at Sekenre, who looked back at me. His dark eyes were unreadable.

I turned to my brother.

"I know all the secrets of death . . . " he said, laughing.

His flesh rippled, and new shapes arose in the tapestry. I saw my wife and children dying, one by one, and I saw representations of my journey hither: of myself lying in a dream in the stateroom of the *Empress Faustina*, meeting Sekenre in the temple of Bel-Hemad, the *Bird of the River*, the colossi, the river pirates, and even, in obvious mockery, a distorted, throbbing image of the Reverend Margos Targeddon as he plunged into the River, his clothing all aflame.

And, as he laughed, I saw the Lady Eudochina Kias, moving within the tapestry which was woven of my brother's flayed flesh. Imagine a candle-flame carried behind a cloth screen. It was like that. Glowing, she passed through him, rising up to kiss his lips, to turn and face me and to mock me one last time.

"Ah, the little brother," she said. "You were always so funny, and, in the end, I think, innocent."

I think I became mad again just then. I drew a dagger I had carried all this time hidden up my sleeve, strapped to my forearm. This was the last malignancy of my own, half-hearted attempts at sorcery. I had learned enough to make this blade enchanted, envenomed, reeking and marked with every possible destructive agency.

This was to be my revenge for the death of my wife, for my children, for the destruction of my *peace of mind* after almost thirty years, when I had so clearly, so deservingly escaped into the sunlit world again.

This. I plunged the dagger into the laughing face of the Lady Eudo-china Kias. I slashed away great swathes of the living tapestry. My brother cried out in agony. Blood poured down over me like a waterfall, washing me off my feet. Yet I clung to my enemy, and slashed and slashed.

And to my amazement, it was Sekenre who was wrestling me away. He seemed very strong, despite his size.

He twisted my arm behind my back. I struggled, in despair, certain he had betrayed me at last.

"Do *not* kill him," he commanded me. "You do *not* understand what you would become if you did." He wrenched my head up, making me see where the dark, pulsing tapestry stretched up through the ceiling of the house, up into the sky, up to where the Shadow Titans themselves gazed down. *They were part of it,* woven out of the very stuff of my brother's flesh. He was one with all of the evil in the universe. I could see this, in the darkness, with some sorcerer's sight which transcends physical sense.

"If you kill him," Sekenre said, "he wins. That is what he wants you to do. Know you not, that when you kill a sorcerer, you *become* that sorcerer, and he lives on inside of you? If his mind is stronger than your own, who do you think will be the master? Now that your brother has become what he is, and gained such power, don't you think he would like to pour himself into the receptacle of a whole, complete body such as your own, which, through sorcery, he could make immortal? Do you think you would be a match for him if he did?"

I relaxed. The my arm went limp, the dagger dangling in my fingers.

Somewhere, far away, my brother was laughing, and all around me, the Shadow Titans drew near, the mouths wide to devour me, their faces too terrible to look upon.

"I am defeated," I said to Sekenre, weeping. "He is a monster who must be destroyed. If I cannot kill him, what can I do?"

Tempted as I might be, somehow still perversely *envious* of my brother's accomplishment, I knew I had not the strength to take my brother into myself, the way a sorcerer would. I could not and retain any trace of my own identity. I would, indeed, be my brother's carriage, his mobile receptacle into which his vileness was poured. I really was a mere dabbler in the black arts, when all was said and done.

"What can I do?" I whispered again, to Sekenre.

"Let me kill him."

And as I watched he made fire with his hands. A white flame leaped, crackling and hissing from the palm of his hand. He held it to the tapestry, which caught fire, like a cloth soaked in oil.

Soon my brother and his lady were screaming. Screaming, too, the Shadow Titans withdrew from the brilliant light of the blaze, the light which was the rising sun, which dispelled the darkness and the faint, strange stars of the deathlands.

Sekenre inhaled the smoke, all of it, sucking it out of the air until there was no more and the fire went out.

He fell down, gasping, choking, speaking in many tongues, *crying out in rage in my brother's voice,* while the castle dissolved around us, and the hordes of *evatim* scurried back into he black water.

Then the sun truly rose, and we were along the edge of the Great River, somewhere deep in Reedland. Sekenre lay beside me, asleep or in some kind of delirium. I took him in my arms — he weighed almost nothing — and waded through the mud until I came to a rise of ground, where I set him down gently among the tall grasses.

I sat beside him throughout the day, while he muttered to himself, and sometimes spoke aloud, or shouted, or even sang in a thousand different voices, in many tongues strange to me. I think I understood what was happening. A very great sorcerer, who contained legions of other sorcerers within himself — for the one who kills a sorcerer becomes that sorcerer, and takes into himself all that other sorcerer has killed, and all *they* have killed, and so on, *ad infinitum* — he was, in time, by the force of his accumulated selves, able to overcome and absorb my brother's spirit into himself, so that Armisdas did not win in the end, but became only another small facet of Sekenre.

And once, after many hours, my brother's voice spoke to me out of the boy's mouth, saying, "Can you forgive me? Can you ever forgive me?"

"No," I said. "How can I?"

"Then how can you forgive yourself?"

I had no answer to that, not that afternoon, not days or weeks later when Sekenre and I, both of us filthy and in rags, staggered into the imperial station in Reed Town. It took all my persuasion to convince the skeptical clerk that I might be mad, but I was *not* a native. I was a citizen of the Empire, to be dealt with as such, and the boy was my servant.

Eventually we were given clean clothes and sent down river on one of the regular barges.

Was it all a dream, then, when I passed through the lower regions of Riverland, when the stone colossi spoke to me in the night?

Was it a dream or a true and prophetic vision when I glimpsed the Reverend Margos Targeddon, Sun Guardian of the First Order standing on the dark shore in Land of the Dead, preaching the gospel of Light and Reason to the very *evatim?* Would he go at last into the ultimate belly of Surat-Hemad and explain to the Lord of Death that he should not, properly, exist?

I think it was in a dream that the five-thousand-year-old boy-child Sekenre explained to me that all had worked out according to his plan, for he could see the future in a limited way, and sought to devour my brother and the Lady Eudochina Kias in the way I had seen, to make their magic his own. For all he had seemed to serve my brother and perhaps made some obscure bargain with him, for all the two of them had conversed many times in the darkness of the underworld, Armisdas would not have allowed Sekenre into his actual presence, but for me. Only for *me* were the gates of the death-castle opened, and if Sekenre entered at the same time, perhaps Armisdas had grown reckless, or he was too arrogant to care.

I understood that the barefoot, untidy boy had been underestimated many times in the past.

All had been to that purpose, he told me.

"*All?*" In a sudden fit of rage, I grabbed him by the hair and held the poisoned dagger — which I still had — to his throat. "Do you mean my wife and children died that way, *for you?*"

He replied calmly. "You don't want to do what you are thinking of doing. If you want to have any chance of becoming a human being again, you must stop now. You must not kill another sorcerer. Then you would be beyond redemption."

I let go of him. I threw the dagger into the river.

"I am already beyond redemption," I said bitterly. "I was damned when I killed Eudochina Kias years ago."

"But she did *not* flow into you," Sekenre said. "Within her soul I see only darkness and void. She is not like the other sorcerers. If she was ever human, she lost that so long ago that she became an apparition made flesh, a *sending* of the Shadow Titans, shaped by them out of darkest dreams, to work the ruin of mankind."

"Yet you have managed to devour her."

"Only because she was already inside Armisdas."

A pause followed.

"You must believe me," he said gently. "I did not *cause* your sufferings. I merely turned them to my purpose once they had occurred, as if I were weaving a tapestry."

Once again, the expression on his face was unreadable.

I asked him if he would hear my sins, and I began to confess.

He protested that he was not a holy man.

Nevertheless, I confessed.

"You are right," he said at last. "You have learned this much, that the way to stop doing evil is merely to stop. You will not atone, you will not set anything right, but at least you won't do any more harm."

I wept. "What chance can I have then? What hope, now, after all?"

"Whatever hope and chance you can find for yourself, and no more."

I think it was in a dream that I finally came to Delta Port once again, and found a travel agent I knew and convinced him that I really was Lord Abernaeven, having fallen upon harsh circumstances after narrowly escaping river pirates. My name was good again. My credit was good. Soon I had a bath, a clean white suit, good shoes, a straw hat, and money in my pocket.

The next day Sekenre and I went to the little square where the toymakers kept pinwheels on a high rack out of the reach of children.

Sekenre looked at the pinwheels, and at me. I understood then that the actual child, the boy who had been Sekenre long ago before ever he became a sorcerer and absorbed so many other dark souls, had somehow survived, and now was manifested before me.

"A bargain is a bargain," I said, placing my hand gently on his shoulder. I handed the vendor a copper and gave the pinwheel to Sekenre.

He ran from me, laughing, leaping into the air, clapping his dirty feet together.

I never saw him again in this world, and only once more, in a dream. On the voyage home, I lay in the delirium of some tropical fever, while the very rational physicians of my own country fluttered and made obscure pronouncements and could do nothing.

They could not see Sekenre as he crouched on the chair beside my bed, with his old blue shirt, ragged pants, and muddy toes, with the pinwheel still gripped firmly in his hand; nor could they hear him when he old me that one day he would be the *last* sorcerer, who would take all the others into himself and survive until the end of time.

"And what will you do then, when time runs out?" I said. (My speech must have seemed more delirious raving to the doctors.)

"I will confront the gods, and demand an explanation for the world's pain," he said.

And in a true and prophetic vision, I saw him, on a plain of darkened glass, when the sun has gone out and the world has died; I saw him at the end of time, exactly as before, his toes muddy, the pinwheel in his hand. I saw him face the gods at last, and the gods were not laughing.

★   ★   ★

THERE IS nothing left for me. I do not think I'll live much longer. Maybe I'll see my home country again, maybe not.

Sekenre knows. On that day when we emerged from the underworld and I confessed my sins to him, he showed me a book he called out of the air, a thick volume in an ancient binding, handwritten in beautiful, ornate, impossible-to-read script. It was a sorcerer's book, he said, which is infinite. You can turn its pages forever and find more of them.

"Is my story there, in your book?" I demanded.

"Yes."

"Then you know how it comes out."

"Yes," he said. "I wrote it backwards, from the ending."

I DON'T think I have much time.

The doctors think I am mad, but my mind is clear. I am visited only by the ghost of my beautiful wife, whom I betrayed before she ever knew me. I am forgiven, she says. The children are with her. We will be reunited very soon.

I wish somebody would —

It is finished. It is begun. I, Sekenre, have written it in my book.

"When you close the sorcerer's book, it is not finished. You are a part of it now. You have closed it on yourself." —Julna of Kadisphon

Printed in the United States
59491LVS00004B/355-360